YOU

Ashley Hickson-Lovence is a former secondary school English teacher. In his spare time, using his experience as a football referee himself, he formally observes semi-professional referees for the FA. His debut novel, *The 392*, was released in April 2019.

'The football novel is back . . . [and] credit to Ashley Hickson-Lovence for seeing how the first black referee in the top flight of the English game could become an intriguing work of "faction".' ***The Times***

'A stirring, stylistically unorthodox novel . . . Tussles with Shearer, together with Rennie's dream of overseeing an FA Cup final, add page-turning drive as well as poignancy to this bold and powerful narrative.' ***Observer***

'Not only is this a thrilling and emotional look at the legacy of one of football's most compelling heroes; it's also wonderfully inventive, detailing a life lived with passion for the game, resilience against racism, hope and integrity. Ashley has written a real tribute to Uriah Rennie.' **JEFFREY BOAKYE**

'*Your Show* remakes the novel as an immersive, defiant, precise work of internal biography. The approach is as compelling and resolute as its subject.' **TOM BENN**

YOUR SHOW

ASHLEY HICKSON-LOVENCE

faber

First published in 2022
by Faber & Faber Ltd
Bloomsbury House
74–77 Great Russell Street
London wwcib 3da

Typeset by Faber & Faber Ltd
Printed and bound by CPI Group (UK) Ltd, Croydon, cro 4yy

This paperback edition first published in 2023

A CIP record for this book
is available from the British Library

ISBN 978–0–571–36680–4

Printed and bound in the UK on FSC paper in line with our continuing
commitment to ethical business practices, sustainability and the environment.
For further information see faber.co.uk/environmental-policy

2 4 6 8 10 9 7 5 3 1

In loving memory of Jermaine Wright
'Mr Hackney Marshes'

'People should write about Uriah Rennie because that's what he wants.'

Kevin Keegan

1997

It's a double celebration tonight, not that many will care about your starring role. You carry the weight of the occasion on your shoulders, take it in your stride. You've worked hard to get here, earned these palpitations, the dry mouth, these uncontrollable jitters: short breaths, thumping chest. You've dreamt of this moment for years now – and what a night to make history. Here, in this, the first competitive fixture at Derby County's shiny new stadium. You, the first black man to referee in the Premiership. You must be the proudest man at Pride Park.

You strut up and down, make your face known, act like a regular at this level, as players from both sides mill about in the tunnel, loiter outside their dressing rooms, laughing and joking, basking in the pre-match buzz before it all kicks off.

Shaking a few hands, muttering a few hellos, you look the tracksuited players dead in the eyes, show them that you belong here, that you're the man in charge.

You look calm, but the nervous energy simmers within, your unsettled stomach a sack of stress, a little uneasy, feeling a little queasy – to be expected of course, becoming the history-maker you are.

Time to get in the zone, get your mind and body ready for the ninety minutes to come. You change from your suit into your training gear in your changing room and head out onto the pitch for a pre-match warm-up as the new all-seater stadium begins to fill up with wide-eyed burger-stuffing Bovril-slurping fans.

The glare of the floodlights is a spotlight and you are the performer about to put on a show.

To start, a light jog around the perimeter of the Pride Park pitch, flanked by your two linesmen tonight: Neil Hancox and Ray Oliver. As a trio, you do a few shuttles and drills to get your bodies match-ready: sidestep star-jumps, high knees, 'open the gate', 'close the gate', skipping, ankle circles, hamstring walks.

Muscles gradually loosen.

First-team coaches in baseball caps, pulled-down socks and Copa Mundial boots bellow throaty instructions at players in fluorescent-coloured bibs who zig-zag through fluorescent-coloured cones. Goalkeepers launch balls from the penalty area to the centre circle. Plump stewards get into position. Everyone has their role.

It looks the part, Derby's new ground: modern, square, neat corners, shiny black and white seats. The playing surface too is in pristine condition, everything seemingly in order already for the Rams to assert themselves as a proper Premiership football club.

You end with a few stretches and then a gut-busting sprint from the goal-line to halfway to show off your speed. You are meticulous with your routine because the devil is in the detail.

You have learned a lot from doing martial arts: *By failing to prepare, you are preparing to fail.*

The words have stuck.

Up to thirty thousand fans will flood into the stadium, you've been told, to see their boys in their shiny new surroundings for this historic Wednesday-night game. Derby have left the old Baseball Ground with all its history, Brian Clough and Peter Taylor, title wins and European nights, they've packed up the boxes, loaded the removal vans and have relocated here to the shiny new Pride Park across the city.

You try to play down the occasion, keep a lid on it, but this isn't just another game. It's taken you eighteen years to get here and you're determined to make the most of it, you're determined to make a good first impression.

Back inside your changing room, kick-off nearing, you thumb through the match programme, see your name at the back in glossy print: U. Rennie (Sheffield). The nerves gush through you, the razzamatazz of the occasion, the first game in this spanking new stadium and you at the centre of it.

You change, you think, you pace, you pretend.

An outer coldness, an inner quickening of the pulse.

Same pre-match spiel to your two assistants, new significance.

Heart pounding, head fizzy.

There's a knock on your door, it's somebody from Wimbledon, he tells you one of their players, Alan Kimble, doesn't have a shirt to play in, they've forgotten it back in London.

You've got to be a people person as a referee, fix things, think fast, think on your feet, be quick off the draw. Not ideal but a plan is hatched, a decision is made, you pretend you have everything under control.

The Dons' kit man goes on the hunt, returns again shortly after, has borrowed a top from a travelling fan. It's a blank shop-bought replica, no name or number on the back. Not ideal but it will have to do.

You've changed, you think, you pace, you pretend.

Sugary snacks and swigs of your sports drink. Liquid courage. One deep breath, then it's time to ring the buzzer, let the players know it's showtime.

You give it a minute, then march out when both teams are lined up and ready. They must wait for you, not the other way around.

In the tunnel, the stench of the occasion consumes you, soaks into your bones: sweat and Deep Heat and bravado.

Take it all in, Uri, quash those butterflies, say your little prayer, not many have made it this far up the footballing pyramid coming from where you have, being who you are. It's all down to you now; at this level, they're expecting you to be good and that you will be, undoubtedly.

The echoing thud, thud, thud of the Wimbledon keeper, Neil Sullivan, bouncing the match ball, mirrors the thud, thud,

thud of your heart. He spits on his gloved hands and claps three times. The sound reverberates: thud, thud, thud.

Last rallying calls from the two captains: rituals and superstitions rife. Everything throbs, new yearnings invade the fibres of your skin, infiltrate your consciousness, as you take those first few steps and saunter out of the tunnel, lead the two teams out of this shiny new stadium. Floodlights glaring.

Your heart pulsing and pulsating.

The roar all-consuming
                        as you blow that first whistle.

Lots of eye contact and furtive waist-down gesturing to your assistant as the ball bounces out of play; getting it right downstairs before lifting your left arm up fully to signal for an attacking throw.

Ray on the line duly follows and hoists his yellow flag up cleanly and clearly. Setting out your stall, singing off the same hymn sheet already. A small thing but a good start: synchronicity. Cogs in a well-oiled machine, one thing leading to another, letting the players know who's running the show.

You use the dead ball time to get into your next position, anticipating where the ball is going to bounce next. You can't give what you don't see, and if you're not in a position to see, then you're not refereeing right.

You swivel, you spin, you sprint, you swagger, you strut.

The Derby keeper, Mart Poom, launches the ball upfield and

you keep shuffling to make the right angle. Ambling and then scrambling along the turf to give you the right vantage point.

Always on the move, always needing to get 'side-on', crabbing left to right to get into a position for you to see the nudging and tussling and shoving, the excessive physical contact, the battle between two opposing players. One desperate for the ball, the other desperate to keep it. Legs and feet scrapping.

No foul, no foul. You play a running commentary of the action as it unfolds in your head, keeping your brain alert, keeping you on your toes, ready to respond at any second.

Wimbledon midfielder Vinnie Jones has a moan, of course he does. Welcome to the Premiership, Uri.

You shuffle into position. You are always shuffling into position to see the next foul, reacting to the next phase of play, spotting the next offence, following the trajectory of the ball as it balloons from place to place.

You break into a sprint, pump your arms and legs like it is a race.

You swivel, you spin, you sprint, you swagger, you strut.

Derby possession, Derby pressure: pushing and probing and passing and . . . goal.

Poise, patience and penetration paying off.

Derby County lead. Ashley Ward scores the game's first goal, heads it past Sullivan. The Pride Park crowd celebrate wildly, make themselves at home. Twenty minutes gone: one–nil.

Wimbledon corner, you get into position, get yourself somewhere to see.

The Wimbledon centre-back, Chris Perry, rises to meet the ball and heads it into the back of the net. The famous ego-deflectors Wimbledon have equalised straight away, a minute or so after falling behind, the score now one–one.

Derby possession, Derby pressure: pushing and probing and passing and Eranio slides in to put Derby back in the lead.

A frantic first thirty-two minutes: two–one Derby.

For a foul, you book Kimble, you know it's him, no name or number on the back of his shirt.

You blow for half-time on the forty-five, swagger and strut down the tunnel, your heart pulsing and pulsating.

A fifteen-minute respite: sugary snacks and swigs of your sports drink.

So far, so good, you think.

Ten minutes into the second half and you reassure yourself you're doing just fine, settling into the rhythm of the second half, the rhythm of top-level football.

Positioning seems solid so far, you're in the right place to make the right decisions. You're getting through your first game as a Premiership football referee with little controversy so far, no hiccups of note here at Pride Park, in this shiny new stadium.

Still over half an hour to go. You give a corner and get into position.

Then . . .
        Darkness,
                Silence sharply followed by ironic cheers . . .
                                boos and jeers . . .
                                        shadows.

All black. Pitch black. Black as the night sky.

Only silhouettes remain. Confusion surrounds you. Players wonder what the fuck's going on. The managers and the fans too. Wonder what the fuck has happened to the floodlights. You're supposed to have all the answers. You wing it. Pretend to be in complete control. Pretend you know what to do.

It goes with the territory that you're going to be a talking point as a referee but this wasn't meant to happen, this lack of light.

You pace and pretend. Speak to your linesmen, speak to the two captains, speak to the two managers, groundstaff and security.

There's only one thing to do, you get the players off. Off the pitch, out of the black and back inside. You have to.

An announcement is made over the tannoy, the fans grumble, puzzled. More boos. The stadium shrouded in nervy confusion.

Twenty-two bodies like baddies in a video game, trudge off the pitch and down the tunnel.

It's nine o'clock now.

The Wimbledon manager, Joe Kinnear, asks what the plan is. The Derby manager, Jim Smith, asks what the plan is. You're expected to know all the answers.

The referee is all things to the players and managers, the wearer of many hats: the police officer, the parent, the teacher, the therapist, the social worker, the confidant, the nurse; judge, jury and bloody executioner.

You pace about, pretend you have everything under control. You're surrounded by hi-vis Derby groundstaff. Staff that barely know their new stadium themselves, trying to reassure you that this is nothing to worry about.

You're told there's an electrical issue.

Someone else says they heard a bang.

Derby: Five minutes, ref, got an electrician looking at it now. Generator problem.

9.15 now. It's getting late, it'll start to get dangerous. It's Wednesday night, fans will need to get home, kids will need to be tucked into bed. The players' legs will stiffen and their muscles will seize up.

They're trying to keep warm and limbered up, you hear them jumping up and down and running on the spot, metal boot-studs peppering the concrete.

Derby: Just five minutes, ref, two failed generator problems.

You give Derby more time, some leeway to sort it out on their special day, provide the light needed to resume the game. You try not to ask too many questions; instead, remain assertive with a series of statements. This is not the time for wishy-washy words, long-winded explanations or beating about the bush. This is not some drama being watched on tele, this is you, right here, right now, with a big decision to make.

Look, you pause to formulate your words clearly . . .

You: 9.30 cut-off.

  Derby: Or what?

You: Or it's postponed, abandoned.

  Derby: Abandoned?

You: Abandoned.

  Derby: 9.30?

You: 9.30.

Pace and pretend and wait.

Pace and wait.

Wait.

You loiter. Club officials from both sides at your 'Match Officials' door.

Wimbledon: Any news? What's happening now? My players are getting restless, ref. Just call it off, this is fuckin' ridiculous.

  Derby: Don't be so hasty, any minute now, we've got a good team on it.

Wimbledon: This is getting silly, how much did this stadium cost to build again?

>**Derby:** The maintenance men have nearly fixed it, we've been told.

Wimbledon: What a joke.

>**Derby:** You can delay it another five, ten max, can't ya, ref?

9.27 – nothing.

9.28 – nothing.

9.29 – nothing.

9.30. You tried, gave them a chance. 9.30 cut-off you said and it's 9.30 now.

Decision made, match abandoned.

Derby: Really, ref? Come off it, we'll get it going any minute now. Just give it another five.

Decision made.

9.33 – light is restored, you hear the ironic cheers from the fans who have remained, but it's too late. Turning back now would make you look weak. You are now a Premiership referee, with Premiership referee responsibilities, you must remain strong, unfazed.

Decision made.

Wimbledon: Well done, ref!

Derby: Rash decision, weak, been bullied, ref, bullied.

Wimbledon: Had to be done. Your hands were tied.

Derby County are embarrassed. The celebratory champagne will have to be put back in the fridge.

It had to be done though; it's hard to be seen as a black man, even in the best of lights.

1972

Positioned at the start line, left foot in front of the right. Big toe wiggling. You ignore the fighting talk from the other boys either side of you, you will do your talking with your legs. You are too busy focusing on the finish line – the invisible white tape between two trees at the far end of the yard – to listen to their big big talk.

You are too busy picturing what winning will feel like when you get to the other side, dreaming about the cheers you will hear and the respect you will get for being faster than them all.

With a quick wobble of the head, you snap yourself back into real life, can't dream for too long, not yet, you have a race to win.

Here, in Jamaica, in Dalvey Pier, St Thomas, you must be good at running, being slow makes you an embarrassment to your area, an embarrassment to your nation.

It's in your blood to be fast, you must run to get to where you need to go, every day to everywhere, bolting it from here to the Blue Mountains, there is no place for standing still or being too slow.

You breathe in heavy through your nose, heavier out of your mouth. You are readier than you have ever been to be a winner.

You are one of the best around, one of the fastest for your age and probably the whole school. You could be everyone's number one sportsman. You run, you race, you bowl, you field, you catch. You play until the sun goes down and your aunt or your grandma shouts, *Uri, where are you, pickney?* for all of Dalvey to hear.

Everything to you is a competition you must win.

A small crowd have come to watch, drawn in by the pre-race noise. One of the younger girls, somebody's little sister, is given the duty to start the contest. She cups her hands over her mouth like it is a megaphone and shouts, *on your marks . . .*

As soon as she says *get set . . .* and *go*, you're off, catapulting yourself forward, running as fast as you possibly can to get to the other side.

You make a strong start, your bare feet pounding into the hard ground as you run a hundred miles an hour like you've been fired from a slingshot. You push out your chest to give you the tightest of leads and the more you run, the more the other boys disappear from the corners of your eyes.

Blood rushes through your body fast like a fielder rushing to the boundary. Sweat drips from your forehead like rain during hurricane season.

You run like you are running to your cousins. Like you are late for school. Like your neighbour's dog is chasing you seconds after you have stolen some low-hanging fruit.

Pushing and pushing, using every bit of your body to make

sure you beat the other boys to be the best. You get closer and closer, the finish line coming nearer and nearer as you stretch out your neck, making every centimetre count, to make sure you finish in first place.

And you have, you've won. The other boys are not even close.

In seconds, you are surrounded, crowded by everyone jumping and dancing like it is a carnival. The other breathless boys mutter their congratulations with half-happy, half-jealous faces.

Even though you are now a winner, your body feels like it is about to explode from the inside and the crowd of bodies isn't helping, so you drop to the floor, collapse back first, spreading out your limbs like a starfish.

Vision is blurry, sky not coming through clear. Your chest heaves up and down, up and down, but soon, as the sound of the children around you can be heard again, your movement becomes more regular, soon it feels easier to breathe. Soon you feel normal. Soon enough you are Uri again.

• • •

Tracing your footsteps in the dirt, leaving your mark in the earth on the road where eventually concrete meets water. All the sounds together make a song: machete-wielding farmers – skinny men with fat voices – yelling across plots; clip-clopping mules tugging carts with crops; noisy birds chirping in the trees.

The sea can be heard from here, twinkling like Sunday-best jewellery, as the sunlight glints off the water in the drum that will need refilling again in the morning. It's your job to make sure it's full for everyone by breakfast.

For now though, you play, hurtling from friend to friend, cousin to cousin, as freely as an old car tyre being rolled downhill past the houses with the old men smoking their pipes in their rocking chairs on their verandas.

Everyone in Dalvey is talking about tonight. A big sound system is being set up: big boxes with buttons and little knobs and flashing lights. Every now and then, you hear the thumping of the bass as they test all is in order for later.

A team of dreadlocked workers from Duckenfield to Golden Grove help put it all together, they smoke spliff after spliff and swig golden-brown rum and laugh and sweat and cuss as they pile everything up, box on top of box. The smell of the kerosene they use to feed the generator makes your eyes sting more than the ganja.

It takes all day to set everything up, and with your own eyes you watch the monster come to life. The many wires like snakes.

You are amazed by the power and energy of something that wasn't alive this morning.

By nightfall, everything is ready.

Little makeshift rum shacks have been built for the grown-ups to drink themselves happy, or angry, or both. And the people eat – jerk chicken, jerk fish – as the youts, younger than you, run and run until they are dizzy, drunk off the fun, the fumes and the extra-loud music.

You like this record, 'Cherry, Oh Baby'. The floor shakes and your ears throb with the dancehall beat as you join the adults shaking their leg in front of the quick-talking DJ.

It doesn't take long, within seconds your body has this great urge to move, like your bones can't be stopped even if they want to. As the record plays, you make yourself the star. Movements start small but get bigger beat by beat.

As the first singer is joined by a second, the track is in full swing. You thrust left, then thrust right with the energy of a famous hotshot superstar. It's a happy tune and the vocals make your insides feel warm. You want to jump and move and dance until you are too tired to dance anymore.

The chorus comes in big and powerful.

You like to dance because you like to move, you like to show off sometimes. You like to be the centre of attention, make people watch, make people laugh, make people admire. You wiggle your hips to the beat. You swivel your ankles, the vibrations sliding all through your body.

You do figure-eights with your hips, swing and spin them, shimmy to your right twice, then allow your left side to copy. You are dancing with rhythm, dancing with heart; the raspy Jamaican tones making your soul feel strong.

Then you switch it up, pick up the pace, start bopping your head side to side: one second this way, one second the other.

Eyesight gets foggy and you start pulling a funny face, the music has you moving mad. You bite your bottom lip and shunt your pelvis forward, then back, and forwards again. You have a little routine going, a little two-step. Hip bones pound the air vigorously.

As a new song starts to play, tiring, you leave the dancefloor for a moment to catch your breath.

Away from the noise, behind the curtain of some trees, you hear some storyteller, an elder, gathering the little ones to tell them a tale. Probably a story with a goody and a baddy and a hidden message – like one of them sermons you hear in church – and an ending that either makes you think, or laugh long into the night.

Cross-legged, you join in to listen for a bit. You like the stories that make you think about what is the right and wrong thing to do in a situation, the stories that teach you things.

The party won't stop till the young ones have been hurried to bed and the adults have run out of rum.

●   ●   ●

The news feels like a strange fruit, weird at first, then sweet. The time has come; enough money has been saved, you and your little sister Joice are moving to Sheffield.

Your stomach suddenly feels tense, like you've just drunk a punch made from a mixture of excitement and sadness. The combination gives you a funny tummy. Your brain feels odd too: memories shifting.

You've read your parents' letters and skimmed through the pages of the *Gleaner* and know a bit about the streets in England that are paved with gold, but not too much about what it will be like when you get there.

Maybe you should have listened more carefully in class when you were learning about the United Kingdom, to know what it's like, how life will be for you when you reach.

Usually, when the grown-ups who can actually read have finished with the paper, you do not really concentrate on the words, instead you like to make kites with them, sharply folded and attached to a long piece of string to run about with out in the field.

You do remember when the Queen came to visit and you saw all the soldiers in their bright red-and-black uniforms marching through town; now you will get to see her and all her guards and the rest of the monarchy all the time when you get there.

You are soon to leave the dirt roads with the junk heaped on the side that cuts up your feet if you don't tread careful. The pile of other people's trash and the sharp-edged stones that can take a toenail off and can only be made better with Bluestone. You are leaving the newly tarred road that gets too hot and starts to melt when the sun shines bright. The closeness of your cousins who live just over the way. The strict teachers who slide a pencil through your hair in the mornings before school starts to make sure your afro's been combed out properly. The macca trees with the sharp sharp prickles. The glass

Pepsi bottles to bring back to the shop for a couple of coins.

You are leaving it all.

No more chicken chasing. No more hearing about Cuba – the bad guys – on the radio. No more Christmas tree making using broken twigs with the bark stripped off. No more library vans with a vehicle full of books, sometimes Penguin ones. No more foraging for fresh mangos, pears, bananas, guineps and jack-fruit picked straight from the tree. No more lemonade making. No more trucks coming round full of ice covered in sawdust, and running home quick before the blocks start to melt. No more hanging around with Benny and Catherine Macpherson from down Morant Bay.

Now, you will probably not be buried with your other family members on the communal plot. The graveyard with Rennies you never met or barely knew.

Your mum and dad, your other brothers and sisters who you have yet to meet, are waiting for you on the other side of the world. They'll pick you both up when you land at a place called Heathrow, where your new life will begin.

It's been three or four years now since you have seen them last, your parents; you can't quite remember the details of their faces, the shape of their bodies and the way they spoke. What their skin smells like.

For the last time, perched on the side of the field hugging your knees, you watch the men play cricket, the lucky players select-ed to represent the parish. Round here, everyone wants to be the number one fast bowler, build up speed, get a good clean throw and show off their wicket by sliding on their knees like showmen.

Sometimes, you look at them doing it wrong, not standing right, not bending their arm correctly as they bowl – or crouching wrong as a fielder, and judge them. Technique is so important; some players should get that right before they start celebrating.

Stepping up to the crease, following a long rub of the ball on his cricket whites, here comes another slow-spinning shot, better looking than the one before.

The batsman looks in trouble. You hear it before you see it, the sound of the stumps smashing and the steady elevation of the umpire's index finger signalling that he is now out. The batsman's half-hearted complaints about the quality of the bowler's delivery are ignored by the figure in the middle. Whether he likes it or not, the umpire's decision is final, and must be obeyed.

Before you know it, sooner than you think, you're driven to the airport by your aunt: you and your sister. It is time to leave Jamaica and head for England, leave your home and everything you know, to go to where you will start a new life in a new place you have never been before.

You kiss your aunt goodbye, not knowing when you will see her again. Not sure when you will see Uncle Tim and Miss Marcia. Not knowing when you will see the sea. Not knowing just how different life will be. Not knowing whether you will make friends like the ones you have here. Not knowing whether you will be the fastest over there.

Each journey starts with a single step. You knew this time would come one day, but didn't know how strange it would feel as you climb aboard the biggest machine you've ever seen, Joice just ahead.

The smell of the plane fuel makes your nostrils tingle.

This is your first time on a plane and everything is noisy and big and busy and scary but you have to be brave as you take off. You are four years older than your sister, so it is your big brother responsibility to look after her like a dad might.

You show no fear, flying within touching distance of the sun, over the blue of the sea, through the clouds, the plane jiggling like an old lady's batty at a ska dance.

From the trolley, the lady stewardess gives you and your sister a weird foil tray that is warm to touch and smells funny. When you peel off the wrapper, you turn your nose up at what you see inside, some strange-looking meat, mashed Irish potatoes, and something else she says are mushrooms. Not keen, you pinch one with your fingers and pull a disgusted face as watery brown liquid drips down the side of your hand.

This is not the food you are used to consuming. You don't like the look or smell of them and definitely do not want to eat things you've seen grow on trees. They are not eaten in Dalvey, they are fungi, you learnt in school.

Are you going to try it? you ask Joice, navigating your fork around the fleshy fungus to get to the meat.

I'd rather go hungry, she says with eight-year-old defiance.

I'll try it if you do, you lie.

She shakes her head decisively as she scoops up a spoonful of potato and shoves it in her tiny mouth. After a few unsure chews, her face confirms it is safe.

Are you hot? you question as she gulps down her mash.

Yes, and my ears feel funny.

You stroke the sweat off her forehead with your thumb and smile. It's your responsibility to make her feel comfortable, even though the insides of your ears feel strange too, like they are growing and shrinking at the same time.

It's going to be fine, you say, it will be colder soon.

As the plane lowers to land, you see your new home get bigger and bigger, nearer and nearer. Soon you will be with your mum and dad and your brothers and sisters in your new home where they already live.

When the wheels touch the tarmac and the pilot slams on the brakes, everyone claps and you're not completely sure why.

With wrist-grabbing urgency, you clutch your sister's little arm, as you lead the way through airport security and the passport control people. It's all knees and bags and people rushing around to meet their families and go to their fancy big English homes.

Suitcases are lugged and tugged from every direction, you feel lost as they bash into you from left, right and centre. You try to dodge them like it's a game but there are too many of them to win and break free.

You are saved by strangely familiar faces, their smiles like lights at the end of the tunnel, your mum and dad.

Life is about survival, and thank God you've made it to your new life in one piece.

• • •

So this is England, the so-called Mother Country. It is July and it is cold.

You join your mum, dad, uncles and aunties, brothers and sisters in a minibus along a long and busy road from Heathrow to Sheffield. It will take over three hours to get there, you have overheard.

Hundreds of motor vehicles, many more than you saw back home, speed past like it is a race they are running.

Unlike where you have come from, the road here has lights and no big potholes and this is shocking to you, details you didn't expect.

You look out the window and see houses that are two storeys tall and have chimneys sticking out of the top of them. In Jamaica, unless you live in Kingston, none of the houses are as tall as the ones that you can see now.

Your other brothers and sisters and cousins play games to pass the time, they are relaxed enough around everybody to try to spot cars with number plates in alphabetical order. You want to be a part of it too, but you're too nervous to join in, and their words aren't coming through clear either, the sounds from their mouths come out all strange like a record that is on the wrong setting and has been sped up too fast.

Your two youngest sisters were born here and they speak like younger versions of the crackly voices you hear on BBC World Service. You don't really catch what they are saying, they are speaking so quickly, your brain has to work hard to understand just a little bit of what is going on. The problem is contagious. When you speak they look at you funny as if you're speaking a completely different language.

At least you are not alone. Inside, you know it will take a while for everything to feel normal, for you two to adjust to your new lives here. For you both to fit in.

Once they get to Z, spotted in the form of a green Ford Cortina, they move on to a game of I Spy.

Peering out still, you notice the grass outside is greener and the fields are big but the clouds are coloured dirty. After a long time, along a long road, you arrive into a city that must be Sheffield. A city that you will have to find your feet in. Somewhere in the background, you can hear the clink clank of machinery.

Everybody is moving back and forth like ants, everybody has somewhere to go, something to do. You see hundreds of people, with their caps and coats, filing in and out of factories at pace.

It will take time for you to understand the routine of it all, where exactly you will sleep, whose clothes you will wear to keep warm. It won't be easy. You've already been told that times were tough when your parents first arrived, sharing the house with friends to save money. Who would sleep where managed in shifts. One couple in the bed in the morning, while the other couple worked.

Here, there are far more white faces than black ones, but this doesn't bother you too much. In Jamaica, the prime minister used to be Norman Manley, a white man who spoke like a regular Jamaican when he addressed the nation over the radio.

You are used to seeing people with white skin, but maybe not so many as you see today though. The girls here, even the black girls, are not as black as the ones from back home and look shinier than you expected.

The minibus pulls up outside your new home, where you will eat, run, play, laugh, work, sleep. The Wybourn is the right place for all of you because of the steel, you've been told. Your parents knew people who settled in Sheffield, worked at the Works: brick, engineering and manufacturing. Unlike your mum's side, which is a bit more middle class, your dad comes from a line of ancestors who have been good with their hands, manual work, farming and that sort of thing, to look after themselves, to survive.

Here, already, in England, in Sheffield, you have cousins who came here before you did and have made it their new home like you must do.

They used to live in Jamaica years ago and want to know what life is like now, want to know what has changed, if anything at all. They ask you questions about people from back home you only vaguely know.

More or less as soon as you park up, outside a house that is smaller than you expected, people from the street have come out of their little houses, to greet you and your sister, welcome you both to your new home, welcome you to the area with their funny voices, smiley faces and cheek-pinching fingers.

Stepping out, the smell of the air is different, harder to breathe in somehow.

As soon as you get inside, your sisters are desperate to show you their toys and teddies. Although you're not really interested in playing with dolls, you're happy they are excited and trying to make you feel at home.

It will only take a little while for the strangeness to feel normal, you think.

Finally, you're a unit now, all together, one family.

And you're going to have to settle here, to survive. There's no flying back now.

1992

You've been crabbing your way up the refereeing ladder. Crabbing and flagging. Flag waving and not drowning, yet. You have risen through the ranks, from jumpers for goalposts, to grassroots, Sunday Junior Leagues, Sheffield County Senior League, Unibond Northern Premier League, Football League line, First Division line, and today, to finding yourself here in north London with the big boys.

No doubt about it, this is the biggest game of your career so far: FA Cup semi-final, Liverpool vs Portsmouth. You, Uri, Linesman. Lino. Man with the flag on the side, assistant to the match referee in the middle, here, this afternoon, down the M1, at Arsenal's Highbury.

A tight little stadium in a small pocket of north London. An old-fashioned stadium, with old-fashioned art deco stands, with the North Bank facing the Clock End. An old-fashioned stadium with no breathing space between the players and fans, between *you* and the fans.

The noise, as kick-off approaches, skin-prickling: back-and-forth chanting between the reds and blues resonates around this little stadium; one team just one game away from Wembley and a cup final watched by millions. And then there's you, a black official, a small part – some might say – on a huge day of football.

As you emerge from the tiny tunnel here at Highbury, there's a carnival atmosphere in the stands of this tight little stadium in this small pocket of north London: singing, bells and all the whistles come together to create a cacophonous noise.

Fans fill every corner of this little ground, not a spare seat in sight, every soul making their voice heard. Red and white seats sat on by red and blue fans. Balloons everywhere.

FA Cup day is, and always has been, a special day in the calendar. Not just your average Saturday, not just your average football match. It's bigger, better, more historic.

One day, you think, as you take in the spectacle of the scene, you will referee the FA Cup final. Be the actual man in the middle, the first black official to have the honour. This is your goal, your era-defining once-in-a-lifetime dream you will strive to achieve.

But first you must earn your stripes, keep your eyes open and your ears to the ground, learn the lessons as a linesman first, in order to be the best referee later.

In every stand, somewhere in the blur of bodies, kids have been picked up and hoisted onto shoulders to get a better view of their shaggy-haired superstars, their idols from their Blu Tacked posters on their bedroom walls right in front of their eyes, in the flesh. Young fans with wide smiles and toothy grins here to see Rush and Barnes and McManaman and Thomas. Fans clambering up metal fences to get a closer look at the players warming up, pinging balls from one side of the half to the other, working up a sweat, getting in the zone.

A day they won't forget, a day you won't either, squeezing the handle of your fluorescent flag tight as you check for holes in the net at the North Bank end.

Liverpool favourites, Portsmouth the underdogs from the Second Division and you, Uri, on the line for this massive massive game.

Perfect cup semi-final conditions, with freshly cut grass for the players to knock the ball about.

You shake hands with the skippers, Mark Wright and Martin Kuhl, witness the coin toss, absorb the last few reassuring words from Martin Bodenham, the man in the middle, and shuffle into position, benchside.

A few last seconds to soak it all up before it all begins, think how far you've come, as you wait for that first whistle. From Dalvey Pier to Sheffield to an FA Cup semi-final. You've plied your trade on wind-strewn public playing fields across the north of England, you've come from being a young black boy from Jamaica living in the Wybourn and barely understanding the words of your brothers, to here, to this, to now.

Being successful back home would have been unlikely, but to be here, as a black man, as an outsider, as a referee – not something many would have predicted. But you must stay focused, the job isn't done yet, the game hasn't even started.

On the line, with your back to them, you can't see their eyes, can't see their funny faces gawking when they see *you* are the man with the flag. A black man. Not that you let what they might think bother you too much. You just do your job, gallop into position, keep your eyes on the field of play and crab down the line to get in line with the last defender.

You'll hear the odd unsavoury comment, whispered words and little jokes made at your expense, you always do, but you take whatever skin-deep slur they want to say in your stride. You've been conditioned to.

From behind you, you hear the rustle of a crisp packet, you hear the muttering and the spluttering and the laughing and every swear word you can imagine, nothing you've not heard before. It's part and parcel of the game, part and parcel of football culture. You're on a mission to the top and their words are water off a duck's back.

All the world's a stage, Shakespeare said, and all the men and women merely players. Football is a pantomime at the best of times, a theatre, a show, and the officials are the villains of the piece, always the villains of the piece. The bad guys. You know that now.

Their words don't hurt as much as a bad performance, so you ignore them and keep your focus.

The Liverpool fans start singing 'You'll Never Walk Alone', and the sounds of that famous song sung in unmistakably Scouse tones make the hairs on the back of your neck stand up.

You jog on the spot, the adrenalin urging you to move. The blue fans chant *Play up Pompey! Pompey play up!* They're all sat at the other end of the stadium to you, a sea of blue.

Union Jack flags and Goodmans-sponsored replica tops bouncing up and down. It's clear their fans are ready to play their part in an upset.

You look across the pitch, look along the line, follow the movements of the last defender. That's the thing about being a linesman, it's an art, and how great thou art; you sort of have to look in three directions at once. It's all fine margins, millimetres. Currently though, you have your eyes on the centre-back, like a supermarket security guard eyeballing a delinquent who looks like he's about to nick something.

Kick-off.

You shuffle left, you shuffle right: stand, skip, sprint.

'Walk the dog.'

You help award throw-ins, corners and goal kicks.

You're in line with the last man, moving a little to the left, then a little to the right, looking to see if there's an offside in the offing. Mark Chamberlain, the black lad from Portsmouth, number ten, has an early pop on goal but drags his shot well wide and you award the goal kick with a whoosh then a jab of your flag.

You shuffle then stand. Step left, step right. Crouch down, squint your eyes, follow the to and fro, players blurred into one, red into blue to make purple. The defender moving out, the attacker advancing. The split-second of a decision. The educated guess.

Tackles fly in, hearts and guts and glory. Martin gives nothing, tries to let this FA Cup semi-final flow.

The ball drops for Ian Rush in the box on the other side of the Highbury pitch to you. He swivels and shoots quickly, aware of the onrushing Pompey keeper putting pressure on, making himself big, spreading himself out, but the ball crashes into the side net. The Liverpool fans groan, heads in their hands.

You shuffle and stand, all action at the other end, Liverpool looking dangerous. Another sweeping move. Another ball whipped in at pace by McManaman, another chance for Liverpool to take the lead in this massive cup tie, missed.

You shuffle and stand, sidle down the line.

The game heats up. You start to sweat as you sprint into a position to spot what you need to see. You shuffle left, you shuffle right.

Martin awards Liverpool a free kick in a dangerous area. Awford tripping McManaman.

You're watching from afar, stood on the halfway line as number five, Ronnie Whelan, prepares to take the kick with his left foot.

Martin gets into position, you hold yours.

The ball is feathered in at pace but the header is scooped over the bar by Thomas. The Liverpool fans, mostly at your end, on their feet behind you, know that was a golden opportunity to go one up.

You shuffle left, you shuffle right. Skip, sprint and crab. Award a goal kick, award a corner, make eye contact with Martin, award a free kick and crab some more. You scurry down the line, get in line with the last defender.

Ball dinked in by Portsmouth, only half cleared. The Liverpool backline have pushed up, but not quickly enough and the ball drops for the Pompey skipper, Kuhl, who is onside, in space in the penalty box. Definitely, almost certainly, onside. It's tight but he's on and in space. He volleys first time, but volleys it too high over the bar.

Portsmouth are matching their opponents stride for stride now and you're just inches away from the action, inches away from another testing cross into the danger area; the Liverpool defence are struggling to hold on as half-time approaches.

Darren Anderton whips it in dangerously from the corner and Liverpool can't clear their lines. You crab left, you crab right, trying to stay in line with the last defender, the ever-changing, ever-moving last defender. The ball lands at the feet of a Pompey player and is backheeled goalwards but Grobbelaar makes an impressive acrobatic save.

The ball drops loose again. It's a melee in the box, bodies and colours blurred into one.

Liverpool cling on, clear a succession of shots off the line. And at the end of all of it, Grobbelaar somehow scoops up the loose ball and Liverpool survive, just.

Into the second half and Martin has some work to do. Rush lunges in late on the Pompey skipper and both players spring up and square up to each other. Handbags at ten paces really, nothing Martin can't handle.

You shuffle left, you shuffle right: stand, skip, sprint.

It's still nil–nil after ninety minutes, the game enters extra time but you've got lots in the tank still, the adrenalin of the occasion giving you all the energy you need.

The crowd still sing and chant, both sets of fans sensing victory, and a big day out at Wembley. Tension felt all round this little stadium, in this tiny pocket of north London.

Nerves frayed, legs tiring.

Portsmouth launch it long through the middle and the ball drops for Anderton who composes himself, adjusts his body shape and strikes the bouncing ball past Grobbelaar and into the corner of the goal.

The blue side of the stadium erupts; the underdogs take the lead in extra time of this semi-final, causing pandemonium in the Pompey end.

One–nil Portsmouth.

You expect with just minutes to go and Liverpool now needing an equaliser to stay in the cup, the action will all be down your end from now.

Liverpool need to score.

Barnes lines up a free kick in a dangerous position, you stay in line with the Pompey wall. You're concentrating hard now, eyes fixed on the last line of defence. Liverpool need something for any chance to get to Wembley.

You shuffle and stand.

The wall edge forward, you crab left.

Barnes' free kick is fizzed goalbound and the keeper scrambles over to his left at full stretch. The ball pings the inside of the post and bounces out, you hear the gasps from the Liverpool fans behind you. They, and you, can't believe that hasn't gone in. But their disbelief lasts less than a second as Whelan reacts quickest to the rebound and has the easiest of tap-ins to score an equaliser with not long left on the clock.

The fans go bonkers in the stands, the magic of the cup very much alive.

Martin looks over, checks with you that Whelan was onside. You give him a little nod and shuffle down the line towards the halfway line and into position for the restart. The goal is good. One–all.

On the full-time whistle, you run from the touchline to join Martin in the middle for handshakes.

You've done it, played your part on the biggest stage in the biggest cup competition in the world. The game ends one–one after extra time, so the tie will have to be replayed in a week or so. Different officials will be appointed.

The game may be finished for today but this contest definitely isn't over yet. This, in many ways, is just the beginning, and not just for the two teams.

1994

Fat, thin, young, old, the due-diligent, the early-wormers, the late-arrivers, the broad-shouldered, the thick-skinned, the potty-mouthed, the shit-spouters, the centre-circle hoggers, the match-fee merchants, the deathly quiet, the ones who won't do this for long; you meet all kinds of refs on the circuit. Very rarely any other black ones though, you're an anomaly.

In the summer, after successful interview, you were officially appointed onto the Football League list, and today, the thirteenth of August 1994, you referee your first official game between two professional teams. An Endsleigh Insurance Division Three fixture between Darlington and Preston North End at Feethams.

You arrive at Darlo's quaint little ground in good time, drop off your bag in the changing room, brief your assistants briefly, have a cup of tea and make small talk with board members in the quaint little boardroom of this quaint little ground; keeping busy and smiling still to try and settle the nerves in the belly. It helps that you've been here before as an assistant; you remember your way around.

Not that you're counting, but you must be the first black official to actually referee in the Football League. Emerson Griffith from Barbados regularly ran the line. And there's Alf

Buksh of Fijian descent and Gurnam Singh from India, but you, you're a bona fide black man from Dalvey Pier, Jamaica; on top of managing the game itself, there's definitely added responsibility on your shoulders.

You've set yourself high expectations but something isn't right already. Two hours until kick-off and there's no sign of the away side.

You inspect the field of play, check the nets, ask for today's team sheets and change.

An hour until kick-off, and the stadium is starting to fill up with expectant fans full of start-of-the-season cheer, and still no sign of the away side.

Communication is sparse, information received in fragmented segments like a game of Chinese whispers.

Word reaches you that the Preston team bus has got lost somewhere along the Yorkshire Dales and is now stuck in heavy traffic on the M62. It looks like kick-off will have to be delayed.

You've got to be a people person as a referee, fix things, think fast, think on your feet, be quick off the draw.

This is far from ideal, this is your first game in the Football League as the match referee and something has gone wrong already.

You pace and think, give yourself another five minutes before making any final decisions, pretend you have everything under control. You skim through the handbook looking for the league rules, acquaint yourself with the regulations in this situation.

The options are limited, you've checked, a game of football needs two teams. Kick-off will have to be delayed by half an hour, at least, it has to be.

Breathe in, breathe out, roll your shoulders back and puff out your armour-plated chest, remind yourself that worse things happen.

Pace and think and wait and nibble on a bit of hangnail and poke your head around the corner and *is that them?* and keep moving, lads, keep the blood flowing through those legs and flick through the match programme again and flick through the league handbook again and wet your thumb then rub a scuff mark off your boot and you're sure they'll be here in a minute and *make sure you're ready, lads, because as soon as they arrive we're kicking off* and stretch and contemplate and keep hydrated and sit down and stand up again and try to forget about the four thousand fans waiting out there and don't forget to breathe . . .

Breathe in, breathe out. The Preston team bus finally pulls up just after three, and thankfully the players have changed already.

This is far from ideal, this is your first fixture in the Football League as the match referee but at least, now nearly 3.30, you have two teams where they need to be and a game of football to officiate.

To get off the mark, just five minutes in, you book Darlington's debutant Ian Banks for a foul on Preston's Paul Raynor who tumbles into the advertising hoardings. You show Banks his second yellow and then the red for kicking the ball away a few minutes into the second half.

Despite going down to ten, Darlo cling on.

Honours even.

Final score: nil–nil.

1974

The colours of your feet are all different shades of brown: really light (sole), medium light (in between toes), medium (top of foot and toes), dark (ankle) and really dark (nail on little toe). Actually, the colour of your nail on your little toe looks so dark it's like the colour of tree bark, feels rough like it too.

You scratch at the surface, chip away, pick at it, bit by bit, as you sit on the toilet playing with your feet, pants hung slack round your ankles. You study the shape of your toes, the ridges and grooves, the sprouting of fine black hairs. They feel alien as you wiggle them, spread them in and out again, push them down on the cold floor to make the blood inside move and change colour, light-brown to reddish.

Sheffield looks on through the frosted window. The shadow of the steelworks looming over like a bully, as it gradually grows darker and darker outside. At around this time of year, despite the Clean Air Act, this part of the city can feel smoggier than usual, there's a filth that gets stuck under your fingernails, sticks to the fabric of your clothes, the collars of your shirts – all that muck that can't be washed off in the tub, no matter how hard you scrub.

You have the perfect record in mind to bathe to, you race across the living room and trawl through the dusty collection till you find the tune you are looking for. When you do, you wipe the sleeve clean and blow on the waxy surface, set the speed and drop the needle down carefully. When you hear those first piano keys of Bob and Marcia's 'Young, Gifted and Black', it's showtime. You run to the bathroom, freeing yourself from your jeans and socks on the way, there is not a moment to waste. You dance in front of the mirror, the frameless square screwed into the wall above the sink, you can't stop staring at yourself as you start to dance, staring . . .

. . . staring at the man hanging limp, looking pale and hungry on that old wooden cross above the altar with nails hammered into his bony hands and feet, blood dripping from his palms. The pain of it makes you wince. You don't like to think for too long about how hard it must have been for Him to die for our sins the way he did in the stories you've heard. His bravery and compassion and generosity makes you desperate to make Him proud in everything you do, in every way you can, to make his sacrifice for us worthwhile.

Every Sunday you come here, just like you did back home, dressed in your best clothes, and your smart shoes you polished until your arms got sore. You owe it to Him to be a good Christian. You like leaving the Wybourn and heading here to Park Hill, heading here to St John's, with the miners and the steelworkers; black and white together like a Newcastle United shirt.

Everyone is welcome for marriages, deaths, christenings, food and a chat. The way you see it, going to church is all about community. Here, even the people who don't have much give what they can, including you. The idea of religion, and the reason you like coming, is because you like helping people who do not have a lot. You, more than most people, know what that feels like.

The church warden, Mrs Blackburn, and Mr Everett the vicar are good people. You're pals with their lad Colin. But sometimes, much like today, the sermons drag on a bit and you get distracted by the prospect of having a kickabout with the other lads when the service is finished. God's words get blurry and boredom sets in and makes your head fuzzy, your eyes begin to close slowly as you continue to stare at the dead man watching over the congregation. To make yourself feel better about Jesus' sacrifice for us, you change your mind, he doesn't look dead, you decide, he looks asleep . . .

. . . fast asleep. Your dad is fast asleep upstairs, recovering from a late shift at Marshall's, sleeping off the stickiness of the sweat and soot and the metallic stench of steel. Sheffield steel. Mum is at the hospital, working. They take the role of being parents in shifts, make regular substitutions to look after you and your siblings. Everyone has their role to play to keep the house ticking over.

You and your brothers have an idea, a competition to pass the time, stop you going stir-crazy at home. There's only so many chores you can put up with. You whip off the tablecloth from the dining room table and dash it on the side, gather a handful of books from the shelf and cradle a pile of the thick-spined ones that'll do the job.

The *Encyclopedia Britannica* is too big for what you have in mind, so you use smaller hardbacks, prize them open at about halfway, and line them up across the middle of the table. Everything is done properly, positioned carefully. You choose your bat, a book the right size, the right weight, and after a few practice swings, the scene is set. You have set up the makeshift table tennis court to the perfect specifications.

You start: a one-handed serve, the ball is hit back by your brother, the tennis ball bounces over the books. Bounces . . .

. . . bounces towards you. Out on the field, the cricket ball hurts if it catches your fingers, the cone-shaped bit of your gloves often does more harm than good. It properly stings. The blue pimples are worn down and don't protect your fingers as well as they should, as well as they would have done when they were bought new thirty-odd years ago. Unlike some of the other lads, you are old enough and tall enough not to look silly in the 'one size fits all' pads. Lucky for you, they fit you well enough without you looking as stupid as some of the smaller boys.

It's a lucky dip what you get to pick from the box, it's all very basic and although some of the other boys laugh and pull faces as they plunge their hands in and fish out some dingy cricket whites, you are grateful to have any equipment at all. Back in Jamaica, you remember having nothing, so having anything at all to protect you from the missile of the red ball bounced to you at pace is a bonus.

When you first arrived from back home, it was rounders everyone played. A different sport altogether. You loved using the wooden bat to hit the tennis ball, was far easier to score runs in than cricket. Most of the time, you didn't even have to hit the ball that far because whenever it looked like you were in danger of being run out, more often than not somebody would drop the ball and it would roll loose, leaving you to run all the way round without too much trouble.

Running, cricket, rounders, no matter what it is, to you it's important to win, important to show off your ability, out-skill your opponent. Living with your competitive brothers is probably why you're so sporty.

You step up to the crease, stand in front of the wickets: wrists, knees and hips angled into shape. The ball is bowled, bounced towards you at a good height, a manageable speed. You hit it, hit it well. The fielders chase the ball which fizzes towards the boundary, they run and run . . .

. . . and run. Run around the makeshift track, the lane lines hand-painted by an old council groundsman with unsteady hands – the surface is uneven and bumpy but you try not to concentrate too much on the floor but instead look ahead, chase down the current race leader, edge yourself closer and closer to the finish line which curves into sight as you pump your arms and legs.

You run in a pair of old plimsolls, feeling every divot as your feet slap the hard grass with each step. Some of the other kids, the ones from money, from other deep-pocketed posher parts of the city, have full tracksuits, Adidas with the right number of stripes and proper running trainers with the proper spikes.

There are coaches from across Sheffield all lined up on the side, with clipboards and stopwatches around their necks, scouting the hottest talent, the runners good enough to represent county. The runners who could go from county to country, then maybe on to the Olympics one day. As you inch into the lead, your heart beats fast, throbs and throbs . . .

. . . and throbs as you head through the Hurlfield school gates and into the main hall. Although, in your heart of hearts, deep down, you know there's not too much to worry about tonight – you think you're a good student, you always try your best, you're a good lad, cause no trouble for your teachers – and that is what you expect to hear. You have your favourite subjects of course, Geography and Biology, Maths too a bit, subjects you can see the point of. Not so much French and Science though, you're not as good at them as some of the other kids are.

In your family, as much as you love sport, education is very important, so you're not one to mess about, get detentions or anything like that. You come from a line of medics on your mum's side, matrons and nurses, so using education to have a decent career has been drilled into you from young.

To you, one of the best things about school is lunchtime. Not for the food necessarily, nobody don't care much for greasy cheese flan, it's the football you love. Come lunch, Monday to Friday, you wolf down something quick and have a kickabout until you're soaking in your own sweat like a miner. You force yourself to have at least half of school dinner because Mum don't want you looking skinny or she jokes she'll send you back home to Jamaica.

The seriousness of Parents' Evening makes you think about the future and what you want to be when you are older. The career you want to have, how you want to earn money to look after a family of your own one day; how you want to be remembered. You know education is important, but going to college will make you soft round these parts. University would be a challenge coming from the school of hard knocks. Not the done thing for a lad like you from the Wybourn. At the gong, it's probably better to get a job first, a degree can come later.

You're from a place that hates the police, the wicked Babylon, but despite what others might think, you've thought about joining the force, helping to make the community a better place, a place to be proud of by being the right arm of the law. You can picture it already, strutting through the Wybourn and advising people doing wrong what the consequences are, a quiet word, a final warning, a chase, a sprint at speed down a ginnel, a chance to apprehend the bad guys. You understand how wrong it sounds to some – a black man in the police force. A snitch, a Bounty bar, a choc ice, a coconut: black on the out-side, considered a white man within, but it's a role that would play to your strengths, you think.

A product of your environment, your new home, the Wybourn, is a tough tough area, everyone in Sheffield knows it – even though it's just a stone's throw away from the city centre, if there's a crime, then everyone says it must be one of the Wybourn lads – but you're a local now who knows better, there's no malice round here, everyone is just busy doing what they can to feed their families. When you think about it, it's not as bad as people think, people have jobs, everyone works either at the Works or cash-in-hand rag-and-bone bits and bobs: scrap metal work, window cleaning, delivery driving.

Some knocks on the door around here are more welcomed than others. On weekends, you always know when the Alpine man is coming because you can hear the clanking of the glass bottles as he clutches them in between his thick fingers, scurrying from neighbour to neighbour. For you, slurping on a glass of Alpine is a special treat, and so is having a bowl of another favourite of yours – fruit salad from the tin with the cut-up apples, peaches, pears, cherries – perfect with a bit of Carnation Milk.

Early on, after moving here from back home, you're told the best places to go, the people you should know, where you're allowed to go, who to avoid, who to make friends with. There's one particular neighbour in the area who likes to drink a lot, and some people on the Wybourn are a bit funny about her, but she has a son your age who's sound, and you don't mind going round her house, because it's wrong to judge people; she's generous and nicer than what most people think.

Actually, to be honest, mostly everyone on the Wybourn is nice to you, gives you drinks and biscuits and things, because you're part of the community and that's important in order to survive in an area that doesn't have a good reputation. You play your part too: when it snows, you and some of the other lads get shovels out to shift it off the old people's garden paths, there's a proper community spirit round here.

Music brings people together too, records are brought over, from Jamaica to the Wybourn via the States: Desmond Dekker – Ken Boothe – Dennis Brown – Harry J Allstars – Freddie McGregor – Phyllis Dillon – Gregory Issacs – The Maytones – Barrington Levy – Bunny Wailer – Delroy Wilson – Derrick Morgan – The Paragons – John Holt – Alton Ellis – Lord Kitchener – Jimmy Cliff – Mighty Diamonds – Toots and the Maytals – Bob Marley. You like scanning the new record sleeves – studying the words and pictures – put them on and start dancing like you are back home in Dalvey, whining your waist and wiggling and . . .

. . . shuffling your feet, swivelling them, drumming a little beat to a hymn on the church floor until you're told to stop and warned that bad behaviour, as you know already, is blasphemous. Even at fifteen, you are learning that lots of things are blasphemous, so you behave, because the thought of disappointing Him and going to hell worries you more than anything else in the world.

But you're getting fidgety, anxious to kick some ball with the other boys. You pray for friends and family's health and happiness, and you pray for the sermon to be done soon so you can be with the boys.

Everyone is desperate for a touch, a second or two to show off, do a skill they saw on *Match of the Day* (but slide tackles are not allowed, not when you have your 'good good' clothes on). No-one wants to be like the Zaire players, not after the World Cup. Even though they are black and it was special to see them on TV, everyone still laughs about how dumb it was that they didn't even know the basic rules of football, how they booted the ball away from the free kick.

When the damage is done, after a few goals have been scored, toe punts and volleys, and there are scuff marks on your good good shoes, you scurry home and polish them up quick before your mums see. Before your dads have to intervene with the threat of a pelt with his belt. You smooth over the damage with a healthy dose of the black stuff.

You play on the street, you play for Hurlfield, you play for Brunsmeer, you play for The . . .

. . . Windsor. In black Patrick boots, you've tightened the studs with the metal spanner that came with them in the box, and carry them around in oil-skin paper from Fletcher's – the same half-plastic, half-paper bag that is sturdy enough to sledge down Devil's Bump with when it snows. At Hurlfield, representing your school, your coach is Bill Nill. He plays semi-pro for Boston United, and gives you pairs of his old boots. Boots he has worn in proper grounds across the country, with cut grass, straight lines and stands with seats. They feel just right now, proper snug, you've been wearing them around the house when your parents have been asleep or working or both. You've moulded them to your feet and now they fit, more or less, perfectly. You are ready to do damage with them, when duty calls, when that first whistle blows.

As far as you can tell, football is a simple game. A working-class game. Working-class men, working-class words, working-class fans, working-class food, working-class drink, working-class venues. You take the opportunity to play football wherever and whenever you can – after school, you play for Brunsmeer: two areas, one name. Your coach is Ron Leech, who set the club up with his wife, Anne, a dinner lady. You can play centre-half, right-back or centre-mid. Your good mates are Rudy, Pat and Mickey, and you're often the best players on the pitch, you all know each other so well that you can sort of predict what each of you are thinking during a game, you all have the same football brain, some might say.

People have said you have a good engine, tall too, and don't mind getting stuck in. There's never any real moaning or play-acting during the matches, nobody's got time for that, you just keep your head down. It's behaviour that makes you tough, tough enough to play with the big boys, the big boys who are real men. Men with wedding rings and calloused knuckles and double chins and protruding bellies and criminal records and the faint smell of extra-strong, extra-cheap ale on their breath. Men that play for the toughest pub team in the area, probably the whole of England, The Windsor.

They swear and drink but always look after you, know who you are and where you have come from – protect you on and off the pitch. They use their chunky frames to win the initial ball and hold it up – outmuscle their opponent and intimidate the referees. The manager is Paul Wilder, his lad watches from the touchline too sometimes, little Chris.

You're playing well one day when semi-professional team Corby Town come calling. You, Rudy and Mickey Caine get given a trial nearly two hours away from the Wybourn in

Corby, which is a workers' town, you're told, a bit like Sheffield but smaller.

It's nice to feel rated, nice to feel like you have potential,
offered an avenue to the top perhaps. On the day of the trial, you pace about the place, meet the tracksuit-and-clipboard
coaches and see the ground – the setup is more professional
than what you're used to: a stand with a corrugated roof and
seats, and a terrace on three sides that has levels for hundreds
of fans to perch on with their pre-match pie and pint.

Corby Town is a feeder club, you've been told, a regular hunt-
ing ground for professional scouts from nearby Northampton
Town. Even though being scouted is good, and so is the idea
of making a few bob from playing the game you love, it's
far from home and you doubt you'd ever be good enough to
become a top player like the ones you see on TV every week.

A couple of the Corby coaches watch on from the side as the
game begins, note-taking and staring. Everyone wants to be a
professional footballer. Everyone is eager to impress. Everyone wants the ball, 'Uri, Uri, Uri!' they all shout like fans
wanting an autograph as you travel into the attacking half
with the ball at your feet, advancing into the space that has
opened up in front of you. You plant your left foot, shift the
ball onto your right and hammer a dropped-shouldered pop.
You strike it with the corner of your foot to give it that extra
curl and as you make contact, it looks good. The ball arrows
towards the top corner and away from the hands of their goalkeeper, but there's too much curl on it and at the last moment
it swerves away from goal and ends up nearer the corner flag.

The Corby coaches watch on from the side, note-taking and staring . . .

. . . and staring; you're staring at yourself in front of the mirror, the frameless square screwed into the wall above the sink, Bob and Marcia's 'Young, Gifted and Black' still playing in the background but fading.

1996

This morning you were on the bench, presiding over cases in court, but by this evening you'll be right in the middle: magistrate to match official.

As you were coming up through the system, you took what everyone said as gospel, you were young and green (and black), doe-eyed and wet behind the ears. Now you make your own rules, referee your own way, have your own style, your own distinctive way of managing a game of football.

You take no nonsense. You haven't got 'mug' written across your forehead. You've basically seen it all on the field of play down the years, no two scenarios are the same but now you more or less know how to handle every potential difficult situation.

You wanted to be a policeman as a lad and you definitely use this drive to help you keep control on the field of play, help you keep your cool when the temperature rises.

Power hungry? Maybe, subconsciously. But you just like doing what's right, being a force for good and keeping people and positions in check.

Fundamentally though, you believe football, like life, is there to be enjoyed and you intend to do just that tonight at St James' Park, Newcastle, one of the biggest and best

grounds in the country. The same stadium used for some of
the games in this summer's European Championships, the
one where football could have come home if we practised
our penalties.

You've crabbed and flagged your way into the big time and
tonight is probably the biggest game of your career so far as
the actual referee, as the man in the middle.

Just two seasons ago, you were appointed to the Football League,
just last month you were refereeing a Division Three game at
Hereford United in front of three thousand fans, but tonight,
you'll be strutting your stuff in front of over thirty-five thousand in the third round of the League Cup.

Tonight, you're a Football League referee, not doing the rounds
in Division One, Two or Three, but refereeing a top Premiership team; you must be doing something right.

It's been a few months since Kevin Keegan's already-famous 'I
would love it if we beat them' rant live on Sky Sports, and even
though Newcastle narrowly missed out on the title last season
to Manchester United, they are still one of the top teams in
the country, 'The Entertainers' they have been labelled by the
press and you can't wait to go face to face with the best.

You don't get nervous, you're aware of your responsibilities
and how important the game is. A creature of routine, tonight
you'll adopt the same style that got you this far; you'll try to
talk, cajole the players, say hello and have a laugh if you can.
If they do something well, then you'll tell them. It's important to establish the right rapport, build the right bonds.

You'll explain a decision when asked, they may not agree but your word is final.

The whole of Newcastle are still celebrating their five–nil win over Manchester United just three days ago. But even though the fans here are still reliving the memories of Sunday afternoon, they'll know they can't afford to be complacent in tonight's game against Oldham Athletic in the Coca Cola League Cup.

You've done your homework, you know the much-favoured home side will want to avoid the embarrassment of this potential banana skin against a Division One outfit. But you can't let league position colour your judgement; like always, you harbour no preconceptions, there'll be no favouritism.

Your appointment is a risk, but this risk has legs. You definitely feel fit enough to be here, among the best; you're six-foot-two, nearly sixteen stone and have been doing martial arts since you were a lad.

Still running too, always running, you train at the Don Valley alongside the Sheffield Eagles rugby league lads, do bits and pieces with the Sheffield City Trust, manage the numerous leisure facilities, use the numerous leisure facilities. You work flat out to be the fittest.

You arrive, drop your bag off, say your hellos, inspect the field of play, look around at the four impressive stands: The Sir John Hall (North), The East Stand (East), The Gallowgate Road End (South) and the Milburn Stand (West). It's quite a stadium, there's quite the energy in the air.

Newcastle United:

Hislop

Barton   Albert   Peacock   Elliott

Clark   Batty   Beardsley   Ginola

Ferdinand   Asprilla

Oldham Athletic:

Kelly

Halle   Fleming   McNiven   Redmond   Serrant

Beresford   Örlygsson   Rickers

Banger   Barlow

A little disappointingly to you, Newcastle's record signing, Alan Shearer – bought for £15 million from Blackburn Rovers – doesn't make the squad. The world's most expensive footballer is rested, or injured perhaps.

He is already a hero round these parts, on the back of many shirts, the subject of many merry songs.

Watching it from home this summer, you saw Shearer shine at the European Championships. And even though England were knocked out in the semis, he still finished the tournament's top goalscorer.

In front of a vociferous Wembley crowd, nearly all singing 'Three Lions' at the top of their lungs, the England vs Holland game stands out. Shearer at his bruising best; striking up a formidable partnership with Teddy Sheringham, between them running the Dutch defence ragged.

After Paul Ince was fouled in the box, Shearer smashed home a first-half penalty to make it one–nil, and then thundered a close-range shot into the top corner in the second half to make it three. Holland grabbed a late consolation, but it finished four–one and England cruised into the quarter-finals.

The one and only Alan Shearer, the all-action darling of the nation's hearts: rugged, well built, physically strong and deadly in the air, you will have to wait till next time, if there is one, to face the great man himself.

For now, you, the justice of the peace, lead the two teams out to the famous sound of 'Going Home: Theme of the Local Hero' blaring and high-spirited Geordie fans cheering, jollying it up in the stands, bouncing and buoyant.

This is a thrill, a rush of blood to the head, you are submerged by a wave of joy. You feel lucky, juggling the eruption of emotion inside, trying to harness the energy of the occasion; it's nights like these, moments like these that keep you going in the hardest of times, in the hardest of games. It's for nights like these that make you want to get to the top: referee at Anfield and Old Trafford and the FA Cup final at Wembley one day maybe.

Kick-off: that first voice is yours.

You award a goal kick with a strong flat hand, keeping signals clean and crisp.

The game has started quickly and not much has happened yet. You jog backwards from the penalty area, always keeping your eyes on the field of play, keeping your eyes on the goalkeeper, just in case; anything can happen, there is no script in football.

You reverse into position like a car might, parallel parking, craning your neck left, then right to see what's behind you, so you don't crash into anyone en route to your dropping zone.

You make the players aware that you are watching. Watching for something illicit, something illegal.

For a team struggling at the bottom of Division One, Oldham have started strongly but it's the home side who go on the attack.

Newcastle's left-back, Robbie Elliott, bursts into the penalty box with a dogged run from the back, the home crowd rise to their feet as one.

He advances into the penalty area. You advance into the penalty area.

He rides one challenge, rides another, dribbles it past the keeper who goes to ground early, gets to the byline and centres it towards Ferdinand waiting in the middle.

The ball in is blocked by the hand of Oldham's Craig Fleming and you have no other option. You point to the spot you're standing on and despite the complaints and the protests, you do not change your mind: penalty.

Peter Beardsley runs up and smashes it home to make it one–nil to the Magpies after just twenty-five minutes.

The Oldham fans sing even when they're not winning. Throughout the second half, you can hear the away fans chant, much louder than the home ones at the moment, as so often can be the case in a cup game.

You give a goal kick and run backwards into position.

You book two Newcastle United players: Philippe Albert and Darren Peacock. Two of the goalscorers from their big win on Sunday.

The underdogs Oldham run their hearts out in the second half but despite their efforts can't find an equaliser and the game ends one–nil to Newcastle, who go through to the fourth round of the League Cup.

You are playfully embraced by David Ginola as you head down the tunnel. One superstar embracing a future one.

After the game, referring to your performance, you hear Newcastle United manager Kevin Keegan tell the Sky cameras: 'You didn't really notice he was there.'

This must mean you had a good game.

• • •

It's December eighteenth weather in Stockport, freezing cold and pissing it down.

Like Newcastle United, you've made it to the next round of the Coca Cola League Cup.

Tonight, you're in the middle for a fourth-round replay between Second Division Stockport County and Premiership side West Ham United; a game that's being broadcast to millions live on Sky Sports.

The rain falls hard at kick-off. The home fans have the lion's share of this lion's den, nearly ten thousand spectators shoehorned into this little windswept ramshackle ground, making their voices heard loud and clear for the people in the back to hear in the most Greater Manchester of weathers.

The pitch cuts up within minutes as the rain falls faster and tackles fly in.

As predicted, Julian Dicks gives the favourites from east London the lead from a corner halfway through the first half.

But just a minute later, down the other end, West Ham United's striker Iain Dowie times his header all wrong as he leaps up and miscues the ball into his own net to make it one–all. Definitely one of the most comical own goals you have witnessed.

The players slip and slide but you remain firm-footed as the rain falls faster and harder on the Edgeley Park pitch.

Just moments after equalising, twenty-seven minutes or so gone on the clock, Stockport striker Brett Angell angles a header home to give the home side the lead.

And through the downpour, and with the roar of the home

faithful behind them from the first minute to the ninetieth, Dave Jones' Stockport County hold on to progress to the quarter-final of the Coca Cola League Cup.

As the Stockport fans sing and stagger their way home, many will wonder how far their little County can go in the competition; but to you, the real question is, how far can *you* go? You have dreams too, you know.

1997

Every step savoured as you inspect the field of play in your smart shoes, suit and tie. You can't help but smile at how far you've come; it's hard not to think about the journey you've taken, when you started from the bottom and now you're here. Real trench baby, you came from the mud: born in Jamaica, grew up on the Wybourn, club linos, cabbage-patch pitches, dirty racist looks and dirtier racist words. Now look at you. Top boy.

Embrace every second, you tell yourself, take in every corner decision, every little throw-in, let your eyes be a camera snapping scenes from the game for your brain to store for later, to remember years down the line. You don't want to forget a single moment in five, ten, fifty years' time.

You're determined to keep the momentum going, get to the very top, be the very best you can be and hopefully it's enough to referee some of the biggest and best games in the country, maybe even the world. You've refereed big games before, your showreel highlights include high-octane top-of-the-table clashes and county cup finals, but this is your biggest game yet, in the biggest of stadiums.

For years now, you've dreamt of receiving news of being appointed as the match referee for a final at Wembley ever since the prospect of it looked potentially possible.

You've had a good season, you're on the brink of a promotion to the Premiership, some are suggesting, so you've earned this, a day out in front of a big crowd in a big stadium.

You were here just two weeks ago, fourth official for the FA Vase final between Whitby Town and North Ferriby United. Graham Poll the referee.

But today is different.

For years now, you've imagined walking out onto the Wembley pitch and breathing in the Wembley turf, hearing the echoing roar of the fans as you emerge from the tunnel, clutching the match ball, and being the black man in the middle of the biggest and best stadium in the country.

Wembley: the home of English football.

Wembley: the Twin Towers, like two Sheffield cooling towers.

Today isn't quite the FA Cup final, no, that day will come. Today is the Second Division play-off final between Crewe Alexandra and Brentford.

The FA Cup final is the best appointment you can get as a ref, the pinnacle of the profession, an honour that can be bestowed on you just once in your career, if you're lucky, if you're good enough.

And that day will come.

It's your goal, the dream that keeps you awake at night, that keeps you going when the pitches are shit and the potty- mouthed players aren't playing ball. It's this thought of walking down Wembley Way on cup final day, marching out of the tunnel with the matchday mascots, shaking hands with Her Majesty, mumbling 'God Save the Queen', that keeps you going.

Brentford fans haven't had far to travel, a couple of tube trains. Crewe fans have had a longer journey but aren't here to just make up the numbers, they have a good young side and will fancy their chances.

Pre-match instructions uttered, boots laced up, smile wide, heart full.

The goosebumps, as you emerge into the sunlight, never lie.

The stands a sea of red, giant flags swishing left to right in great swathes, New Labour, Tony Blair, D:Ream 'Things Can Only Get Better' red.

You shake hands, share smiles and stand authoritatively with your hands behind your back and the match ball at your feet.

Dario Gradi, the Crewe manager, is in good spirits, as is the Brentford manager, David Webb; the omens look good.

A little smile and a little wave to Roseanne and little Crystal in the crowd. This is your moment to make all of the Rennies proud, show them that the sacrifices you've made, and they've endured down the years to get here, have all been worth it. There are tears in your eyes that need holding back.

Your legs feel a little heavy as you plod into your starting position; the weight of the occasion, this big game in this big stadium.

You count the players, give your assistants a thumbs-up, and with a big intake of breath, blow that first whistle to start.

The game is tight, neither team wants to over-commit, let the other team in, let the other team win.

Gaps are appearing though, areas for the opposition to exploit.

Crewe grow in confidence, have settled into the game, warmed up under the north London sun, beguile Brentford with a couple of nice touches.

Another dangerous-looking ball is whipped in by the Crewe right-back, a gliding cross aimed towards players at the back post.

The ball is floated over and headed down into a dangerous area.

Any action in the box keeps you on your toes, has you on high alert, but no need to run, you are in a good position, slotting in somewhere to see, just outside the D, thinking outside the box, watching as the ball bounces into space.

The hapless Brentford keeper has no chance as Crewe's left-back Shaun Smith smashes the knocked-down ball into the roof of the net to give Crewe the lead after thirty-four minutes.

The Crewe players run off to celebrate; they are on their way to the First Division and their fans delight in the possibility of promotion.

Into the second half and Brentford need something and know it but, just when they begin to look a threat, you show Brentford midfielder Brian Statham a second yellow card, and then the red, for a wild foul on Steve Garvey in the seventy-third minute.

Not an easy thing for you to do in a play-off final, especially at Wembley; you don't want to steal the show, but you do what you have to do, apply the laws how you see them.

You must be only one of a handful of referees ballsy enough to do it. You don't want to ruin anyone's big day, or make a name for yourself, but laws are laws.

Tensions run high after the red card, so you do your best to keep calm and in control, stay one beat ahead, get in position, not let standards slip on this big stage.

Crewe come again, with just minutes to go; look for that second goal to kill off the game using the extra man and the extra space to try and double their lead. The ball breaks to their athletic striker, their number eleven, Dele Adebola, who latches onto it at speed.

He outpaces the Brentford defender who is busting a gut to put pressure on, to get back in time, to stop his team's dream from ending prematurely.

You sprint your diagonal, make your angle.

Adebola waits until the time is right and lays the ball off to his Crewe teammate to swipe a leg at it, but the effort is a tame one and is easily blocked by the Brentford central defender who has retreated to the goal-line.

The last real action of the game. One–nil is the score it stays.

You entertain a few last touches then blow the final whistle. Crewe are promoted to the First Division. You, the match referee, have refereed a big game at Wembley, managed ninety minutes of football in the best stadium in the country.

As you thumb your memento, finger the inscription, you hope this is just the beginning, you hope you'll be back here again.

You soak up the surge of pride that courses through your body before scuttling off the pitch, letting the players wallow in their congratulations or commiserations.

No, today isn't quite the FA Cup final, but that day will come.

• • •

Heard through the grapevine, amongst the whispers and rumours, letters and text messages, significant news is received.

People can say what they like, sticks and stones, but you are now a Premiership referee. You have risen through the ranks, from jumpers for goalposts, to grassroots, Sunday Junior Leagues, Sheffield County Senior League, Unibond Northern Premier League, Football League line, First Division line, to reach the summit of the English footballing pyramid.

You've made it to the top division and today you're at Elland Road for Leeds United vs Crystal Palace.

Dirty Leeds to some, but not to you.

You watched them growing up, glued to *Grandstand*. Billy Bremner. Johnny Giles. Joe Jordan. Eddie Gray. Norman Hunter. Peter Lorimer. Leashless bulldogs with their tails up.

Soldiers.

Gods.

You wouldn't say you supported them, wasn't really allowed where you're from, but there was always something special about watching them as a lad. You couldn't help but be wowed by the way they bullied their opponents, fought for every ball, left a leg in, kicked every shin, brushed off every challenge; their famous never-say-die spirit.

Champions back then, now England's sleeping giants.

Now, here you stand on the hallowed turf of the Leeds pitch, black on green, suited in your finest, about to make history, properly this time.

Fifth-placed Leeds might not have the same pedigree as the team from the seventies but today that doesn't matter. They could play the reserves come kick-off and this day would still be one to remember, one to tell the grandkids.

Here you stand, take two – the first time at Derby County with the floodlight failure didn't count – history-maker, toeing the centre circle of Elland Road, one of the greatest stadiums in the country. Encircled by the East, South, Don Revie and John Charles stands, with their brightly coloured navy-blue and custard-yellow seats.

Thirty thousand fans will soon flood through the turnstiles, singing their hearts out till their throats are sore and the veins are throbbing in their necks. And in certain moments – a contentious penalty appeal, a potential red card, a handball on the line – all eyes will be on you, the match referee.

Then, for those in the stands who hadn't noticed already, they will see who the man in the middle is. Some, not many, will know who you are and the significance of the day.

You better hurry up and get changed, history-maker.

Paul Warhurst heads the visitors in front.

Lombardo doubles Palace's lead.

The Leeds United fans grumble, they know this is not good enough.

But nothing is your fault, you run where you need to go, give what you need to give.

The games ends, without a floodlight failure (or the need for floodlights).

Final score: Leeds United nil, Crystal Palace two.

You issue four yellow cards.

All you think, as you head back into your dressing room, down the same tunnel as some of the footballing greats that have graced this pitch in the past, is *phew*, you're officially a Premiership referee with a full game under your belt finally. *Fucking phew!*

• • •

Next, to Highfield Road, the home of Coventry City. Another Premiership game to build your reputation, assert your name as a top referee in the top division of English football. Another fixture to control, twenty-two professional players and TV cameras to contend with and close analysis on *Match of the Day*.

Des Lynam and Alan Hansen.

Sky Sports' Andy Gray and Richard Keys.

You get the game going and the home side start strongly.

Coventry waste chance after chance but eventually, midway through the second half, make it one–nil. The goal scored by their summer signing, Trond Egil Soltvedt.

Three bookings: Williams for Coventry. Lundekvam and Johansen for Southampton.

Another game at this level ticked off, in front of just under twenty thousand fans. Another important ninety minutes of experience, acclimatising to the faster pace, the better players, the greater stakes.

The twenty-third night of September. A Tuesday. A trip to the brand-new Reebok Stadium to referee Bolton vs Spurs. Only your third game as a Premiership referee. Another game to make a name for yourself, be someone the FA can trust, show the players you mean business.

You will not change your style too much from the style that

got you here: you will smile and try to let the players play and only intervene when you deem it necessary.

It is a style that is working again tonight, so far, as Nathan Blake is fouled by Justin Edinburgh in the Spurs box and you award the home side a penalty.

A momentous decision, if Bolton score from the spot, this will be, at their third attempt here, the first ever goal at their brand-new stadium.

Alan Thompson steps up, strikes the ball left, Ian Walker dives right and it's one–nil Bolton after twenty minutes. The home crowd go wild, a goal that will go down in the history books.

Chris Armstrong equalises for the away side on the seventy-first minute.

The game ends one–all. You caution five players: Vega, Sellars, Fox, Mabbutt and Bergsson.

Next, down to London for Ruud Gullit's Chelsea vs Martin O'Neill's Leicester City. Third against sixth. Assessors in the stand to please, criteria to meet, numbers to crunch: competencies and weightings.

You must be doing something right, to get a game like this; you've clearly made an impressive start to your reign in the top league.

You blow, you run, you glare, you brandish, you blow again. Chelsea win one–nil, the home side get a late late winner through Frank Leboeuf, and you dish out a modest three yellow cards: to Celestine Babayaro, to Frank Sinclair, to Muzzy Izzet.

You're grateful for the opportunity to show everyone what you're made of, show everyone that you're good enough to be at this level. You are not some show pony, you're Uriah Rennie.

Then it's back to Pride Park, where in many ways it all began, to referee the rearranged game from your first fixture of the season between Derby County and Wimbledon. You pray for a decent clean game of football, you pray you make a good impression to the assessors and more importantly, you pray for the floodlights to work.

1977

Quick run round the block, fitness is key, head starting to feel light already, only a mile deep, you keep your head down, eyes to the floor – skip – over – dog – shit – you're leaning a little to the left, swaying to the edge of kerb.

Spirits are high in the city because it's the Queen's Silver Jubilee and every window and shopfront and little kid's face is red, white and blue (there ain't no black in the Union Jack). Street parties have been planned: sausage rolls and pork pies and cups of tea using the fine china for the adults and polystyrene ones for the kids.

In the backdrop, like a headache, the forge from the steel factory pounding. The lava-orange sparks are blinding even with masks on. Through the eruption, what the metal will become is not yet clear.

Sheffield steel, a thousand types, bent and moulded with gloved dirt-black hands. High-grade steel of the highest degree of purity, bent and moulded in fire-red furnaces.

Turn into Norfolk Park, jog through the gates, spot a tramp sitting on the bench up ahead, he looks at you all rough as you run past, the cheap cider got him feeling woozy – *oi you, lad, you an Owl or a Blade?* You don't respond, it ain't derby day, he don't need to know.

You're fluent in football, you play football, you coach football, play away games and come back to home-cooked meals bunged in the oven to keep warm and George Best is drinking again and Clyde Best don't play for West Ham no more and everyone's already getting excited for the World Cup next year down in Argentina.

The boundaries of Bramall Lane have been pushed in: the cricket has gone, football is king. Round here, football is life, football means freedom, football means keepy-uppies to a hundred, a bent crossbar drawn on alleyway walls with heavy-handed white paint, shirts versus skins till sunset, five-a-side, Wembley, two in net till teatime, your dads like cricket and Viv Richards, but this ain't Jamaica no more – none of you support Liverpool, but you all chant 'You'll Never Walk Alone' when you win – *if this is the Commonwealth dream, somebody wake us up already*, you heard an uncle say at the 56 bus stop.

Don't think about running, you're trying not to think about running, but you can't stop thinking about running – East Bank Road, building works, you're coughing up the dust – you see the claw of the digger curled like a cat's paw, nudging old chimneys over, most of the rabbit-hutch pebble-dash houses have been condemned – and there's that lad you know, lives on the Manor like, enemy territory, saw him the other day in Woolies – you run faster, work muscles harder: thighs and groins and hamstrings, you have a sweaty belly.

Your feet creep in and out of view beneath you – right one, then left – your thumbs are sticking up and you're not sure why, your fists are clenched and you're not sure why – why's he looking at you like that? You ain't no nig nog, this ain't *Love Thy Neighbour*, you're not Rudolph Walker's lad – *KBW* painted over with the wrong colour paint – you drink the wind up like it's water, it's nice but not so fresh – really running you are now, each step feeling a little too heavy – the surface underfoot tough, bits of brick from the building site have rolled onto the pavement, rocks and rubble, men with hard hats who read the *Sun* and smoke B&H till the morning haze blows over (but it won't).

Your legs know a route, up and down the seven hills of Sheffield, past the grumpy shopkeeper – this ain't Belfast but the headline today is about some trouble in Northern Ireland, you wouldn't wanna live there, there's always trouble in Northern Ireland – running helps you forget what you do not yet understand.

You're a young black man hoping 'A Change is Gonna Come', not just for you, but for the people of the city who are worried about their jobs, worried about the future, but remain, through it all, ever hopeful. Not everyone round here is fleecing a living, people do what they need to do to get by, to put fritters or fish fingers on the table on a Friday, salt-of-the-earth people, who would give you their last pound and a penny to survive another day, and being black amidst all this uncertainty is a struggle sometimes, you have to work twice as hard just to be seen. That on top of everyday slum-dwelling makes it hard to keep calm and carry on day to day in a tough tough place like the Wybourn.

After years of scrimping and saving to earn their daily bread, squirrelling away enough money to survive from a Sunday to a Sunday, everyone just wants their time in the sun, riding pedalos in Millhouses Park or having a picnic on the green with 99 ice creams and Flakes and a bunch of fresh bananas from Bulbrooks and bottles of Hendo's and Lucozade in orange wrappers to make them feel better when they are poor(ly).

Your old school, Hurlfield, has a strict uniform policy, it's part of the fabric, so students get their gear for the new school year in good time, like you used to, from Fashion Focus on Manor Top. The school bus, the 656, from the Wybourn to Hurlfield via Whites Lane, Manor Oaks, Boundary Road, up Southend Road, down Manor Lane, before turning onto City Road. Woodthorpe vs Wybourn is like United vs Wednesday, a real red-blooded rivalry, so simmer down and pucker up. Years of avoiding silly spats and playground scraps with the Hurlfield big-hitters at the school gates.

Eight under one roof living cheek by jowl. Years of topping and tailing with your brothers, fighting for the hot spot in the middle, feet in mouth, toes touching teeth, and nothing but crumbs in the biscuit tin. Paper-thin walls, paper-thin dreams. Going through puberty in poverty certainly wasn't easy.

Up the stairs and under the underpass. The forge from the steel factory still pounding.

On Friday nights you'll find booze-fuelled fights in Fiesta by fellas in flared trousers. Pride of Yorkshire: Yorkshire Tea, Yorkshire TV, Yorkshire Bank. Free banking for school leavers, wise banking for wise people. The regeneration of the city continues, bricks and rubble and dust and dirt and hopes and dreams, flattened. Unfulfilled shovel-ready ambitions. Even the hardened Sheffield stoics, resolutely Christian, shudder at the prospect of the future.

Matey there has lost his job and all the money he has to his name on the horses. And there was another power cut last night, and the cornershop are selling off their frozen food before it all goes off, and matches are needed to navigate your way round the dark, torches and paraffin lamps just to be seen when the sun goes down, just to know where to go. A black man during a blackout is far from ideal.

Sheaf Works is not a place of work to most as it once was. Sheaf View Hotel doesn't have the best views no more. Tom, Dick, Harry and John Smith drink pints of John Smith's and Stones Ale and toast to dreams of a better future, an upturn of fortunes, a couple more pints now and one for the road. Everyone's working hard today to see tomorrow. Continuing (for now) to make steel for the factory, steel for the home, steel for other industries until they are told to make no more. Just there, over the road and then on a bit, a cough and a spit, the craftsmen have been making cutlery for centuries. Made in Sheffield. Made in England. The forge from the steel factory still pounding.

Your arms are working hard now, pushing you forward – you run past parked cars and chase moving ones – the Morris Minors and Minis, you won't find a Jag round here, this ain't bloody Buckingham Palace! The sun-tipped trees turn colour quickly – you quicken the pace – Manor Oaks Road – what's he looking at? This ain't Barnsley, son, this ain't Rotherham you know, we're not in Doncaster, ahkid – you feel it – it's hard to escape their gaze, the way they eye you up – some know you, seen your face around, Whatshisface's son – from the Wybourn with the others so you're tough like – you don't have much money, no-one does, so you gotta fight your own battles – those who leave don't usually come back, why would they?

Roll your sleeves up, it takes a brave soul to just saunter into The Windsor Hotel, face the men – and women – guzzling pints of Tetley Bitter, because even when a punch-up ensues the police are wary of intervening when the fingers are pointing and the arms are flailing and the kids round here don't feel the cold, not even when it snows, not even when the warmth of the furnace switches off for the last time. Men round here work all the hours they can and look forward to fish-and-chip suppers and fags from W.H. Smith while you admire the watches in H.S. Samuel and think about how life could be in the future, and you look down, and the soles of your shoes look loose and a trip to House of Barrington is in order, and outside, toddlers in prams are crying to their headscarved mums for a coin to feed the 1p gumball machines, wanting a sweet treat to shove in their bulging-cheeked gob.

It's on your shoulders, the weight of being black. Always looking, listening and learning, trying to carve out your own identity in this gritty city. The Jam on the radio, on the tele too, *The Old Grey Whistle Test*, and now rudeboys roam round town in black monkey boots bought from Timpson's humming 'In the City'. Trumped-up Teddy Boys who only like your kind sometimes, when it suits them to. The older men, the ones from down t'pit, neck pints that never quench their incessant thirst, the same men who pigeon race on the weekends to get out the house for a bit.

Another new Tesco is opening and another old cornershop is forced to close. The Future are the new kids from these parts and music is needed to lighten the mood and lift the gloom. Everyone, especially the young girls and the older girls, and all the girls really, love The Osmonds too and spend all their pocket money on their records, and David Essex posters and mums neck Babycham because they've got to work, look after the kids and make sure dinner's on the table by six.

Hadfields are in trouble, you've heard. The steel industry is struggling, you've heard. Everyone who works there says their jobs are in danger, the city's economic lifeblood under threat. Many men are saying they will soon be on the dole, begging, cap in hand to the government and the cornershops, hoping to get a loaf of bread and a pint of milk on tick. And even though the women are putting the bunting up, the men feel duty-bound to put food on the table: mince pies and sliced Spam.

Prepubescent paperboys, cheap labour, fling copies of the *Star* or the *Morning Telegraph* at the crack of dawn, people not from round here always think you hardwired Wybourners are always out on the fiddle, earning your coin through dodgy means, especially since the ever-rising inflation rates. But what do they know? Wybourners work their fingers to their bare bone. Always on the run, trying to escape decimalisation and discrimination. The forge from the steel factory still pounding.

And Star Walk competitors pound it down the high street, keeping one foot on the ground at all times, as boys and girls, brothers and sisters, perch on walls to see the walkers waddle past, shimmying their hips towards the finish line. Men with pints at hand cheering them on with slurred words of encouragement. When you fancy it, craving something sweet, you go to Bill's and binge on Curly Wurlys and Refreshers and bars of Fruit & Nut. Everyone in the city has gone snooker crazy, the waistcoat-wearing players have turned into superstars overnight ever since the championships at the Crucible, ever since Spencer vs Thorburn, it's all Embassy cigarettes and snooker halls rammed with young men with wispy moustaches, and now cues are actually being used to pot balls in pockets and not to wrap rivals round the head with when they get pissed and fancy a scuffle. In snooker, unlike in pool, you're allowed to pot the black.

Stumble onto the number 9 rumbling along Manor Lane to Manor Park. Pond Street Bus Station is busy again and Sheffield Sheaf Valley swimming baths is as loud as ever; black kids need to learn how to swim because not enough black kids know how to swim. You're a young black man, with rhythm and pecs and a picky head and a fearsome attitude and darker skin and a wide nose and long limbs, rooting for Kunta Kinte in *Roots*, even after the slave owners chop off his foot. And black and white minstrels on the TV, and you have to laugh or else you'll cry, and Lenny Henry is doing impressions on the tele and making black people proud and all the while there's Charlie Williams telling jokes on the TV, making light of being black.

You're black, they can't see right through you. You want to go to France one day or Spain and drink fancy red wine and have a nice cottage somewhere in the feather-bedded posh part of town with a beautiful wife and two lovely kids who go to a good school. You want a wife one day that looks like royalty but speaks normal and makes you think of that Hot Chocolate song, the one about love and death. Her straw-coloured hair is long and flowing. When you're out in town showing her off, she swishes it about like she's in Miss World. Her nails are long like little claws. Her veins are blue around her wrists and flesh-coloured everywhere else. When you first meet, like a game of tennis, you take it in turns to make moves. She plays with her hair, you lick your lips, she flutters her eyelashes, you try to touch your toes. At first, there's something naughty about your feelings for her, like a scary story from the Bible. She says she prefers Cadbury over Nestlé. She says she prefers Dairy Milk to Milky Way.

Sheffield is not all smoke and chimneys, you're more than just a black man from the wrong side of the tracks. You see more black faces every year, you see more hatred too, it won't be long before the country has a riot on its hands. But despite the uncertainty hanging over the city, you kick ball and hope for the best, you run round the block and see beauty still. The forge from the steel factory still pounding, for now.

Last little bit, still breathing, hear your name being called from somewhere, born Uriah but called Uri by most, down your road and breathe, you've made it back home, Uri.

1998

Trial by fire, it's been a busy season so far. Last December, you gave your first red card as top-flight referee. The victim, Crystal Palace's Marc Edworthy in their draw with Leicester City. You saw what you saw and laws are laws.

In February, back at St James' Park, you oversaw Newcastle United's defeat to West Ham. Stan Lazaridis scored the only goal, thundering a shot into the top corner from over thirty yards.

It's March, you've already refereed fifteen Premiership fixtures and despite some highly competitive games you feel at home here, at the top, refereeing some of the best names in world football. The players know who you are. The managers certainly do. Even your average Joe down the high road knows the name Uriah Rennie.

And this feels like just the beginning on the road to becoming the best referee in the country, refereeing the best games: relegation six-pointers, top-of-the-table clashes, the Champions League, FIFA internationals perhaps, the FA Cup final?

Another appointment, another matchday: today you're back at the Reebok. Black at the Reebok. Bolton Wanderers vs Leicester.

Another ninety minutes of top-flight action, another *Match of the Day* appearance.

Football is a popular and passionate game, especially this one. You have to send off Bolton's Gudni Bergsson in the twenty-ninth minute and Leicester City's Robert Ullathorne in the fortieth.

If the Premiership didn't know you before, it certainly knows you now.

The game finishes two–nil to Bolton, Alan Thompson scores a double.

• • •

Dual carriageways turn to motorways, indicator, overtake, fast lane, slot back in, slip road, roundabout, traffic lights, stadium car park.

Sleepless nights, long journeys, missed birthdays, missed turnings, running late, running in the cold or dark or both, sodden Saturdays, torrents of abuse, hurtful racist abuse, shit changing rooms, shit blocked in the bog, shit pitches, shit players; all of it, you've put up with it all, for moments like these, days like these.

Today, you referee at Old Trafford, home of the best team in the country. Top-of-the-league Manchester United play New-castle United in fourteenth. It's a great appointment, one you feel you deserve, a marker of how far you've come in your first season refereeing in the top flight of English football.

Today, you are the black man in charge. You've been here before, the Theatre of Dreams, back on Boxing Day for United against Everton. But today is a bigger game, an even bigger contest for you to take control of. Today, you're given the responsibility of taking charge of a top game between two top teams, to make big decisions that could impact the title race in the biggest of leagues.

Look at you go, top of the pyramid, top dog, top boy, top man. The history-maker is not just here to make up the numbers but to show everybody what you are made of, ready to make a name for yourself, be the best in your field, be the best on the field, be the best in the world.

It's the tail-end of the season, squeaky-bum time. Manchester United need points; their nearest competitors, Arsenal, have two games in hand and are breathing down their necks for the league title. They sense blood after beating the Red Devils here just last week. Marc Overmars with the only goal. Alan Wilkie the referee.

It's a huge game, a sell-out, but there's a strange feel to Old Trafford this afternoon, a nervous energy in the stands, in the changing rooms, in the tunnel. Everyone on tenterhooks.

Manchester United:

Schmeichel

G. Neville   May   Pallister   Irwin

Beckham   P. Neville   Butt   Giggs

Cole   Sheringham

Newcastle United:

Given

Pistone   Dabizas   Albert   Pearce   Barton

Lee   Speed   Batty

Shearer   Andersson

Ten minutes in, Newcastle go on the attack, the Manchester United defence too slow to push out. Batty dinks one towards Speed, who has made a clever run into the penalty area, he could be offside but your assistant keeps his flag down.

The defenders are static, haven't followed Speed's run; he now has all the time to nod it towards Andreas Andersson, who is onside and slots the ball past Peter Schmeichel to give Newcastle an early lead.

The goalscorer is quickly embraced by his strike partner Shearer as the home team players look at each other in despair, look at you and your assistant for answers, but no explanation is needed, both players were onside and the goal stands. The team who need to win the most go a goal behind after just eleven minutes.

To compound the hosts' ill fortune, United's keeper, Peter Schmeichel, is forced off, injured five minutes after falling behind, and has to be replaced by substitute Raimond van der Gouw.

The home team respond, forge out a few half-chances. Sheringham has a shot that's well blocked by Barton.

Urged on by the home crowd, Manchester United come again.

The ball is played out wide, you advance towards the penalty area, await the ball in. Giggs' cross evades most of the players in the box, but Beckham arrives at the far post to meet the ball with a diving header that nestles into the corner of the net to make it one–all.

To the relief of the home crowd, the home team have their equaliser, thirty-eight minutes gone on the clock.

As Beckham runs towards the fans, punching the air in delight, hopes of the home side winning the title resurface, renewed belief reverberates around the Theatre of Dreams. It's game on, but the hosts go into the break still needing a goal to keep their Premiership ambitions alive.

Into the second half now, the Old Trafford crowd want a winner, they're desperate for one. The title depends on it. Every cheer, every groan, every sigh amplified.

Cole chance, saved.

Scholes chance, saved.

With ten minutes to go, it's all or nothing. Manchester United manager Alex Ferguson makes an attacking substitution, defender Gary Neville is replaced by striker Ole Gunnar Solskjaer.

Manchester United pressure, pressure, pressure, pumping balls into the box from left, right and centre.

Into 'how long's left?' territory, Beckham whips one in at pace but the ball is headed clear. Newcastle hold on. Hold strong. Eighty-nine minutes gone. The home team have everyone forward as the ball is curled in again, as the ball is headed clear away from danger, as the ball soars towards a black-and-white shirt.

It falls for Newcastle United substitute Temuri Ketsbaia and he is fouled as he controls the bouncing ball, a slide tackle from behind, but you hold your whistle, you let play go on, play the advantage, you're relieved you do, he has set Rob Lee free. He has acres of space in front of him. He has sprinted from his own half to retrieve the ball and now has it at his feet.

Lee sprints
Ole Gunnar Solskjaer sprints
You sprint

Lee runs and runs, you chase and chase, afterburners on. You're going like the clappers, stretching every sinew to keep up with play: inches from them both, inches from the ball, inches from making a decision.

Solskjaer, Manchester United's young striker, is sprinting back to put pressure on the Newcastle midfielder who is bursting towards the United goal at speed.

You, just yards away from the impending contact, Ole Gunnar Solskjaer busting a gut, sprinting to keep up, sprinting to put the pressure on Lee who is tearing hell for leather towards the penalty area.

Lee sprints (just ahead)
Ole Gunnar Solskjaer sprints (just behind)
You sprint (just behind him)

Then, as clear as day, the United player scythes down Lee cynically with a lunging tackle from behind just outside the box denying him the opportunity to have a shot on goal.

The hammer's up, it's a cast-iron decision, he knows what he has done. Guiltily, he's already walking towards the tunnel before you even brandish the card from your back pocket. It's the epitome of 'taking one for the team' and he knows it. You show him the oval-shaped red card within seconds of the foul being committed.

The appeals from the Manchester United keeper, Raimond van der Gouw, are only half-arsed, only half asked. Everyone knows there was only one thing you could have done.

A clear DOGSO: Denying an Obvious Goalscoring Opportunity.

The home crowd applaud their hero as he walks off down the tunnel at the corner of the Old Trafford pitch like he has just scored a hat-trick. They know what he has done and why he has done it, the ovation is rapturous.

A referee would never get a reaction like that.

Gary Speed blasts the resulting free kick over, a last chance for Newcastle United to take home all three points but the game ends one–all, and Manchester United have dropped two precious points at home, the title now out of their hands.

Nothing you could have done of course, you just applied the laws.

•   •   •

Your first season in the top league ends with a game in east London, a clash between two mid-table teams: West Ham vs Leicester, final score four–three.

And as you walk off the Upton Park pitch, change, chew, chat and drive up the M1 back up to Sheffield, you think about your first season as a top-flight referee. You've refereed nineteen games in the Premiership in some of the best grounds in the country: Old Trafford, twice, White Hart Lane, Stamford Bridge, St James' Park, Elland Road, Villa Park.

You're a big black history-maker from Jamaica telling some of the best footballers in the world to behave themselves.

Communication has been key. Not just what you say, but the 'non-verbals' too. The words unsaid, the loaded silences and such. The spaces in between. A stone-faced stare, a tilt of the head, a raised eyebrow, a strong hand. The Premiership moves too fast to stop and chat to every player every other minute.

Sportsmail awards you Whistleblower of the Year. The history-maker is now also an award-winner. The British Michael Jordan, this season's MVP, no, this season's MVR – Most Valuable Referee.

You're the first black referee to referee in the Premiership, and even though this is only the start of the journey, you couldn't be prouder of yourself.

• • •

The difficult second album. The difficult second book. The difficult second season: 1998–1999.

You feel the pressure, everyone does, it's to be expected when you did so well last year, firmly found your feet in front of thousands every week. There's no doubt about it, you've become a household name: the players, the managers, the groundstaff, the season-ticket holders, they all know who you are. Obviously, your face is one all the fans in the pubs recognise, talk about over their Boddingtons bitters. Liked by some, respected even.

They're not all unreasonable, your run-of-the-mill football fans, you're sure many of them acknowledge being a referee isn't easy and appreciate your no-nonsense style. Equally, you know there are others who hate the sight of you, judge the type of person you are based on snippets shown on *Match of the Day*. This is not something you let affect you. In the eyes of God, you're doing the job that you were born to do.

You're back. You do West Ham vs Southampton at Upton Park on a Monday night in east London. It's September now, and Southampton are bottom of the league and need points to survive.

Into the second half, an hour gone on the clock.

Skittering into position as the ball is knocked about, then

whipped in from the left: always watching, always on the move, always in the mix ready to make a decision. The ball is centred for Ian Wright – now in the claret and blue of West Ham United after seven record-breaking years at Arsenal – who has been given too much space in the penalty area.

He adjusts his body and dives to head the ball towards goal and it's one–nil to the Hammers.

As Ian Wright wheels off to celebrate, his gold tooth glistening under the Upton Park floodlights, he runs towards one of his teammates pointing excitedly. His Hammers hobnobber, Neil Ruddock, has rushed forward from the back to join in on the celebrations, it's clear they have some mischievous routine planned.

They rush towards each other, Ian Wright now brandishing an invisible red card in his right hand as if he is sending Ruddock off the field of play.

As the 'red card' is flashed, Ruddock reacts playfully and shoves Ian Wright in the chest causing him to tumble onto the turf and roll to the ground in an over-the-top fashion.

You see it now, see that they are reenacting the incident which made all the back pages of the Sunday papers: Sheffield Wednesday's Italian striker Paulo Di Canio shoving your colleague Paul Alcock over after being sent off in Saturday's game at Hillsborough vs Arsenal.

It would take someone very strong and very stupid to push you over, Uri.

You contemplate your options, question whether their celebration is an example of unsporting behaviour. Should you caution Ruddock? Should you caution Wright? Should you book both? Thinking about it for a second or two, you decide to do neither. You will let the FA take retrospective action if needed.

Game resumed, Southampton, still losing, are bottom of the league and need points to survive.

Le Tissier whips in the corner, you take up a position to see the bodies in the box. A West Ham player is pushed, it looks like Dicks. You see something and give it. To Southampton's dismay, you disallow Ken Monkou's volleyed finish which cannons in after the whistle, your whistle.

And annoyingly for them, West Ham manage to hold on and win it one–nil.

After the game, Dave Jones, the Southampton manager, lambasts you, says the goal should have stood. Of course he would. Football is a matter of opinions and yours always seems to be wrong to some.

West Ham's Julian Dicks comes out to the media, you hear, praising your performance. Confirms he was pushed in the incident that prompted you to disallow Southampton's goal.

He felt what he felt and you saw what you saw.

• • •

The big games come thick and fast.

It's December now, a few weeks until Christmas and you drive down to White Hart Lane in north London to referee Tottenham vs Manchester United.

Two teams that played here just over a week ago in the League Cup quarter-final that Spurs won three–one. Peter Jones the referee.

This is some sight: two of the four officials in this big game, between two big teams in the top division, are black men. You, in the middle, and Trevor Parkes, from Birmingham, on the line.

This is more like it, you think, more like how it should be. An historic moment for sure. This is the future. You are the future.

Manchester United, knowing they can go top with a win, start strongly.

But with just under ten minutes gone, Ginola goes on a jinking run on the left and is hacked down by a rash slide tackle by Nicky Butt. There is uproar in the stands by Spurs fans who demand a yellow. And, despite the United protests, led by their tough-tackling shaven-headed captain Roy Keane, with David Beckham and Ryan Giggs in close quarters for back-up, a yellow card is brandished.

Laws are laws.

It's end to end: you run and blow and wait and stare and glare and point.

Sinton's ball in is headed clear and United have a chance to break.

They counter at speed, gangly-legged Giggs advances into the Spurs half and you're right there, up with play, as he lays the ball right for Beckham who takes a touch to control it, looks up and curls one into the penalty area at pace. Giggs' header is well saved but the rebound falls for Solskjaer who prods it home to make it one–nil to Manchester United after just eleven minutes.

You're on your toes to see what's afoot as the away side come again. Keane chips it to Butt, Giggs gets involved, the ball is played right again to Beckham who looks up, picks out his target and curls it in towards Solskjaer who makes it two: déjà vu. Eighteen minutes gone on the clock, the away side in complete control.

Gary Neville is the next United player in your book, a reckless studs-up lunge on Allan Nielsen on the halfway line.

Tottenham might be two–nil down but continue to show fight, the home crowd urge them on, bang their drum, sing their songs, their defender Luke Young goes on a surging run and has a pop, Schmeichel saves, Armstrong is first to the rebound, Schmeichel saves again.

Spurs need a goal, Ginola receives it and looks to attack down the left again; he dribbles and then pauses, weighs up his options, toys with the Manchester United right-back for fun. With a show of pace, he gets the better of Gary Neville, who clumsily tumbles into him to impede the Frenchman's run.

You have the upper hand, you hold all the cards. The decision is clear, the punishment is too, ten minutes after he received his first one, you show Gary Neville a second yellow and then a red: an early bath.

Into the second half, Spurs are two goals down but a man up and looking to take advantage.

David Beckham, following his sending off at the World Cup for England in France this summer, continues to get taunted by the Tottenham fans; it's clear he's starting to get wound up, and it's no surprise, as proactive as you try to be, when he takes his frustration out on Spurs' Andy Sinton with a late foul near the touchline, earning himself a yellow card.

Sinton seeks retribution seconds later, committing a crude challenge on United's number seven. And now, despite your best efforts to prevent further misconduct, Sinton and Roy Keane square up and you have to intervene, in the same way a boxing referee might.

You usher Keane away and book Andy Sinton for the retaliatory tackle.

Minutes later, Manchester United's Ronny Johnsen fouls Ginola from behind so you award Spurs a free kick. The Norwegian's not happy, talks himself into the book, is cautioned for dissent. The sixth United player to see a card, having already taken the names of Nicky Butt, Teddy Sheringham, Gary Neville (twice), Phil Neville and David Beckham.

Keeping your head and waltzing into position, you scour the penalty area for anything illegal.

Darren Anderton's ball in, Sol Campbell's head and with

twenty minutes left to play, Tottenham have a goal back, it's two–one.

The home side push and probe and pressure but the away side are holding on. Just.

Ninety on the clock, you decide two minutes of stoppage time is to be played. Tottenham might just have one last chance left, if any at all, to nick a point. As Stephen Carr motors down the touchline, he is fouled by Jesper Blomqvist in a dangerous area.

From the other wing to their first goal, Anderton looks up, picks out his target and curls it in again towards Campbell who rises and heads it in to make it two–two at the death: déjà vu, part two.

After the final whistle, despite earning a point that sees Manchester United go top of the league, you hear Fergie has locked himself in the dressing room and refuses to speak to the media, unhappy at your decision to send off Gary Neville apparently.

You can't please everyone.

Nine yellow cards and one red in all, you did what you had to do.

1979

Observing from the sideline, for the first time you're not really watching the action like a football fan might, not studying the players' techniques or the playmakers' darting runs made down the middle, not interested in the mechanics of the match from a player's point of view; instead, you're absorbed by the referee's movements, the shuffling and side-stepping, the effortless decision-making, the dynamics of power, the confidence of the figure at the centre of the action.

Responsibility at his fingertips, with short blasts of his whistle, everything stops and starts again.

You're a sponge, anything involving sport you like to mimic, try your hand at, see if you could be good at it too, and now you begin to wonder, as Brian, the man in the middle, scurries from corner to corner, if you too would make a good referee.

You've never really paid much attention to referees before, haven't yet learned what their story is, worked out what they're up to when not in shot, figured out what type of person has the guts to make potentially match-changing decisions but this is an eye-opener.

Brian Coddington, just four years your senior and already on his way to becoming a Football League linesman, is refereeing a youth match and you're utterly engrossed.

Afterwards, as he gathers up his stuff on the side, you ask him about how you can get involved, you tell him you would like to have a go to see what it feels like to be the man in black.

As part of your FA coaching course, you learned a little about refereeing, did the Laws of the Game exam, which gave you a taste, but now you think you're ready to do it properly, be a proper referee.

Watching Brian at work, and wanting to try your hand at something new (like you always do), you sign up to do the basic FA Refereeing Training course properly, parting with £1.50 for the pleasure.

The sessions to be a proper football referee take place at Sheffield Polytechnic, and through the sleet, snow and sludge, and the worst winter weather you have ever seen in Sheffield since arriving, you make sure you attend every class, do all you have to do to be a qualified referee, and be good at it too.

The Laws of Association Football, the *LOAF*, is your new Bible.

A lot of the other wannabe referees can't make all the sessions as the weather worsens, but you can, it's just a short walk from the Wybourn, and when the weather does get better, and classes are resumed, with everyone in attendance again, you are retaught what you already know to comfortably pass.

Whatever happens, whatever you decide, whether you wish to pursue this properly or not, at least now you have another qualification, another sporting string to your ever-growing bow. A new badge of honour.

Now qualified, within days you have a message from a referees' secretary of a local league who's given you a midweek evening Working Men's Club game at Concord Park, behind the golf course to the north of the city.

In the days leading up to your first fixture as a qualified referee, the match is all you can think about: as you eat, before you sleep, when you wake; when you do forget about it for a moment, you remember again seconds later, remember that in a few days, you, a fresh-faced twenty-year-old, will have to face twenty-two other grown men on your own. Men with short tempers maddened by the prospect of Thatcher getting into power and their jobs being on the line.

Riddled with self-doubt, questions flood your brain: will the teams behave? Will you have to send someone off for ungentlemanly conduct or for using foul and abusive language? Will you cope with the responsibility?

You make yourself feel better by reminding yourself it's just a game of football, the game you love, the game you know, the game you're good at. Last year, Viv Anderson became the first black man to play for England. Anything and everything is possible.

You ring back and confirm that you are available (but maybe not quite ready).

The big day nears and you're gifted a pocket watch by your dad to fulfil your duty as timekeeper, Law 7. You think you have everything else you need, you pack your bag yourself – a habit you're keen to get into if you decide to stick with it, if the game goes well – you have listed everything you have to remember on the day on a bit of card.

You change into your kit in a cubby-hole, the same space where the nets and corner flags are kept. And as you pat yourself down to check you've got everything you'll need, tucking your spare pencil into your sock, you can't help but think that already the role is not at all welcoming.

You're alone now, no other soul to talk to, to confide and console in before your baptism of fire. No-one there to help and support you: no teammates, no linesmen, no friends to assist you with the big decisions. The feeling of isolation hits you smack in the face suddenly.

It's mind over matter, your legs feel heavy and your brain feels dizzy as you take that long walk to the pitch. Everything everyone says, you take personally and it's only their eyes that are talking. You are not in a position to be anyone's chum today even though you recognise many of the faces – either from playing for Brunsmeer or The Windsor – and they certainly know you too. Have seen your face around, played against you, played with you – and now you've done the course, now you're qualified and got the badges to prove it, they are expecting something different.

Your unsettled stomach simmers as some of the players snigger and smirk when you drop your bag on the side of the pitch in your new kit, all black of course, with bright white laces on your black boots to match your shirt collars.

You jog around the outside of the pitch, stretch your legs, try to look official, like you were taught, and as you check the nets are securely in place, like you were taught, make sure there are no holes, like you were taught, some of the players think it's funny to kick the ball at you and then pretend they were aiming for the goal.

All you can muster in reply is to glare back weakly.

Your heart's beating out of your chest knowing it's your job to try and control the twenty-two who stand before you.

You are ready to kick off but everything you have learned on the course and told to do pre-match seems to be a sticking point, already making you an enemy.

It was meant to be a six o'clock kick-off and it's already five past. You ask for the team sheets, but they're not ready yet, the home team don't even have eleven players, there's a player who's in the toilet and another, Pete, who must have missed the bus.

When you ask for the match ball, it rolls to you unsmooth, and you know before you control it that it will need pumping up before you can start.

You feel far from relaxed as you keep a mental note of all the things you will need to report back to the county FA after the match.

Brian has given you some tips, little things to give you the upper hand from the off.

For example, he says, when you bring in the two captains for the coin toss, have your notebook in your hands, give the players a glimpse, fiddle with it, open it up and close it again, he says, let the players know immediately their punishment if they fail to comply, where their name will end up if they choose to misbehave.

Secondly, he adds, when the ball goes out of play for the first time, keep the whistle to your lips as you signal for the throw. That way, everyone can see you with your special tool, your whistle – so when players look up at you, they know *you* are the referee, the man with all the power.

With the heartbeat of a hummingbird, you march into the middle, Brian's words ringing in your ears, nerves worsening.

As soon as you blow that first whistle, you're getting paid, good money too, to provide a service.

As soon as you blow that first whistle, you know it's you versus them.

Already, there's a small crowd gathering around the edges of the pitch, assembling from all angles to see some action.

'Yes please, skippers!' you shout, your voice cracking just a little.

1999

New year, same season.

As millions around the country nurse hangovers, your head is also spinning, dizzy at the thought of what it means to be a referee. When you think about it, in the grand scheme of things, in the bigger and broader picture, you feel no pressure.

Knowing you can't provide for the family or put food on the table, that's real pressure.

To go to Old Trafford or Highbury or St James' Park and referee games is not pressure, it's an honour.

You know if you worry too much, you won't referee with confidence, so it's important to shut it out, have ice in your veins, embrace positive energy, think positive thoughts.

You want to deal with every potential possibility on the pitch because you want to demonstrate that you are good at your job. Every contentious decision is welcomed. You can't ever think 'I don't want this to happen or that to happen' because you want to deal with every situation possible to come out the other side bigger, better and stronger.

January, February, **March** . . .

Less than two months to go until the end of the season and you're at Goodison Park for Everton vs Arsenal.

You apply the laws as you see them.

Off the ball, Everton's Don Hutchison and Arsenal's Martin Keown tangle, Hutchison's elbow isn't where it should be. He has done something he shouldn't. There are no other options. You send him off. Loft the red card high for all of Goodison to see.

You apply the laws as you see them.

At half-time, as you walk down the tunnel, the home crowd boo you. You hear it loud and clear. But football is a theatre, a pantomime, and you are the actor playing the villain. The baddy. No matter what you do.

You try not to let their jeers affect you, you run where you need to run and give what you need to give.

Petit: a loose first touch, a dangerous lunge, a late tackle. Yellow.

Petit again, a loose first touch, a dangerous lunge, a late tackle. A second yellow. Red.

Petit slams his shin pads down and mumbles something that sounds like 'That's me finished with English football' as he trudges down the tunnel.

You apply the laws as you see them.

Come the end of the season, the numbers have been counted and verified: you have booked more players than any other Premiership referee.

You apply the laws as you see them.

• • •

A new season: new hopes, players, dreams, ambitions, ticket prices, kits, stands, managers, assistants, fans.

There's a different spirit when you travel this far north up the A1, unbridled, raw passion.

The atmosphere in the North East can be toxic if Newcastle aren't playing well; a stray pass or a shit shot isn't good enough, not here, not this season.

Like most of the north of England, a lot has changed in the city recently, but love of the beautiful game never wanes. Even through change, football remains. There's a bounce in people's step when the Toon win. The ship builders and the glass makers and the motorcycle assemblers are dying, heavy industries losing to lighter ones, but both young and old, from South Shields to Blythe, you'll find the most loyal Geordie fans necking cheap pints in The Strawberry on a matchday like today hoping for a much-needed three points.

Newcastle lost the FA Cup final a few months back, and seem determined to challenge for the top trophies again. Ruud Gullit, who you know well, a figure who graced the game as a player and used to manage Chelsea, is under pressure to perform and the season hasn't even begun yet. Finishing thirteenth, as they have for the last two seasons, will not be good enough this year.

And when you get there, lay out your kit like you always do, fish out your boots and tuck them underneath the bench before inspecting the pitch, there's a palpable anticipation about the place, more so than you've encountered before.

A game of football is a game of football. You approach every one the same, you can't let the atmosphere affect you, you never have done and you never will, but you are aware of the significance of the first game of the season. Especially here, today.

This is a team in transition, new manager, new players, new half-built stand, new hopes. Newcastle have spent money, big money, bought in quality players: Marcelino, Goma, Dyer, Dumas. Highly thought-of footballers to help forge a team that should help them compete this season. The fans are expecting.

Villa have spent big too: new signings George Boateng and David James are in the team today. Names you know. Players you have refereed before playing for different clubs.

It's cloudy but dry, JCBs and cherry-pickers soar above the stands of this roofless stadium as you inspect the field of play.

Newcastle United:

Harper

Barton   Marcelino   Goma   Domi

Dumas   Speed   Solano   Serrant

Shearer   Ketsbaia

Aston Villa:

James

Delaney   Southgate   Calderwood   Ehiogu   Wright

Thompson   Boateng   Taylor

Dublin   Joachim

In the Officials' Room, an hour to kick-off, you skim over the team sheets, make sure everything's in order, the numbers, names and colours.

The Villa assistant manager, Steve Harrison, comes in, as does Newcastle's Steve Clark, a chance to make your expectations clear. New season, new interpretations of laws, new inconsistencies to be ironed out.

This pre-match chat is witnessed by your two assistants and Jeff Winter, your fourth official today. There are firm new FA directives and edicts to follow, you begin. You will explain the decisions you can, you say. You will be watching aerial challenges closely, you add, knowing you have been reminded by the FA over the summer to keep a closer eye on illegal use of the elbows and clamp down on any misdemeanours by club officials in the dugouts. These are your expectations and you expect them to be followed, you end with.

Another thorough warm-up, *by failing to prepare, you are preparing to fail*: high kicks and higher heart rates and making your face known and a brief word with a couple of the players as you jog around the pitch.

You watch the keepers' kicks, see where they land, observe where you will have to stand in the ninety minutes to come.

You lead the two teams out to the roar of the St James' Park faithful. Walk out of the tunnel to the saxophonic sound of 'Going Home: Theme of the Local Hero' blaring and topless blind-drunk Geordies cheering. The expectant black-and-white magpie crowd.

The game is a scrappy one: new season rustiness.

Tackles fly in, from both sides, in all areas of the pitch. You have to be strict, you have to be strong, you have to be Uri. Brave.

A clenched-fist signal to your two assistants means you have a real game on your hands, means keep your eyes peeled, means get ready to get involved.

Newcastle are just on top, keep possession, prise out chances.

Carl Serrant crosses the ball into the centre and Goma heads it onto the bar.

Speed goes close.

Solano goes close.

Both teams have eleven men each but sometimes, on a day like today, the home crowd make it twelve, and in the middle, it's just you. Alone and outnumbered.

Jeff beckons you over to the touchline, wants Villa manager John Gregory binned from the bench. He has said things he shouldn't. You don't have to be told twice, laws are laws and John must have pushed the boundaries. Keeping communication concise, you send him to the stands.

Back in the middle, you're working hard to keep the players in check. All around you, emotions run high, swaying and swirling, you're refereeing out of your skin, getting wider and wider, like a second-hand car that keeps pulling to the left, to make sure you have the right angle to make the right decisions.

The ball pinballs from end to end, hoofed one way and then the other, and for a moment you're a spectator watching the action from afar, behind a glass screen, unable to get a grip of the game, when you should be like a conductor coaxing the players, orchestrating and conducting the rhythm of the match, controlling the temperament of the players.

You're always up with play though, remaining eagle-eyed just inches away from the action.

Thirty-eight minutes in, your hand is forced, you book Shearer. England and Newcastle United captain Alan Shearer. A cut-and-dry decision. Guilty of backing in, doing something he shouldn't, catching Colin Calderwood in the face with a flailing elbow. You deliberated a red. You gave yourself nano-seconds of thinking time. Firm new FA directives and edicts to follow. You choose yellow.

You get booed. Called names. Grandads and grandsons casting aspersions and conflating conclusions, about you, the man in the middle, when you're just doing your job.

You're doing your best to keep a lid on it, refereeing by the book and then some.

It goes from being scrappy to feisty quickly. A game that needs controlling. A game that needs cards.

You book Goma.

You book Barton.

You book Speed.

You book Delaney, Thompson and Ehiogu.

Another long ball punted forward, you saunter into position and get 'side-on', give yourself a better chance to see any pushing, shoving, elbows, illegal levering.

A gallop turns into a sprint.

At this level, you've got to get from A to B without thinking about your lungs and your legs.

Honestly, and you will die on this hill: good fitness should be a given. You need to be able to focus solely on your refereeing, not whether you're going to make it from one box to another without conking out or collapsing.

The ball pinballs about, ricocheting from place to place, and you're in the middle, trying to grab the game by the scruff of its neck, your mind going a mile a minute.

Players flop to the floor, wriggle and writhe on the turf. Another Aston Villa player goes down clutching his head, there are shouts from his teammates, they edge closer with their arms in the air all akimbo.

Another coming together, another scrimmage, another bloody battle, another war. This is no easy game, every decision disputed.

Another long ball punted forward, Shearer the target man, Calderwood leaps, as does Shearer, but something isn't right. Something isn't right so you blow. Instantly.

Why wait when you have seen what you have seen? Shearer can't believe it. But you know what you saw and you think you know what Shearer was doing.

It didn't look like a normal attempt for the ball, an aerial challenge between the defender and striker that you've seen a million times. There was movement there, an action that shouldn't have been. Not just 'backing in', not just a harmless coming together, but something more sinister.

Who can't hear, will feel: a Jamaican proverb.

On another day, in another game, with another referee perhaps, he might have got away with it. But not today, not with you in charge, you've caught him bang to rights; laws are all about interpretation, and are subject to the referee's opinion and you saw what you saw.

No means no in anyone's language and your expectations were clear. You do what you have to do, do what you think is right and brandish him a second yellow, then the red card for persistent use of the elbow. He has been guilty too many times and laws are laws.

Ian Taylor, the Villa captain, has his hands on his head in dis-belief but that's happened before – players from the opposition shocked at a big decision in their favour.

What's done is done, there's no turning back, no backing down; the decision, your decision, hotly disputed or not, has been made and your head will not be turned. You are no shrinking violet, no shirker; you are a guardian of standards.

He's off, Shearer, trudging down the tunnel, muttering a few words you can barely hear as he charges past Jeff Winter and back towards the changing rooms.

The home crowd can't quite believe it, there's venom in the air, fury emanates from all four corners, and again you are the villain of the piece for doing what you think is right.

Action resumes and Villa have the bit between their teeth, they know there are points to get here.

Fifteen minutes to go in this opening game of the season. The mood is fractured, tense. The home team are a man down and the away team are in the ascendency.

You stroll into position, the award of the red card niggling in the back of your mind still. A decision that you are reminded of by every Geordie in the stadium as you award every throw-in, free kick or corner. But you do what you have to do, give what you have to give.

Newcastle, now Shearer-less, are struggling, and to make mat-ters worse, far worse, Mark Delaney, the Villa centre-back, crosses the ball in for Julian Joachim who glances the ball into the bottom corner to make it one–nil Villa in the seventy-fifth minute.

Newcastle lack the manpower to respond, down to ten they face an uphill battle up the sloping St James' Park pitch.

Before long, you blow the final whistle and boos ring around the stadium, the incomplete, half-finished stadium.

All eyes on you, the home faithful's performing monkey.

Football is rarely black and white but today it is, here in Newcastle, with you in charge. Black ref. Black-and-white shirts. Angry white fans.

You will get some stick for this, no doubt about it. It doesn't help matters that Villa win the game, but you saw what you saw and you did what you had to do.

Before they ask, you reaffirm to yourself that not for one moment is this about Shearer or trying to make a name for yourself or trying to make a point. This is about right and wrong, foul and misconduct, dangerous play.

You remain defiant; difficult days, difficult games, make you a better referee.

You hear this was a special occasion for Shearer too, his one hundredth game for Newcastle but you did what you had to do.

As you prepare to walk off, Ruud Gullit charges onto the pitch, locks swooshing, shouting something he shouldn't: pointed fingers and plosive sounds.

He says what he saw was 'incredible'. Meant negatively, you imagine. You think it shouldn't be that hard to refrain from making knee-jerk replies. You could easily come out, post-match, and start slating players for missing a sitter or splaying a pass out of touch, but you always manage to hold your tongue.

After the game, mood strange, sending off Shearer is already proving to be quite the cause célèbre, the chief steward comes into the dressing room, your dressing room.

Gentlemen, he says, there is quite a crowd outside, and in the best interests of your safety, it is best not to go out the front door. We will go out another way, he suggests.

The four of you – you, Dave Babski, Russell Booth and Jeff Winter – are escorted to your people-carrier through a side exit off the club shop.

Snuck out round the back like A-list celebrities avoiding the paparazzi.

Shearer has his say later that day: I challenge anyone to watch on television the incident which got me sent off from any angle and at any speed and if, after total scrutiny, there is the slightest foul I will accept the decision without further comment. If, however, it is proven beyond all doubt that no foul was committed I would hope that something could be done.

You saw what you saw and laws are laws.

• • •

Seven days later, after a week of endless headlines and telephone calls and second thoughts, you're sent back to the North East, but not to referee Newcastle United this time sensibly, instead it's Sunderland against Arsenal at the Stadium of Light.

And, as you take to the field for your pre-match warm-up, something strange happens.

Something that's never happened to you before, or many other referees in the world, you imagine.

The referee is usually always the bastard in black that people love to hate, but today, all of the Sunderland fans get to their feet and applaud you as if you are some god: Uriah the Messiah. For the first time in your career, you are given a round of applause and a standing ovation.

Your decision to send off Alan Shearer last week has gone down well on Wearside, here at Sunderland, Newcastle's fiercest rivals.

You're trying not to smile at the ridiculousness of it.

You needed a quiet-ish nil–nil and you get one, sort of, just the six cautions, three for each team.

Despite the scoreless draw, it's a whole month till you're given another Premiership game.

You do your best to get on with it, forget about Newcastle and St James' Park and Alan Shearer and persistent use of the elbow.

You ignore, where you can, the newspaper reports, the unnecessary nationwide reaction to applying the laws of the game.

There's nothing else to it: you saw what you saw and laws are laws.

If you say it enough times, you might just believe it.

• • •

It's October, a midweek game in the Midlands. Division One's Birmingham City are at home to Premiership side Newcastle United in the third round of the Worthington Cup and guess who's the referee?

Like the first game of the season, it's a team from the North East versus a team from the Midlands. Like the first game of the season, you are the man in the middle. Like the first game of the season, Alan Shearer starts.

Ruud Gullit resigned a few months back, just five games into the new season, and has been replaced in the Newcastle dugout by Bobby Robson. The living legend Bobby Robson.

You are booed by the away fans, songs are sung and swear words are uttered as you run and blow and wait and stare and glare and point. You expected it, it was only a few months ago you sent off their hero.

After just four minutes at St Andrew's, you have a big decision to make.

The Newcastle fans think you hate their club but you do not hate any club; to their surprise perhaps, you emphatically award them a penalty when Silvio Marić is fouled by Darren Purse in the box and Newcastle have the chance to take an early lead.

Shearer steps up, the one and only Alan Shearer, but his penalty is missed; saved by the Birmingham keeper, Ian Bennett.

Nearly half-time, a crucial point in any football game, a goal now changes the second-half dynamic, shifts the perspective. In the forty-fifth minute you have another big decision to make, you send off Newcastle United's goalkeeper, Steve Harper, for a foul on Andy Johnson that leads to a penalty.

The Newcastle fans think you hate their club. This couldn't be further from the truth, you have no gripe with any particular team, you're just there to do a job. You are employed by the FA to apply the laws, and that's the long and short of it.

O'Connor strokes the ball home on the stroke of half-time to make it one–nil to Birmingham City.

Deep into the second half now, a corner is taken by Gary Rowett and met by the head of Darren Purse who nods it into the net to make it two–nil to Birmingham City.

Newcastle United, down to ten men now of course, offer little in the way of a response and the game ends two–nil.

You've refereed two Newcastle United games already this season and have sent off two of their players and overseen two Newcastle United defeats.

The Newcastle United fans think you hate their club but it's not like that at all; laws are laws, you see what you see and give what you have to give. That's the long and short of it.

2

The darkest man in the room: darkest eyes, darkest hands, darkest nails. The pint-drinking pauses as you walk into the spit-and-sawdust pub, look for a corner to sit in. Quiet whispers. Loud eyes. A figure of suspicion. Followed by the security guard in Asda. Cause people to cross to the other side of the road. Can I touch your hair? My best mate's black. I'm not racist but . . . Flash needed for the camera. Are you from Jamaica? Do you like Bob Marley? The cabbie worries you'll do a runner. Dark skin, white teeth. A beast. A brute. Biggest cock in the changing room. Biggest *cock* in the changing room. Product of the welfare state. From the wrong side of the tracks. Baseball cap, hoodie-wearing, spicy-food loving, weed-smoking, national anthem not-knowing, council-flat renting, gym-going, benefit baby.

Things black men **don't** have:

the innocence   the better pay   the equal opportunities
the tools to break through the glass ceilings   the right
not to remain silent   the freedom   the free reign
      the voice to be heard   the love   the crack of the
whip   the protection from the whip   the arm around
 the shoulder   the second chance   the same finances
      the nicer car   the detached house with a sun-warmed
south-facing garden   the corner office with the leather-
bound books   the power to be free   the uncomplicated
relationship with their father   a barber based outside the
big cities who can cut black hair   the lot

Unlike an away fan lying low in the home end, you can't hide your true colours, you're the only black referee in professional English football, you stick out like a sore thumb. They say the best referee is one you don't really see, but everyone notices you, Uri, you're hard to miss.

To too many still, you are a black referee, when all you want to be is a referee who happens to be black.

It was only ten years or so ago that John Barnes backheeled a banana thrown at him off the pitch.

There are still only a smattering of black fans in the stands.

White man. White man. White man. White man. White man.
White man. White man. White man. White man. White man.
White man. White man. White man. White man. White man.
White man.   White man.
White man.   Black man (you).   White man.
White man.   White man.
White man. White man. White man. White man. White man.
White man. White man. White man. White man. White man.
White man. White man. White man. White man. White man.

You are an ambitious man and want to be seen on the world stage. You still regard refereeing as a hobby, but a hobby you take very seriously.

Come hell or high water, you will be back.

The bastard in black.

The bastard *is* black.

Demoted? Not bloody surprised!

He just then did everything by the rule book and didn't use any common sense

Too big for his Fila-sponsored boots, had his own website devoted to all things Rennie

He hired an agent to deal with the press and began extended Kung Fu type warm-ups on the pitch before games in full view of all

His demonstrative style did not go down well in some quarters and Premiership bigwigs

Taken out of the Premiership firing line and restricted to games in the Nationwide League

Card issuing style: frequent

In my picture book dictionary under 'showy referee'

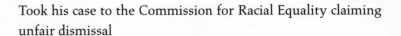

Took his case to the Commission for Racial Equality claiming unfair dismissal

Even stuck his tongue out to the faithful that night when they took the piss out of him for some bizarre incident

Rob Harris and Paul Alcock have also been demoted

Continuing his international career after a breakdown in communication between the football authorities

The only black ref in the Premiership got demoted (and for what?)

His martial arts warm up before a match was excruciatingly toe curling. The penny never dropped that the match wasn't about him

It just so happens that the Premiership have decided not to use him

Only being allowed to referee the lower leagues after some questionable refereeing displays

I dislike intensely how referees' punishment is demotion to our league, they ought to be suspended for three games as per a players' punishment

One minute he was being hailed as the first black ref, the next

It was the wrong decision, but he gets himself noticed – he always has done – and I think that's one of the reasons he was demoted from the big league

Should never have been allowed to officiate a Premiership match in the first place

Many managers felt had he not been black, he would have been demoted sooner but the authorities did not want to ditch such an obvious standard bearer

Giving him a whistle serves about as much point as airlines giving one to passengers in case they end up floating in the ice-cold Atlantic

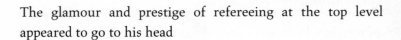

The glamour and prestige of refereeing at the top level appeared to go to his head

Demoted and also the only black referee in the league, which added to the controversy

"Relegated" to officiating Nationwide matches due to poor performance (too many complaints)

Legend has it, he would wait until the stadium was almost full, and then begin his warm-up

He should NEVER be allowed to ref top flight games again. His arrogance on the pitch towards the players is just unbelievable. He does not talk to the players he just looks away

He should have been chucked out years ago

Every time I have seen him this season he has been mentally off the pace by about five years, producing displays littered with unnecessary stoppages, inconsistent disciplining and bizarre decisions that serve only to make him the centre of attention

Rumors that Rennie is in fact a Malteaser sellotaped to a bag of marshmallows have yet to be confirmed or denied

= worst ref in the top flight, easily

You can argue he's consistently bad . . . No matter what league he's in. Getting him to ref five-a-side might sort him out

Shouldn't be officiating in the Premiership. He just can't perform up to the standards required

I cannot believe anyone on here has a good word for Rennie (apart from ****) he is a fat, useless, biased, clueless, spineless, lump. And I hate him more than I hate Styles (not much more, but still more)

Will find himself in the wilderness again if he continues to perform as poorly as he did

I thought he gave a master class today, on the role of the fourth official

Was getting some stick from the Stokies that night due to the
fact he'd been "relegated" from the Prem

Is actually a Magistrate and has a keen sense of justice that he
never really brought onto the pitch, unfortunately

He is married to his whistle

Impregnable self-confidence soon became interpreted as arrogance

I avoid discussing referees whenever possible. They get far too
much attention as it is. I am, though, aghast that one Premiership referee, Uriah Rennie, has his own agent and a sportswear
contract. He'll be dating one of the Spice Girls next

Was it perchance after Rennie sent off Edworthy at Leicester
for tripping over an opposition players legs whilst running
down the wing for a ball? That was a ludicrous decision too
. . .

Rennie is a joke, and he has the right name really, he gives me indigestion everytime we have him at our place, a complete and utter joke

Rennie, when he was on his way up, was by a good margin the best ref outside the premier division. Its why he got promoted. Unfortunately when he did get promoted it seemed to go straight to his head, and he seemed to change overnight and had some nightmare in the prem

Uriah Rennie + Sky Cameras = An excuse for him to prance around and turn the game into a "look at me show"

'Urinal' Rennie. What a ponce he was!

Muscular Roboref who avoids dialogue with the players and dispenses justice with grim relish

He features on billboard advertising and is believed to have his own agent

Some said that it was just desserts because of his pre-match high kicking antics and his boot deal with FILA. Others pointed

a self publicising website (which we haven't found yet – if it ever existed outside a journalist's imagination) and his use of an agent to deal with the press

Never said he was biased pal – simply inept

2000

Half a year or so into the new millennium and the only bug you have is the bug to keep going.

Like Wimbledon, Sheffield Wednesday and Watford, you have been relegated from the Premiership, taken off the list, removed from the top after just two seasons, but you're not crying over spilt milk, not down in the dumps, not heading for the hills to hide somewhere.

Wounds licked, you've stiffened up your upper lip, hunkered down and weathered the storm. After the initial disappointment of being demoted from the big league, you've dusted yourself off, jumped back in the saddle, remained focused and headstrong, kept your cool, not lost your rag, not taken the decision to heart, but instead pulled your socks up and had the balls to continue.

A few months back, without a word of warning, the news of your demotion down the divisions was leaked to the press before you were officially informed yourself, wasn't ideal but it's done now. Water under the bridge. The past is the past, you have scaled the ranks before, you can do it again.

In God you trust. You will return to the top league one day redoubled, you're sure of it. They can't keep a black man down, the more they try to erase you, the more you will be right there.

It is August, the start of a new season and even though you are no longer a Premiership referee, you are not sent to Rushden & Diamonds or Dagenham & Redbridge but Georgia, a country you have never been to before.

As a FIFA referee now, officiating in UEFA competitions, you are appointed to referee a Champions League game. A proper Champions League qualifier.

A good appointment: the second leg of a second-round qualifier. The home side, Torpedo Kutaisi, are four–nil down from the first leg. It will take a miracle for them to overcome the deficit but this is not your problem, you will do your job regardless of the final outcome.

Your fourth official is Mark Halsey, a good ref, someone you have got to know well over the last few years. The home team play Crvena Zvezda (or Red Star Belgrade to you and me).

You fly to Tbilisi, the capital city of Georgia. You are shuttled to the ground in a sticky minivan, sweat dripping from every pore as you rattle along the bumpiest of terrains, every divot in the road a jolt through the body.

Over dinner you hear crashing and banging, shells and gunshots, close enough to be heard but not near enough to be of any real concern to your hosts apparently.

'Nothing to worry about,' you are told. 'Just rebels in the hillside. It's normal.'

You relish the occasion, the opportunity to referee new faces with different backstories in a country many miles from the

UK. You wonder what they think about you, as you walk out onto the field of play, as you blow to award a free kick, or a corner, the man with the power. You are the only black referee to referee in a top-level division in Europe.

The game itself finishes two–nil to Torpedo, not enough to get them into the next round, to overcome the four-goal deficit, but a decent effort nonetheless.

You caution three players. Names seldom heard in Sheffield. Lots of 'i's.

Then out of the blue, coming as a bit of a shock to you, you are appointed to referee the Charity Shield between Manchester United and Chelsea at Wembley. Considered a glorified friendly by many, an insignificant start-of-season curtain-raiser, but this is a big game to you and you're thrilled to have the opportunity to show the decision-makers they've made a mistake removing you from the top.

But your excitement is short-lived, more or less at the last minute you're taken off it. There's been some kind of mix up it's said, crossed wires somewhere, you are demoted (again) to the role of fourth official, the reserve referee, instead. Made to stand on the side and watch Mike Riley referee as Manchester United lose two–nil to Chelsea.

Demoted from the top league maybe, but you are certainly not out of favour with UEFA.

October now, and you are sent to France to referee France U21s vs Austria U21s. Sent to Brittany to referee a European

Under-21 Championships match likely to feature some of the continent's brightest talents.

France, the favourites, have players that play for Lyon and Paris Saint-Germain, world-class French teams.

Tonight's game is just across the Channel, not too far from Blighty in Brest, right in the corner of the country. To you, it doesn't matter where the game is, you're chuffed to get another European appointment as the only black referee officiating in European competitions. History-maker.

The game finishes two–one France. You book seven players.

• • •

Like you've said, to go to Old Trafford or Highbury or St James' Park and referee games is not pressure, it's an honour, but so far this season, demoted from the Premiership, you've done:

August:

22nd: York City 1–5 Stoke City (League Cup – First Round First Leg)
Attendance: 2,035

26th: Bolton Wanderers 2–0 Preston North End (Division One)
Attendance: 19,954

September:

5th: Peterborough United 2–2 Luton Town (League Cup – First Round Second Leg)
Attendance: 4,286

16th: Norwich City 0–0 Crystal Palace (Division One)
Attendance: 16,828

18th: Derby County 1–2 West Bromwich Albion (League Cup – Second Round First Leg)
Attendance: 2,899

23rd: Huddersfield Town 0–1 Burnley (Division One)
Attendance: 14,016

30th: Northampton Town 2–2 Wrexham (Division Two)
Attendance: 5,595

October:

15th: Fulham 2–1 Blackburn Rovers (Division One)
Attendance: 15,247

18th: Grimsby Town 3–1 QPR (Division One)
Attendance: 4,428

November:

11th: Hartlepool United 3–1 Kidderminster Harriers (Division Three)
Attendance: 2,726

18th: Crewe Alexandra 1–2 Stockport County (Division One)
Attendance: 6,099

December:

2nd: Portsmouth 2–0 Norwich City (Division One)
Attendance: 13,409

10th: Millwall 0–0 Wycombe Wanderers (FA Cup – Second Round)
Attendance: 7,819

23rd: Wycombe Wanderers 2–1 Swansea City (Division Two)
Attendance: 5,001

2001

January:

1st: Scunthorpe United 2–2 Macclesfield Town (Division Three)
Attendance: 3,168

6th: Morecombe 0–3 Ipswich Town (FA Cup – Third Round)
Attendance: 5,923

Now this is a turn-up for the books. Following your demotion, you've been doing the rounds in the lower leagues, taken the playful abuse from the fans in the stands who sing jaunty songs about you being removed from the Premiership. But you've kept your head down, kept going and got on with it.

And you must be doing something right, because although you find yourself refereeing in Division One and Two, sometimes Three, no longer a top referee in the top league, you've been given some good games across Europe: Champions League qualifiers in the middle of Georgia, competitive internationals in France, and today back on home soil, you referee the first leg of Crystal Palace vs Liverpool in the Worthington Cup semi-final in south London.

It's a good appointment, cup semi-finals always are. Maybe you're back in favour, back in the good books, maybe you'll be back in the big league before too long.

You approach the game like you do any other, with belief that you are one of the best, with belief that you could do this game and any final you might be appointed to in the future. Including the FA Cup of course.

Liverpool start strongly here in chilly south London, here at Selhurst Park: chase everything down, close down the spaces, pile on the pressure.

But with the home fans in full voice, the home side are a threat.

Palace launch it forward, you get a shifty on, scamper into a position of credibility.

The high ball loops down and is only half cleared by the Liverpool defender, Stéphane Henchoz. Palace pick up the loose ball and spread it left. You spread yourself left. Follow the Palace winger, Rubins, as he takes one touch to set himself up, and a second one to blast it into the back of the net.

Underdogs Palace go one up and the Selhurst Park crowd go wild.

Pass, pass, pass: one–nil up Palace grow in confidence. Find pockets of space on the left wing, the Liverpool defenders are chasing the ball, playing piggy in the middle.

You adopt an advanced position. The ball is crossed into the penalty area, the Liverpool defenders are slow to react. The ball is laid off for Clinton Morrison, who, just a few yards from goal, smashes the ball home into the top corner to make it two–nil to the First Division side. The home fans roar with delight as Crystal Palace double their lead.

Liverpool get their act together belatedly, show a bit of fight, exhibit a bit of their Premiership quality. Just a minute after, down at the other end, Šmicer grabs a goal back with a tidy finish. A vital goal, a late lifeline.

Despite renewed Liverpool pressure, the score stays two–one to Palace as you blow the final whistle. The south London side have a slim lead to take back to Anfield in the second leg.

It's all to play for though, one team now just ninety minutes away from the final.

You have played your part, for now.

• • •

10th: Crystal Palace 2–1 Liverpool (Worthington Cup – Semi-Final First Leg)
Attendance: 25,933

27th: Aston Villa 1–2 Leicester City (FA Cup – Fourth Round)
Attendance: 26,383

February:

3rd: QPR 1–1 Bolton Wanderers (First Division)
Attendance: 10,293

17th: Grimsby Town 1–0 Burnley (First Division)
Attendance: 6,044

March:

14th: Birmingham City 0–2 Blackburn Rovers (First Division)
Attendance: 29,150

18th: Wolverhampton Wanderers 3–1 West Bromwich Albion
(First Division)
Attendance: 25,069

31st: Preston North End 0–0 Gillingham (First Division)
Attendance: 13,550

April:

28th: Watford 1–1 Tranmere Rovers (First Division)
Attendance: 16,063

• • •

Another big day, another big game. Not quite the FA Cup final, that will come, soon. If you continue to work hard, Uri, do what you do so well, that will come.

Today, it's your turn to referee the Football League First Division play-off final. Bit of a mouthful. Doesn't quite roll off the tongue. Doesn't quite do it justice.

That won't matter when you strut out, ball in hand, leading both teams out in front of over fifty thousand fans.

It's winner takes all: Bolton Wanderers vs Preston North End. One team just a game away from the Premiership. Ninety minutes from a season with the big boys.

Promotion to the Premiership would be a massive achievement for them both, a precious gift to the people of each town.

Before you know it, before it sinks in, you're in. Not Wembley, not today, that's being torn down and built back up again, but the Millennium Stadium, Cardiff, Wales.

Here you stand, all kitted up and ready. Shirt tucked in, boots laced up.

The biggest game of your career so far and you're trying your best to take it all in, soak it all up. You remind yourself to remember the day as you live it.

You meet Big Sam and David Moyes, exchange light words, make small talk. Big Sam is already chomping on a wedge of gum.

In the dimness of the tunnel, waiting, you and the players contained like animals desperate to be set free.

Your heart is beating in your face.

You've done big games before; you hope there'll be bigger games to come still.

Players stretch and sniff behind you like restless dogs. They get in the zone, you're already in it.

In the dimness of the tunnel, waiting. Heart racing.

You get the signal and it's showtime.

The brightness blinds you; the roar, all-consuming. But you're ready, you have to be.

National anthem sung. Hands shaken. Pleasantries done.

You blow the whistle and everything that was still comes alive: legs, lungs and hearts.

Middle of the pitch, just outside the centre circle, you award a Bolton free kick.

Early-game sluggishness shaken off; you stroll into position, no need to rush.

You get into the right area, watch for the pushing and shoving and nudging and levering, illegal use of the elbow, all of it at once. You get into the drop zone, where you think the ball will land.

The ball is lofted in, finds a blue Bolton head. Gardner gets a leg in first from the knock-down, then falls to floor as if he's been caught. Contact? Trip? Push? Penalty? Muscles flinching, your inkling says no. Your inkling is usually right so you don't blow, you don't point, you stand unmoved.

But there's no time to dally, no time to contemplate, barely any time to think. You think in full stops. Not long rambling sentences.

The ball in is only half headed, only half dealt with. It falls to a Bolton player, their central midfielder, Farrelly, just outside the D, who hits it sweetly, with the laces of his boot.

The drilled shot nestles into the bottom corner. The hearty roars from the Bolton fans in raptures overwhelm you, the incomprehensible sound of unbridled joy. The Bolton players rush to celebrate, one foot in the Premiership.

Into the second half and Preston have come out rejuvenated, reinvigorated, revitalised. They've come out hungry.

They spread the ball about in the Bolton half, they need a goal if they want to play against the big boys in the big league next season.

Their centre-back, Rob Edwards, desperate to do something, desperate to take charge from the back, charges through the centre and straight towards the Bolton defence.

He is faced by a wall of Bolton blue, an impenetrable wave.

You shuffle out of the way, turn on the spot, as the defender becomes an attacker.

There aren't many options but he sees a slither of an opportunity, and dissects the Bolton defence with a threaded clever eye-of-the-needle ball with the outside of his foot.

He has spotted a runner motoring from midfield. You have spotted the runner motoring from midfield.

The receiving player, number eight, Rankine, has a chance to make the Bolton keeper work, a chance to equalise, a chance to restore parity.

You wait and watch, you are far enough, you are close enough.

The angle skewed, Rankine has an ungainly swipe and the ball soars very high and very wide into the stand, a golden opportunity to equalise, missed.

Tired legs are kicking in now. The pitch here in Cardiff is a big one, and the players are struggling to keep the ball, struggling to string passes together, struggling to find the right man.

Little passes don't work so the ball is booted downfield by Preston in hope. Macken the usual target. He runs on to the long ball, gets a touch.

You run and chase, watch and wait.

Outside, outside, inside, he's now inside the penalty area. Macken protects the ball from the Bolton defender, uses his strength to shoulder him out the way; you sprint to where you need to be, getting closer and closer to an area of credibility, ready to award a penalty if needed.

The Bolton defenders have got back in numbers.

Macken is desperate to do something, muster up a bit of magic to get his team back in the game. Somehow the Bolton defender ends up on the floor, legs flailing. *No foul, no foul.* Macken, off balance and with his back to goal, lays the ball off, with the outside of his foot, for his strike partner, David Healy.

Healy adjusts his body shape, eyeballs where he wants the ball to go and curls one towards the bottom corner. The shot looks good and for a brief moment, you contemplate the possibility of extra time but before you're allowed to think that far, the Bolton keeper, Clarke, has dived to his left, and at full stretch, has got fingertips onto the ball and stopped it from entering his net.

It's a fantastic save, a save that keeps Bolton Wanderers in the lead.

The Bolton defenders remain resolute in the face of increasing Preston pressure.

You're where you need to be, keeping control, keeping calm amidst all the excitement and drama.

From the resulting corner, you watch the swell of bodies to-ing and fro-ing, making sure everything is kept clean and tidy.

It's all Preston. Persistent Preston passing, persistent Preston pressure. They knock the ball about, keep possession, try to unlock the Bolton defence with through balls and long ones over the top.

They pile bodies forward, there isn't long left and legs are running on empty.

But Bolton are quick to break with acres of space to play with, the Bolton midfielder sees an opportunity ahead, knocks the ball first time to the substitute, Michael Ricketts.

The game is wide open now, and you break into another sprint to get into a good position.

The ball to Ricketts is a good one, pinpoint, the striker takes it into his stride, lets it roll across him and now is one-on-one with the Preston keeper.

The Preston defender, the tired Preston defender, can't catch up, Ricketts is too quick, too fresh.

The keeper comes out, makes himself big, spreads himself out like good keepers are taught to do. Ricketts is calm and composed though and seems to have this (the ball) under control, seems to know what he wants to do.

He drags the ball left, around the clutches of the goalkeeper who has crumpled to the floor, and now the goal is gaping, and now the Premiership is within touching distance.

There is a Preston defender tracking back, desperately sliding in, but he is too late, Ricketts stretches along the turf to tuck the ball home in front of the already jubilant Bolton fans.

The gradual crescendo of noise reaches maximum roar as they celebrate their impending promotion.

With just seconds left, within seconds of kick-off, Preston lose the ball again, and now the Bolton winger, Ricardo Gardner, goes on an enterprising jet-propelled run.

He's pacey, a Jamaican international, so you, even in the ninetieth-plus minute are forced to burst into a sprint. You chase your fellow countryman as you might have done back in Dalvey as a little lad.

He has so much space to run into, the Preston players look like they've given up, their legs certainly have, but the Bolton players want more, sensing blood.

He runs and runs. You chase and chase. He's just outside the Preston penalty area and skips past a white shirt with ease.

He now has just the keeper to beat; he now is well placed to smash the ball in with his left foot, and that's what he does, right into the bottom corner to make it three–nil with more or less the last kick of the game.

Game well and truly over, Bolton back in the Premiership, you the man refereeing their return.

At the full-time whistle, you shake the hands of Football League officials and other various representatives and collect your memento as the Bolton players continue to celebrate and their fans sing and cheer euphorically.

While down the Preston end, teary men and women are consoled by loved ones and lifelong pals.

You know you've had a good game, you know you haven't done anything to directly influence the final score and you can afford a little smile as you walk down the tunnel and back into your dressing room.

No cautions, no red cards.

Job done, Uri. Job done.

·   ·   ·

Pre-season over: new season, new players, new teams, new grounds, new goals. You're keen to make your mark for all the right reasons, get given the best appointments, be the best referee you can be in every game you are given.

After a difficult season, a season spent in the lower leagues in places like Portsmouth and Peterborough, you want to take every opportunity you can get.

Over the coming weeks, heard through the grapevine, amongst the whispers and rumours, emails and texts, news is received of a significant development, a shake-up to the system: referees in the top division will become full-time Select Group officials.

Philip Don, the referees' manager for the newly formed group, has told the press that these new arrangements have been designed for the best refs to continue to improve the standard of refereeing. He has called it a priority.

It will enhance the status and standing of referees within the professional game both at home and abroad, Don added.

And you know, if you want to referee that FA Cup final, if you want to be the best referee, refereeing the best players in the best league, you too must be selected for the Select Group and get yourself promoted back to the Premiership.

And soon enough, one fine day, heard through the grapevine, amongst the whispers and rumours, emails and texts, the news received is good. After just one season, you've done it, you're back in the big league.

It's confirmed, you, Uri, are to be among the twenty-one of the country's elite full-time officials. The vanguard of a new movement reshaping the face of English refereeing.

You will earn a basic salary: thirty-three grand a year, plus match fees of £900, plus performance-related bonuses.

But it's not about the money, it's time to get your arse in gear, this is a second chance to put your stamp on the league, a second chance to impress.

The Steadicams, the sound booms, the scrutiny, the cama-raderie, the journeys to and from stadiums in blacked-out people-carriers, the matchday buzz, the late nights, the early starts, slaloming between world-class superstars; after a sea-son away, you've got a second wind, you're back in the big league with the big boys and you're raring to go. The limit is the sky.

You are the only black referee in the Premiership, and this time, you're more determined than ever to not let standards slip, you have an FA Cup final to referee one day, one day soon hopefully.

Refereeing, something that you initially did on a whim, is now something that you will do professionally. Something that was first just a pastime to try your hand out, a hobby, some-thing that started out as an activity to get out of the house and make a quick buck, something to cover the coaching insurance, something to keep fit, will now be your full-time job.

Ex-Sheffield Prem ref Keith Hackett calls you 'the fittest referee we have ever seen on the national and world scene', a quote the press seem to love, but going full time means conditioning, more training sessions, diets and data scrutiny: technology, technology, technology.

God helps those who help themselves, and you're more than ready to do what you will have to do.

You are among twenty-one members of the country's Select Group referees. You and Chris Foy, Dermot Gallagher, Phil Dowd, Alan Wiley, Steve Bennett, Rob Styles, Barry Knight, Matt Messias, Mike Dean, Neale Barry, Mike Riley, Graham

Poll, Andy D'Urso, Jeff Winter, Graham Barber, Paul Durkin, Peter Jones, Steve Dunn, Mark Halsey and David Elleray.

You suppose it is fair that, now you are officially a professional, you should be expected to keep raising your standards. It's not just about the current Select Group, you think, it's about the legacy you will leave behind when you will have to hang up your whistle one day, it's about ensuring that the standard of refereeing in England is better than it was before you turned pro.

The aim is to be better referees, you tell a journalist for the PFA, make fewer mistakes, drop fewer clangers; you are now more accountable for your decisions than you once were, the systems are more transparent too.

Despite what people might think, you don't get above your station, you don't live in an ivory tower. There are no delusions of grandeur; you have a job to do if you want to be the best.

Of all the referees on the elite panel, you have experienced the effect of increased accountability, the hardest being having been demoted to the Nationwide League once already. Experienced the full gamut of emotions dropping down the divisions and fighting your way back: inner conflict, self-doubt, uncertainty, vulnerability, the works, as you bounced in between the leagues.

Character built, you're a better person now, a better referee you think too, a bellwether, you could say.

You have come a long long way from the Wybourn and tough tough games at Concord Park, tough tough games in the

Unibond Northern Premier League and tough tough games at Boothferry Park. From a standing start to a superstar.

• • •

September now, back on European duty, you are appointed to a UEFA Cup game in Poland. A great appointment. A first-round game between Polonia Warsaw and FC Twente of the Netherlands.

You are a black man, a black referee taking charge of a European game in Warsaw.

There are nerves before you leave the UK, before you arrive in Poland, but more so, a surge of excitement gushes through you.

A new stadium, new languages to try to interpret, but this is what being a FIFA referee is about, new challenges from games you normally do, in stadiums you normally go, this is the honour that comes with the badge.

As the ball is knocked about, and the home fans bounce up and down in the stands, you allow yourself a second or two to let it soak in. Like a photographer with a wide-angle lens, you zoom out for a moment and imagine observing the scene from afar, before zooming back in again to blow that first whistle.

You, a black man from Dalvey Pier, St Thomas, rural Jamaica, a black man who grew up in the Wybourn, Sheffield, refereeing a European game here in Warsaw, Poland.

Some black men, you know, would be too scared to even visit Warsaw for a city break, would be too put off by the stares and the comments they might get walking down the street. But you're not just walking, sipping on cheap beer in the main square, or visiting the local museum and checking into the local hotel in the evening, you're controlling, dictating, instructing twenty-two professional European footballers. History-maker.

The home side lose two–one, you dish out two cautions. Names you cannot pronounce.

2002

Deep down, you don't want to be centre of attention all the time, but sometimes you find yourself right in the thick of it.

In some places you go, controversy seems to follow.

It's not your fault. It's part and parcel of being a football referee sometimes.

But it shouldn't have to be this way. You're not a traitor, you're an arbitrator. You're there to make a decision when there's a point of dispute. Not there to trip the players up.

The black man dressed in black: black top, black shorts, black socks, black boots, two black watches, black skin.

You're the appointed match referee and that's your job. Peacemaker, mediator, firefighter. And usually, when players appeal it must be because they genuinely feel aggrieved by something. Or, they genuinely feel they haven't done anything wrong. But it's up to you to say 'yes, you have'. Because usually, you're right.

It's in the job description: you live by the sword, you die by the sword.

It's battle after bloody battle. If you put yourself in the public eye, stick your head above the parapet, you're going to take some hits. It goes with the territory.

It's noon in north London and you're back at Highbury for an FA Cup quarter-final replay at Arsenal. Today, the Gunners play Newcastle United and you are the referee in the middle.

It's a big game for both teams, it's a big game for you. Both teams are just two games from a potential final. You, Uri, are just two games from a potential final.

This is the furthest you've been appointed in the FA Cup as the ref in your career so far, and the final feels like it's within touching distance. You pray the referee committee, the power-er brokers at the top, think you're the man for the job come May.

It would feel different to refereeing a normal match, you're sure of it, the cup final. You can picture it already, arriving into Cardiff on the Friday night, given a tour of the stadium – not that you'll need one – do TV interviews and be the guest of honour at the Referees' Association Eve of Final Rally dinner. You'll say a few words, thank your friends and family for their support, and then take pictures with referees of all levels, from the FIFA-listed to the lowly Level 7s wearing wide-necked shirts and oversized stripy ties.

The goosebumps, the dry mouth, the inability to speak, the uncontrollable shakes, the butterflies. You can't buy those feelings.

You can picture it now, that important first decision, a throw-in, something straightforward to ease you into the game, get a feel for it.

Then making sure if you get a decision wrong, you get the next one right.

For now, back to today, back to about to referee Arsenal vs Newcastle United. It finished one–all back at St James' Park a few weeks back – Mark Halsey the referee – but there must be a winner by the end of play.

Arsenal:

Wright

Luzhny   Adams   Campbell   Cole

Ljungberg   Vieira   Edu   Pires

Wiltord   Bergkamp

Newcastle United:

Given

Hughes   O'Brien   Dabizas   Distin

Solano   Acuna   Dyer   Robert

Shearer   Cort

Tight sloped tunnel. A glare at the end of it. The two captains – Tony Adams and Alan Shearer – shoulder to shoulder. You, just a step ahead of them.

Having been to the final twice in recent years and losing them both, Alan Shearer must be desperate for an FA Cup winners' medal; you just want to get there.

The journey here, the pre-match checks, the polite small talk all done, and finally it's time to do what you do best, time to boss it.

Do well today and you're in with a shot for the final, maybe.

All Arsenal to start. Bergkamp is fouled, but has the ball still. You let the play continue, let the play go on, hoist both arms up in front of you and shout 'Advantage!' as you run towards the penalty area.

Bergkamp slides it left to Pires who slots it into the corner of the net and with just over a minute gone on the clock it's *one–nil to the Arsenal.*

The Gunners come again, Newcastle not at the races. Just outside the box, Bergkamp receives, shimmies, turns and curls one towards the top corner.

It thunders off the crossbar and Newcastle United scramble the ball clear.

The earlier favour is repaid between the two Arsenal players involved in the first goal. Pires slides it across for Bergkamp this time round and now it's two. Too easy.

Newcastle muster the odd chance but look unlikely to score. O'Brien misses a sitter. Heads the ball wide from a yard or two out.

The Highbury crowd want a penalty. Bergkamp tussles with

O'Brien in the box. Not enough for you, you're in charge, no penalty.

Shearer chips just wide from far. An audacious effort from the one and only. But Newcastle's saviour can't save the day today.

Pires is injured (badly), and has to be stretchered off by a team of concerned medics.

Ljungberg shot. Given save.

Free kick Arsenal. Bergkamp cross and Sol Campbell makes it three just minutes into the second half.

Fifty minutes gone, game over.

Arsenal go for a fourth. Bergkamp tries a chip again, again he hits the crossbar.

Final score, three—nil Arsenal.

A walk in the park. The home side easily into the semi-final, Alan Shearer's Newcastle United out.

In your changing room, after the game, as you undress, lather up and let the water wash over your skin, you sing 'Shackles' by Mary Mary and treat yourself to the brief thought of refereeing the cup final.

A brief moment, a snapshot, a dream, appearing and disappearing again as you towel yourself dry.

• • •

Another pre-season over: new season, new players, new teams, new grounds, same goal.

Back in the North East, back at the Stadium of Light: Sunderland vs Manchester United.

In position as the corner is taken short by the away side, but the attack is scuppered by a Sunderland block and the ball balloons skywards.

You monitor the aerial challenge which is won by the blue shirt of a Manchester United player.

The Sunderland backline haven't pushed up quickly enough and Ryan Giggs has found too much space in the penalty area.

Two touches: one to deftly control it, the second to slide it into the bottom corner. United take the lead.

Seeking an equaliser, Sunderland string a few cute passes together, one-twos and triangles around the static Manchester United defence.

The Black Cats have a throw-in in their attacking half.

You're watching and waiting, stood to attention.

The ball is played towards Claudio Reyna, you sidle out of the way as he plays a clever ball forward towards Jason McAteer who has evaded his man, snuck into the penalty area, rounds Roy Carroll in goal and angles the ball goalwards.

The first shot is blocked. With a hand? It's hard to say, it's hard to see. Bodies have infiltrated the box in numbers.

The ball pinballs about but eventually falls for Flo, Sunderland's lanky Norwegian, who cannons the ball into the roof of the net to make it one–all.

Seventy minutes played. It's heating up in the North East. Jason McAteer loses control in the United half and is hounded by Roy Keane from behind.

You adjust your position, you could have a decision to make here, you need to be somewhere to see everything as it unfolds.

You get side-on. Always getting side-on.

Roy's nicked the ball but McAteer isn't giving up easy.

Roy has the ball at his feet and is bursting into the Sunderland half. But Jason stays tight, has got a fistful of his shirt, stopping him from running. Roy doesn't react at first. He holds off. Holds off until he suddenly snaps.

They both tumble onto the turf. Limbs flailing. Elbows and knees.

Roy's reacting now, fury in his eyes, head's gone.

This feud has history. Messy Irish history. Messy World Cup history.

Grab Roy, save Jason? Only a moment to think. You take matters in your own giant black hands with a cliff-edged fearlessness. You get in between the two. You do what you have to do, to stop it escalating, going too far, from turning into a twenty-man mass brawl.

You grab Roy, grip onto his shirt like you did a few seasons ago at White Hart Lane, but tighter this time. Roy Keane and Andy Sinton then. Roy Keane and Jason McAteer now, you in the middle of it again.

You don't follow FA protocol. You throw away the rule book and intervene early with action, words won't do, stopping Keane from doing something he shouldn't.

You stare Keane dead in the eyes, still clutching a fistful of his shirt. Beckham gets involved now, helps usher his captain away from the scene with a gleeful grin, his blonde locks like curtains.

Manchester United's John O'Shea gets involved too.

Messy Irish history. Messy World Cup history.

Keane is fiddling with his captain's armband as you try to reason with him. He's only half listening, facing you but eyeing up the Sunderland player who has retreated behind you to safety shouting something seemingly relating to Keane's new book.

Although he might not be showing it now, maybe in his own reluctant way, he respects you, Roy Keane: your literal handling of the situation, matching force with force, fire with fire.

When you referee at Plymouth, and you make a decision like you just have, maybe five thousand people are watching, referee a game like this in the Premiership and the whole world can see. It's a theatre. The stage-trained players are the actors and you're the director.

Director and star with the leading role.

This isn't the end of it though.

In a separate incident, in the last minute of the match, Roy Keane elbows McAteer straight in the face. Straight red. You have no choice.

• • •

You replay the moment in your head. Over and over. The colours, the sounds, the actions. Your actions that are now under scrutiny from the FA, from the media, from ex-players, from the pundits in their slim-fit silver-tongued suits and cosy television studios. It's an onslaught.

Some people are calling your handling of Keane yesterday heavy-handed, too involved, too busy.

But in your eyes, and you will stick by this until the day you die, you just did what you had to do. You did what you did to keep control.

You have been scrutinised before, you will be again, but you just did what was right at that time. Nothing more to it.

You replay the moment in your head over and over.

Couldn't do that in a Dog and Duck game on a Sunday at grassroots level, many have said.

The phone rings, it's Keith Hackett, he has his say.

Your boss, Phil Don, has his.

Former ref Keith Cooper has his.

An inquest: the jury's out, opinions are split, the verdict non-unanimous. You've heard referees from the lower leagues question the physicality you used, but you stand by the fact, again, that you did what you had to do in that particular situation on that particular day.

Your actions are the talk of every football fan in the country, even some nimble-fingered keyboard warriors from across the world, who voice what they think on the BBC Sport website.

The fact that Rennie is now marked for possible disciplinary action is both ridiculous and a wrong precedent to send out. Refs are only human, and they react in different ways to different situations. Punishing a ref for dealing with a situation in the best way he thought possible is as good as saying to them 'you are just there to observe, we'll take the major decisions thank you'. I think the fact that it was even mooted at all is ridiculous and if I were Rennie I would quit.

Biodun Gaffar, Nigeria

The fact that McAteer was not even booked is conveniently overlooked by the anti-Keane mob. Keane clearly felt that an injustice had been done and went about seeking revenge in his own way. I do not condone Keane's behaviour but the referee and McAteer's behaviour (faking injury / abusing Keane etc...) were deplorable.

Chris Oxford, Dubai

Rennie is by no means my favourite referee. His sending off of Alan Shearer against Villa was a joke. His failure to notice the elbow on Michael Owen by a Leicester player was also a sign of his uselessness. However, had he not done anything to stop Keane thumping McAteer, then he would also have been criticised. It's great isn't it, the FA drags its heels in punishing Keane, but Rennie gets it around the ear almost straight away.

Simon, Germany

As a Sunderland Fan, I thought he did the right thing; he used his common sense in preventing an incident getting out of hand. For Uriah to be hit with disciplinary action for using his head is a disgrace. Let's be honest he's had his fair share of criticism in the past.....but this time its hats off to Mr Rennie.

Matthew, England

Rennie had to step in, however he should not have manhandled Keane. We all know he has a fiery temper and I'm just glad Keane didn't whack him too; otherwise he'd probably get a life ban.

Alastair, Northern Ireland

Uriah Rennie is the most improved referee in the Premiership. He is perceptive and uses good old fashioned common sense in his approach to refereeing. To discipline him for taking quick and decisive action to defuse a potentially volatile situation would be completely off the mark. Get these idiots out of their ivory towers and in touch with the views of supporters. Well done Uriah Rennie and keep up the excellent standards you have attained in the past season. If only they were all that good.

Iain Mackie, England

Why should it be "a dangerous precedent to set"? Boxing referees split up two fighters, why can't football refs split up two players. If he hadn't, both would have been in a fight, then sent off. Both Keane and McAteer should praise Rennie. He stopped the whole situation getting out of hand.

Nick, London

This just proves what a joke the people who officiate the game in this country are. No decent human being can stand aside and watch someone get attacked – why is Uriah Rennie any different? He's a human, before he's a referee.

Drags, England

Uriah Rennie's intervention probably stopped a serious fight starting that would have landed Keane in even more trouble.

Fair enough, Rennie probably should have booked McAteer earlier, but would this really have stopped Keane elbowing the Sunderland player later in the game? I think the ref must feel very disappointed that his prompt action to avert a fight on the pitch has been rewarded by a ticking-off from the small-minded authorities.

Simon Miller, England

I was at the game on Saturday, and am convinced that if Rennie had not got between Keane and McAteer, Keane would have ended up with an assault charge against him.

T Baker, UK

Uriah Rennie did the right thing in stopping Roy Keane from reaching Jason Mcateer, as he saved a very dangerous situation. Roy Keane was completely out of control and could have caused a lot of trouble...as usual! Well done to the courageous Uriah Rennie!

Anthony Calleja, Malta

If a player if touches a ref then that player is punished, so why should it be any different when it is the other way around?

Mark Smith, England

Fair play to the ref for stepping in and preventing an ugly clash. I don't particularly like Roy Keane, but the ref done him one hell of a favour. Who knows what he would have done to McAteer on the spur of the moment, because he was up on his feet a lot quicker than him. 10 out of 10, Uriah!

Gareth, Ireland

How can the FA even think of punishing the ref, when he possibly stopped a complete riot. Keane was looking for McAteer from the moment his late tackle went in. I say "well done, ref".

Phil, UK

With the exception of failing to book McAteer, I think Mr Rennie had a very good game. By preventing Keane from attacking McAteer he may have seriously damaged Keane's book sales, although Keane himself set that straight in the last minute by securing the headlines with a shocking off-the-ball attack. Mr Rennie should not be reprimanded for his actions, but neither should it become common place for referee's to manhandle players.

Jon Hewitt, England

I think that a ref stepping in to pull a thug off another thug in order to maintain the peace is simply a case of him doing his job. It's unusual for a ref to do his job properly, so why are people criticising him for doing it for once?

Ian, UK

There is no way Uriah Rennie should be punished. Have the people thought that if he had not handled Keane, then we may have had 22 players battling? As a referee myself, I was taught early on that at potential flashpoints, identify the troublemaker and deal with them there and then.

Stewart Smart, United Kingdom

I agree that refs should not grab players, the same as players should not touch refs. In doing so, Rennie seems to have totally missed the fact that the tackle that started the issue should have resulted in a booking!

Lez T, UK

I don't think Rennie should be punished. It's about time we saw referees stand up and show that no matter how big a player is, he cannot abuse the referee. Too many times have we seen players get away with things because the ref has been scared! Good on you Rennie.

Jez, UK

Opinions are split, but you did what you had to do in that particular situation. You stand by that. You wouldn't advise young refs to do the same but at that moment, in that particular context, with those particular individuals, you did what you had to do to maintain control. Stop a potential mass confrontation.

In the week that follows, McAteer tells the media you did the right thing; you tend not to read the back pages of the paper but you're relieved to have his support.

Face saved, this too shall pass.

• • •

October now and you're back at Goodison for Everton vs Arsenal. The away side are unbeaten in thirty games and have started the new season strongly.

Last time you refereed both these teams here, because laws are laws of course, you sent off Don Hutchison and Emmanuel Petit. That was in 1999, it's 2002 now, and no two games are the same.

Ljungberg gives Arsenal the lead on the eighth minute.

Radzinski equalises for the hosts after twenty-two.

With the game tied, Everton attack with only minutes to go; the ball is hoofed forward by Thomas Gravesen towards their teenage striker, Wayne Rooney.

Always on the move, you jog into position to see the teenager cleverly control the dropping ball over his head.

With his back to goal, he turns on a sixpence, the Arsenal defenders retreat, as Rooney looks up, picks his spot and rifles one towards the top corner.

You're right behind it, know it's a goal as soon as it's hit.

Seaman is beaten all ends up, as the shot thunders off the underside of the bar and Everton have got the winner it seems in the eighty-ninth minute of this match.

Just yards behind it, you're honoured to witness such a special moment: a special goal by a special talent.

There's clearly a fire in his belly.

*   *   *

Christmas with only some of the trimmings, no pigging out on pigs-in-blankets, you have a game tomorrow. Family. Presents. Queen's Speech. Dinner. Pack bag. Bed.

It's Boxing Day, and you've been sent to the Reebok Stadium to referee Bolton Wanderers vs Newcastle United.

Bolton, a team you know well from last season's play-off final and last season's stint refereeing in the Nationwide Football League. A team that need points to boost their survival hopes.

You and Newcastle have history too, obviously. You and Alan Shearer have history, obviously. You approach the game with some trepidation but these anxieties are quickly quashed, you have to believe in your ability to referee the top players in the top league. This is just another game for you to excel, show *them* what you've got.

Like any game you do in this league, you have to be on your guard, you are aware you are not a fan favourite with the Newcastle following, but there is no vendetta or agenda; just the laws of the game and your Fox 40 whistle.

You came across this the other day, your record refereeing Newcastle United games:

1997–1998: West Ham (h) <u>lost</u> 0–1

1997–1998: Man Utd (a) drew 1–1

1998–1999: Chelsea (a) drew 1–1

1998–1999: Wimbledon (h) won 3–1

1998–1999: Leeds (a) won 1–0

1998–1999: Leicester (a) <u>lost</u> 0–2

1999–2000: Villa (h) <u>lost</u> 0–1

1999–2000: Birmingham (a) <u>lost</u> 0–2

1999–2000: Leicester (h) <u>lost</u> 0–2

2000–2001: None (demoted)

2001–2002: Arsenal (a) <u>lost</u> 0–3

2001–2002: Blackburn (a) drew 2–2

2002–2003: Man City (a) <u>lost</u> 0–1

Bolton Wanderers:

Jääskeläinen

Charlton   Bergsson   Whitlow   Barness

Frandsen   Okocha   Djorkaeff   Gardner

Pedersen   Ricketts

Newcastle United:

Given

Griffin   O'Brien   Caldwell   Hughes

Solano   Dyer   Speed   Robert

Ameobi   Shearer

You, in the dressing rooms of the Reebok. You, taking off your suit trousers and hanging your blazer on the peg. You, loosening your tie till it's off and unbuttoning your shirt. You, wiggling your head through the hole of your black referee shirt. You, wiggling your legs through the holes of your shorts. You, filling your pockets with your cards, your coin, your notebook, your spare pencil. You, now ready to referee twenty-two grown men and their managers.

The game starts frantically, furiously fast-paced. Your legs gallop into position: a dark horse, black beauty. Cantering on, you blow, run, sprint, point. Jockeying into position, going where you need to go, giving what you need to give to keep a tight rein on the game, gliding across the turf like a tree-trunk-legged figure skater, a black Christopher Dean doing the *Boléro*.

Fifth minute: Newcastle's Kieron Dyer loses possession cheaply, dwells on the ball for too long. Gardner seizes onto it and centres for Jay-Jay Okocha to give Bolton the lead. One–nil.

Eighth minute: Nice build-up play between Dyer and Solano and predictably, Newcastle's saviour Shearer equalises, drives the ball home, squeezes it past Bolton goalkeeper Jussi Jääskeläinen. One–one.

Ninth minute: Newcastle's Caldwell blocks Bolton's Ricketts and you give the free kick in a dangerous position. Gardner breathes in, breathes out, runs up and smashes the ball past Given at the far post, Bolton restore their lead. Two–one.

Forty-fifth minute: Just before the half-time interval, the Newcastle defence fail to clear their lines and Bolton striker Michael Ricketts makes it three–one with a header.

Three–one is the score it stays as you blow the half-time whistle.

Sixty-third minute: Ricketts scores again for Bolton, capitalises on a Gary Speed error, and races away before finishing past Given. Bolton in complete control, the home crowd cheer rapturously again, they can hardly believe it. Four–one.

Seventy-second minute: The ball pinballs from goal to goal like the football scene from *Bedknobs and Broomsticks*. Advancing from the right, Ameobi skips into the box and drives a low effort towards goal. The shot deflects off Dyer's boot, Jääskeläinen is wrong-footed and Newcastle have a goal back. Four–two.

Seventy-eighth minute: Newcastle free kick. Dangerous area. Robert touches the ball for Shearer who in typical Alan Shearer fashion, like you've seen him do so many times down the years, rifles the ball home from twenty yards. Four–three.

Ninetieth minute: You book Lomano LuaLua for diving. Simulation. The Bolton defender, Mike Whitlow, didn't touch him; the Newcastle United substitute play-acted, displayed over-the-top theatrics. Shearer attempts to intervene, gives his two pence. Captain or not, his remonstrations are taken too far. No player is above the law, so you show Alan Shearer a yellow card too. It isn't well received.

Stoppage time: For the last few remaining minutes, Bolton keep the ball in the corner. Do everything they can to cling on to a much-needed win.

Okocha dribbles the ball down the line, cuts back once and then again, does step-overs, dainty flicks, Cruyff turns and clever crowd-pleasing backheels, O'Brien is left totally bamboozled. The Nigerian wins his team a corner. The home fans cheer with less than a minute to go of stoppage time.

Full time: The game ends four–three. Another eventful Newcastle game you're in the middle for. A chance for Newcastle to reaffirm their European hopes, lost. This game in hand was meant to be a gimme for the Geordies, but football is not played on paper.

Post-match: In the dressing room, your dressing room, as you undress ready to wash off the sweat which has dried white on your forehead, someone knocks on the door, your door.

After a second, Shearer comes in, kitted up still. Your shorts are off but you keep your top on for now. Despite scoring his 350th career goal this evening, there's a clear annoyance in his manner, a bubbling irritation his eyes are unable to hide. He stands, so you stand too. As you expect, he questions the yellow you gave to LuaLua, and then to him, in the last minute.

I thought it was the captain's prerogative that you could go up and speak to the referee, he says. Whitlow admitted he did trip him so there was no reason to book Lua.

Of course he is allowed to feel aggrieved, no player likes getting yellow cards. You didn't know it at the time, but by getting booked tonight, Shearer has reached five for the season and will miss the next game through suspension. But what's done is done, is what you think, but do not say. Instead, speaking with the honesty needed in this situation tell him, almost apologetically, Once I had it out, I could not put it away, I would have looked foolish.

Your answer seems unsatisfactory to him though, his reply is instant and forthright. I thought I was being very polite. I thought the captain could ask the referee questions. That's what you're there for, he says. I don't think I had one free kick in ninety minutes today.

There's not really much to say to this, you think. You have reached an impasse. Is every player entitled to at least one free kick every game? Obviously not. You saw what you saw, gave what you gave, and did what you had to do. And now, have said all that needs to be said.

Before he leaves the dressing room, your dressing room, he fires one last parting shot to mess with your head: he suggests that it's something personal.

But it never is.

As he leaves, you want to say, Close the door on your way out, like some line from some movie, but you don't.

2003

The clock is reset. Everything starts again.

Everyone's conditioned to make goals at the start of the year, set targets, achieve more than they did in the last twelve months: get fitter, stronger, smarter, kinder, richer.

This year, you still just have the one resolution, to referee the FA Cup final in May.

Your long-standing quest to do just that resumes today, you have a game in the third round at Manchester City's Maine Road.

A few days into the new year, a Sunday, the kids are back to school tomorrow, and Kevin Keegan's Manchester City play Gérard Houllier's Liverpool.

Liverpool have not won a game in their last ten.

A minute into the second half, just as the fans dribble back to their seats having downed their pints and scoffed their hot dogs, you award Liverpool a penalty.

Šmicer's cross hits Foé's outstretched hand so you point to the spot. The City players aren't happy, no team ever is when they concede a penalty, but you saw what you saw.

And Murphy's law, Danny Murphy dispatches it to make it one–nil and that's the score it stays.

Liverpool go through to the fourth round.

Manchester City aren't happy. Kevin Keegan isn't happy.

'I never talk about Uriah Rennie except to say I don't like him as a referee – never have, never will, end of story,' he says, you hear.

'He's a law unto himself. Ask his agent if you can have an interview', you heard was added.

You don't take it to heart, you can't.

It's definitely been difficult at times. There's certainly a feeling among players, managers and supporters, that because you're professionals now, you're going to be perfect.

That's clearly not the case. You can never be expected to make correct decisions all of the time, that's not how life is, not just refereeing.

Referees make mistakes, you make mistakes, you are not God. But when you do, it's not about saying 'Oi, Uri, you've made a mistake, you're out', it's about saying the right things in the right way. Referees do not come ready-made or pre-programmed.

If only more people understood that shattering a referee's confidence is no good for anyone.

• • •

Like last year, you yo-yo up and down the leagues. Referee where you are told to. Go where you need to go.

It's all swings and roundabouts: you do Peterborough vs Notts County in Division Two one week, then Middlesbrough vs Spurs in the Premiership the next.

Different grounds, different budgets, same scummy pre-match cups of tea.

You travel the miles, run your diagonals, brandish the cards. You reel through the pre-match instructions, eat up the yards, eat up your post-match meal, then drive home after another job well done.

Your last Premiership game of the 2002–2003 season takes you back to Highbury for Arsenal vs Southampton.

On paper, a dead rubber, Arsenal can no longer win the league and Southampton will probably want to remain injury-free and save their legs for the FA Cup final next week.

Their opponents: Arsenal again. The referee: Graham Barber.

This is just the dress rehearsal for another FA Cup final you've not been appointed to.

Always the bridesmaid.

The game ends six–one to the home team, a non-event.

Arsenal's young winger, Jermaine Pennant, scores a hat-trick on his Premiership debut. Looks like the real deal.

• • •

Just over a week later, you are the referee for the final of a FA competition, but it's not the FA Cup at the Millennium Stadium in front of eighty thousand fans. Instead, you are the man in the middle for the FA Trophy final – the FA Cup for non-league clubs – between Burscough and Tamworth at Villa Park in front of just under fifteen thousand.

Not the one you wanted, obviously, but a final is a final and you are still proud of your appointment.

The big one will come soon, it must do.

The underdogs, Burscough, win it two–one.

●   ●   ●

A plush principality, a playground for the super-rich living tax-free, the Grand Prix, casinos and sexy celebrities. Is this what making it feels like? You, Uri, a European cup final official: AC Milan vs Porto in the Super Cup here in the south of France, here in Monaco.

OK, you're the fourth official, not quite the man in the middle, the main referee, but this is a big one, Uri. This is a big appointment. A black man and a European cup final, unheard of before tonight, but here you are, yet again, the history-maker, watching and waiting from the wings ready to come on if and when needed.

It could be you in the middle soon, could be you showing the world what you're made of. A European cup final, and you the referee in the middle.

That day will come, with God's grace it will come, maybe even next year, you never know.

Not today though, Graham Barber and the Dave Bs – Babski and Bryan – are in charge today. You're behind the scenes. The manager of the managers, the sideline mediator of Carlo Ancelotti and José Mourinho, the handler of the substitution boards, the writer of shirt numbers, the can of Coke-getter. A sponge soaking up each manager's jibes, protests and queries.

A runner standing still between the two benches.

You wear a green-and-blue jacket emblazoned with 'UEFA'. You're one of the big boys now.

Little Uri. Big Uri.

You would much rather be in the middle, stepping out of the shadows into the spotlight to be the star of the show, but you must bide your time, wait your turn. Apply the laws and wait. They say good things come to those who wait.

Today you watch Shevchenko, Maldini, Seedorf, Deco, Benni McCarthy from the sidelines.

In this game, more than most, here in the Stade Louis II, you're acutely aware that you earn just a fraction of what these superstars around you do. Not that this bothers you of course, you're not in this for the money obviously, you never have been. You just want to be the best referee that you can be, and if that sees you reach the top, the pinnacle, lauded as one of the best in the game, then that's an honour you're prepared to carry on your stress-resistant shoulders.

You want more of this and you have it in you, you know you do.

Final score: AC Milan one, Porto nil. Andriy Shevchenko with the only goal after ten minutes.

• • •

Just like four years ago, in that now infamous game where you sent off the famous Alan Shearer, your first game of the new season takes you back to Newcastle United's St James' Park.

Every time you come back here, the stadium gets a little bigger, a little more spectacular; a better stadium means greater expectation. And now, with all the work that's been done, it's the second biggest stadium in the country behind Old Trafford.

Jeff Winter from nearby Middlesbrough was fourth official then, Jeff Winter from nearby Middlesbrough is your fourth official again.

Today, Newcastle United play the Premiership champions Manchester United. The mighty all-conquering Manchester United, who have won more league titles of late than you can count. Who have some of the best footballers in the world at their disposal: Scholes, Giggs, Van Nistelrooy . . . Roy Keane.

To you, this is a massive game, a game involving two massive teams. A chance to show the big boys at the top what you can do. A chance to prove to the Geordie faithful you're up to the job. A chance to start the new season on a high, hit the ground running, throw your name in the hat for even bigger games. The cup final namely.

Newcastle United:

Given

Griffin   O'Brien   Bramble   Hughes

Bowyer   Dyer   Speed   Robert

Shearer   Ameobi

Manchester United:

Howard

P. Neville   Ferdinand   Silvestre   O'Shea

Solskjaer   Keane   Djemba-Djemba   Giggs

Scholes

Van Nistelrooy

You know you're no fan favourite round these parts but you are not here to make friends, you are here to apply the seventeen laws, to keep the game under control, to keep the players safe, to get through the ninety minutes and head back home to Sheffield knowing it has been another job well done.

Round here, you know your name isn't on the back of any shirts. There are no fans in the crowd with placards and signs that say 'I ♥ Rennie'.

A referee shirt with your name on the back in big block letters can't be bought in the club shop.

Four years is a long time in football, but you know the fans will never forget when you dismissed their hero from the field of play. On that day, he – Alan Shearer – wasn't wheeling away with one arm aloft jubilantly. Instead, you saw his arm being used illegally to fend off Villa defender Colin Calderwood.

Elbow met head and you showed him the red.

You can't be everyone's friend, it's not in the job description. People see things differently, it's human nature.

Are you shit, or are you just doing your job? Are you a cheat, or are you just doing your job? Are you a blind bastard, or are you just a human being doing your job?

Your name is still uttered with scorn around these parts, in the nearby pubs, at the school gates, on radio phone-ins and fans' forums. It's probably not the best idea to rile them up too much, so you decide against warming up on the field of play, you don't want to incite, maybe even excite, the home crowd with your high knees and high kicks and jogs around the pitch. Not today.

Despite what people think, you are not here to be centre of attention, some dastardly ball-chasing, wall-marching pedant, you are here with a job to do and that is what will be done.

You count the players, you nod, you smile. You know you will have a challenging ninety minutes to come, but for now you grin.

The away side string a few passes together; you watch your step, pirouetting from penalty area to penalty area.

Van Nistelrooy shot, deflected, corner.

O'Shea header, Given save.

Ameobi turn. Ferdinand tumble. No penalty. Play on. Definitely no penalty.

Shearer dives in on O'Shea, right by the corner flag, right by your assistant. It's a little naughty, a tester, late and untidy but just a free kick will do, for now. You're in no mood to cause a riot.

Silvestre dives in. Djemba-Djemba dives in. Griffin dives in from behind on Van Nistelrooy, recklessly. His first offence or not, you know what you have to do. You reach for your book instinctively, no need to think.

The home crowd whistle and jeer, atmosphere vitriolic, they know a yellow is coming. He says he got the ball, they always say they got the ball. They always think they are the victim of some apparent miscarriage of justice. He gestures his defence, makes a ball shape with his hands, they always make a ball shape with their hands.

Some of the Newcastle players surround you, make what they think of your decision clear, Shearer included, but your mind has been made up, and with only ten minutes gone, Andy Griffin is the first player whose name goes in your book.

It's relentless, no let-up, end to end. Tit for tat. Kick for kick.

Keane dives in on Shearer. Free kick given. The crowd cheer, ironically. The Irishman isn't happy.

If it wasn't obvious already, it's clearer now, you have a game on your hands.

Giggs cross. Given impeded, free kick.

Twenty-three minutes in. The away side come again. A long ball forward and Giggs nods it past O'Brien, beats him for pace and charges towards the Newcastle goal at speed.

O'Brien, the last man, lunges in with his long left leg. The home crowd hold their breaths, go quiet momentarily.

With your whistle to your lips, you look over to your assistant, Russell Booth, who doesn't signal. O'Brien got a toe on the ball, he must have.

Giggs is livid, races to you as the ball goes out for a throw-in by the benches. Keane joins in too, of course. They wanted a free kick, they wanted a red card. But O'Brien timed the tackle perfectly, got the ball completely, he must have.

But you see from the corner of your eye, the edges of your vision, as Neville lines up the long throw, that United boss Sir Alex is incensed.

He's fuming, face flaring, gnawing on his gum furiously.

You can see Jeff trying his best to keep the irate United manager calm. But he, and you, aren't Sir Alex's favourite referees, you don't think, if indeed he has any.

Jeff has clearly had enough and beckons you over. You march towards the dugouts, potential reprimands running through your head as you approach the Man United manager.

Jeff whispers in your ear, he's had enough and wants Fergie binned, removed from the technical area: out of sight, out of mind.

Listening to what Jeff has said, keeping communication concise, in your best softly spoken tone, you send Sir Alex off, down the tunnel, to the stands, away from the field of play, to the home fans' amusement.

Not ideal, you are no homer, but laws are laws.

Play resumes, Fergie-less, mood fractured.

Scholes handball. Robert with the free kick, and who else but Alan Shearer towering tall with the bullet-headed finish, right into the top corner to make it one–nil Newcastle.

The St James' Park faithful celebrate yet another big goal from their hometown hero. Their goal-notching maestro. Their Gallowgate giant.

You watch him wheel away, that famous arm hoisted high, feeling something you can't quite describe.

Back in the Officials' Room at half-time, Jeff gives you the lowdown.

You, like any other referee, don't like your integrity being questioned; at the best of times, it's all you've got. To most, if not all referees, the word 'ch**t' is worse than the word 'cunt'.

You did what you had to do.

Into the second half and the away side are the better team.

Van Nistelrooy misses a sitter.

Scholes hits a four-yard shot straight at the keeper.

But then Keane leads from the front and slides it forward. Van Nistelrooy turns and tucks it home and Manchester United have their equaliser.

Manchester United come again: Keane cross, Scholes' chest and from being one–nil down, the away side are now two–one up.

Under fifteen minutes to go, Manchester United bring on Cristiano Ronaldo, their newly signed Portuguese talent. He gives away a free kick for shirt-pulling within seconds of entering the field of play.

Looks like a player though, ghosting in from the left, dragging the defender who snaps at his heels out of position.

You are relieved as you blow the final whistle, you are relieved to get through a testing first game of the season. But yet again, you cannot seem to go a ninety minutes here at St James' without it being shrouded in controversy, without being at the centre of some headline-making decision involving you and some god-like footballing figure, first Shearer, now Fergie.

• • •

A DJ doesn't just turn up to a venue, press play and walk away. They need to provide the revellers with an experience. In many ways, refereeing is the same.

Rightly or wrongly, every man and his wife's heard of you. Their mum and dad, their nan, their uncle, the old man in the boozer, every Tom, Dick, Harry, butcher, baker and candlestick-maker in the country. Every niece and nephew know the name Uriah Rennie. The only black referee in the Premiership.

Are you too quick to retort sometimes? Maybe. Do you mean to be rude? Certainly not. You do what you think is right, you say what you think is best at that time to manage particularly sticky situations.

It's just who you are, and you are probably too old to change now. You demand respect because the role dictates it.

Some might say otherwise, but you've tried to keep a low profile since reaching the big time.

Some will probably want to know more: what the D stands for in your middle name (it's Dudley obviously), what your kids look like, how you spend your Sundays, but you won't let them in, won't give them the satisfaction. Your family are too important to be ogled at in some double-page spread in *OK!* magazine.

Are you really a black belt? Wouldn't they like to know. Away from football, you're a private man, offering no more than just a broad-stroked outline of who you really are to the wider public. A gun-metal black silhouette. Just the way you like it. This is not an episode of *This is Your Life*.

Your children are Crystal and Jordan. Their mum is Roseanne. Jordan's godfather is Albert Smith, a good friend. And despite some tricky days and mistakes made, you love them all dearly, and that's all that matters.

It's mid-October, tonight you find yourself in Sweden, you fly from one far-flung place to another: town to town, city to city, country to country.

This occasion's different though, bigger, probably your biggest UEFA appointment as match referee: first round, UEFA Cup, Malmö vs Sporting Lisbon, second leg. Two established European teams with European pedigree, you the man in charge of them.

It's a good appointment, no doubt about it, and this is an image to be proud of, you leading out the two teams onto the Malmö Stadion pitch. You've gone from U. D. Rennie (Sheffield) to Uriah Rennie (England) at the back of the match programme; in many ways you're like a national team player representing the nation now. 'God Save the Queen' plays in your head.

The strut into the middle is longer than usual, the pitch here is encircled by a running track like the lines of a record on a gramophone.

The stadium is a modest one, but a stadium that has been used for big games in the past. A stadium used for the World Cup in the fifties, the one where Pelé burst onto the scene as a teenager, the Euros in 1992, and now it is the scene of this momentous occasion, momentous for you at least anyway.

The away team tonight, Sporting Lisbon, lead by two goals from the first leg, meaning Malmö need a big performance to overcome the deficit, to get into the next round. Facts you need to be aware of, facts needed to read the tensions of the game, the fluctuating temperature, the give and pull, the ebb and flow.

Right from kick-off, the game is played at a quick European pace.

But you're on top of things, running where you need to go, being where you need to be to give the decisions you need to give.

Body language in European games is even more important than in England.

It's easier in many ways, refereeing abroad. Cards are expected in Europe, the players expect it, the coaches expect it, and most importantly, the UEFA delegate watching from the stands with their beady eyes and notebook in their hands, expects it.

So, as expected, you caution a Sporting player on the forty-first minute.

So, as expected, you send off a Malmö player, Jon Inge Høiland, right before half-time for a second yellow card.

Laws are laws, in England, in Sweden, anywhere in the world.

Going down to ten men will make the unlikely Malmö come-back even more unlikely, but laws are there to be enforced and you saw what you saw. Control will not be lost on your watch.

Four minutes into the second half, the player you booked just before half-time, Liédson, scores for the visitors to make it one–nil to Sporting Lisbon on the night, three–nil on aggregate.

Even though Sporting's lead has been increased, you mustn't switch off. You have people to impress, European standards to maintain, you want to continue wearing your UEFA badge with pride until you're forced off the list at forty-five, having worked so hard to earn it in the first place.

A few more yellow cards later, the game ends one–nil. Malmö are knocked out of the UEFA Cup, Sporting Lisbon progress to the second round and you are on a flight back to England, head held high, proud of yourself.

2004

Anything can happen in a game of football; just a few months ago at The Valley, the last minute of the ninety, Blackburn Rovers keeper Brad Friedel, up from the back for a corner, swept home a last-minute equaliser with the deft touch of a striker to make it two–two against Charlton Athletic.

Always a special sight, seeing the goalkeeper score.

His joy was short-lived though. Down the other end, just a few minutes later, Claus Jensen volleyed home a stoppage-time winner for the hosts.

Anything can happen in a game of football.

It's April twelfth and today, you're a black man in the Black Country. At Molineux for Wolves vs Bolton Wanderers.

You're into the last few minutes with the away side winning two–one.

Been tough at times to manage, this has.

As the game enters the dying seconds, tensions are fraying and the crowd are baying for your blood. You can sense it from here, feel it too, the Wolves manager Dave Jones is far from happy with you, again.

You don't even need to look over to see he's fuming. He wanted a penalty, probably two. Most of Molineux did too.

Appeal 1: Stelios 'trip' on Kennedy, no penalty.

Appeal 2: Thome 'tug' on Miller, no penalty.

You saw what you saw and, as always, as it should be, your decision is full and final.

The crowd are livid. Their fever-pitched anger, palpable, rippling through the stands of the orange-and-black-clad fans. Not a friend in sight.

Into stoppage time now and from the corner of your eye, the edge of your vision, you see a figure running towards you. But something isn't right.

You sense something strange as the figure comes closer.

Not a player, or a coach, or a mascot or another official, not a steward or a police officer. Not dressed in civvies like that he's not.

Not naked enough to be a streaker.

The figure is getting closer and closer . . .

It's a fan.

There's a fan on the pitch striding towards you, all fire and fury. Denim jeans and a blue trucker cap. He's a supporter. An angry supporter. He's coming closer. Closer and closer. You're not scared but alert. Always alert. It would take a lot more than one madman to put the fear of God into you.

He's coming closer.

You must keep your head.

He's even closer.

You must stand your ground.

He's close.

You're big enough and ugly enough to look after yourself, you know kickboxing and aikido, you've done martial arts since you were lad, you've done shoes and socks off and sticky bare feet on gym hall floors and piling the gym mats back in the corner, but this a football field, and not the time or place for such physicality . . . surely?

The stewards are too slow. It's fight or flight. This finger-pointing fella is just a couple of yards away now.

And just as things look a bit hairy, the Wolves captain, Paul Ince, intervenes in the nick of time, shepherding the rage-fuelled fan – who's effing and blinding, pointing and shouting – away.

Eventually, belatedly, the stewards catch up with him and he is frog-marched away.

The final whistle, which can't come too soon, is met with a chorus of jeers, you are loathed and lambasted.

Boos are bellowed in unison, from all stands of the stadium.

Every game you do, someone somewhere has something to say.

You are surrounded by stewards; you're at the centre, enveloped and encircled by groundstaff in hi-vis.

The Wolves players and their coaches are outraged, you're harangued and castigated by the whingers and whiners. They shower you with swear words.

For a moment, it feels like you are watching yourself from above, besieged, like a helicopter hovering over a fleeing felon; trying to escape is futile.

After the game, dust not yet settled, Wolves manager Dave Jones is again vocal about your performance to the media, undoubtedly oversteps the mark, says things he will probably regret.

It's a one-way salvo, a hot-tempered tirade, a no holds barred barrage.

Dave Jones: He's arrogant in the way he behaves. He's there to referee the game in a manner that's acceptable and I don't think he did that . . .

. . . As for talking to him afterwards, you can't get a word in with him. He's probably too busy putting lip salve on. I'm not blaming him for the predicament we are in or the goals we conceded but we should have had two penalties. I'm not a vengeful man but I can be vindictive and he was crap . . .

He says things he will certainly regret when the FA (hopefully) slap a fine on him. A fine that will probably do little to deter him from saying stuff he shouldn't in the future, in the heat of the moment.

You hear what he has said in fragmented snippets, not in full, but you've heard it all before, no manager ever says anything new about you.

But you don't take it personally.

Certain managers are very astute, much more than people would imagine.

Sometimes what they say to you away from the cameras can be constructive, even beneficial to your progress as a referee.

There are managers who people may think are not interested in your development, but in reality, they often take time to come to your changing room after a game and speak one-on-one.

What they suggest stays private of course, never enters the public domain, but is always taken on board, provided it is appropriate and delivered in the right manner.

People want to be praised, you like to be praised, you don't want to hear on *Match of the Day* that you're the worst referee in the world, but it is essential that any praise is deserving and sincere.

It's unfortunate Dave Jones isn't happy with your performance, but you brush it off, you have to.

And to be honest, you'll probably outlast him, you'll outlast most managers in fact.

Managers in this game, at this level especially, will come and go, but the referee, the man in the middle, you, Uri, will still be there, doing the job that they say you can't do.

• • •

Are you religious? Yes. Are you practising? Yes. Do you go to church? These days, only sometimes. Is this what He wants from you? Undoubtedly, it's all part of the plan.

You fly to Ireland, buzzing, a welcome break from the usual duties. You fly to Cork for a European tie, the quarter-final second leg of the UEFA Intertoto Cup, and you're the referee, you, Uri, the man in the middle.

The landscape is both familiar and foreign: a palette of greens and greys.

The houses here look different, the skies too. Even the air has a newness to it. A freshness.

As the wheels hit the tarmac, you know this is likely to be your last game as a FIFA referee at forty-four years old, soon to be forty-five, so you do your best to take it all in your stride and enjoy it.

As you reach the hotel, you can't help but reflect on the opportunities refereeing has given you. You think back to refereeing in Switzerland, Sweden, Italy, Egypt, Georgia, Poland. You're very grateful, but you can't help but feel slightly disappointed too; what could have been maybe.

Growing up, you remember hearing stories of signs that said: *No Blacks, No Dogs, No Irish.*

There's definitely a strange affinity between the Irish and black people, you think: the outsiders, the non-belongers, historically hated, mistreated. Both God-fearing people who like a tipple or two from time to time.

As of four o'clock this afternoon, you're told tonight's game is a sell-out. The home fans know if Cork can get an early goal, then their unlikely dream can continue.

The home side have kept themselves in the tie with a late goal in the first leg in Nantes but they have a huge task ahead of them, even with the home crowd behind them.

You're in yellow. UEFA yellow. You look the part, feel it too. This game is the talk of the city; a big game for you, but an even bigger game for Cork who are three—one down in the tie.

You lead the teams out flanked by your two assistants, match ball in hand. The noise from the eight thousand fans in the crowd as you march out makes your flesh prickly.

You cross the white line and onto God's green pitch, you swivel to face the main stand, plonk the ball down between your legs and take it all in, soak it all up.

Most of the home crowd will recognise you, of course they will. You're you; the black face of English refereeing.

You let the atmosphere of the occasion penetrate the fine fibres of your skin and invade your bones.

You line yourself up ready for the handshakes, your first chance to look every player in the eye.

Nantes start nervously. Cork throw-in in a dangerous area of the pitch, right in the corner, you're well positioned, a panoramic view of the thrower and the bodies in the box.

The ball is launched in and flicked on by one of the Cork City attackers. A green shirt latches onto the ball in the corner of the penalty box, flicks it over the hapless Nantes defender and drills it in at pace into the danger area.

The ball is cleverly diverted goalbound by a green shirt, number seventeen, and the keeper has no chance as the ball deflects off the Nantes defender and into the back of the net.

After just five minutes, the boys in green, Cork City, take the lead. It's one–nil on the night, three–two on aggregate, already they have one goal of the two they require to get through to the next round.

The home side seem spurred on by the early goal, the Nantes players haven't started yet and give away a succession of cheap free kicks in potentially dangerous positions.

You're in no mood to take any nonsense, you use your body language to show the culprit of a blatant trip that you are unimpressed, and niggly tackles will not be tolerated tonight.

You follow, run, stop, chase, dummy, point, shout, signal.

At your age now, this is probably your last game as a FIFA referee and, like always, you're going to apply the laws of the game as you see them, properly.

The home team want to take a quick one from the resulting free kick, they know they have the French side on the ropes, but laws are laws and you make them take the ball back a few yards and take the set piece from where the offence took place. The words exchanged are brief, no time to dally.

You follow, run, stop, chase, dummy, point, shout, signal.

Nantes have warmed into the game finally and are beginning to show their quality and pass the ball about with increasing confidence. You follow, run, stop, chase, dummy, point, shout, signal. Perform a combination of verbs to keep everything under control.

As Nantes play 'keep ball', whistles and jeers from the home fans circulate around this tiny little stadium. The majority of the crowd do everything they can to put them off, rattle and intimidate, but Nantes attack again undeterred.

The Cork City winger plays it forward and is caught late, right by your assistant. Another mistimed tackle by Nantes' number eleven. You stroll over, decision already made, hand dipped into your pocket, fingering the yellow card ready to be brandished. You call the guilty player over, words sparse, pleasantries avoided, and hoist the card up high. The culprit shuffles back into position without complaining, a continental mentality.

You follow, run, stop, chase, dummy, point, shout, signal.

The Cork City full-back plays it forward into the attacking half and is caught late, right by your assistant. Another mistimed tackle by a Nantes player. Another yellow card, another chance to demonstrate to the players your tolerance level, how *you* want the game to be played, what is and what is not allowed on this field of play, your field of play.

The culprit claims he slipped, but you do not tolerate blame-shifting excuses.

The Nantes captain, number eight, remonstrates from afar, so you call him over ready to read him the riot act, make an example of him, show him in no uncertain terms that he might be the captain but you are the boss.

You follow, run, stop, chase, dummy, point, shout, signal.

Nantes switch the play, ping it long from left to right, pin-point passing from one touchline to the other, try new tactics to break through the Cork City defence. You swivel one way, jog into position and do the same thing over and over.

The ball is played in and bounces out. The last action of a busy half.

Second half, focus sharpened, legs rested.

It's anyone's game, both teams fancy themselves to get a goal.

You strut, shuffle, swagger across the turf.

You follow, run, stop, chase, dummy, point, shout, signal.

Nantes keep coming, find gaps to exploit. The ball is played forward through the middle. The striker receives, cuts inside and looks to shoot. The Cork City keeper rushes out bravely, smothers the ball at the striker's feet. The striker looks at you imploringly for a penalty but you're not having any of it.

You follow, run, stop, chase, dummy, point, shout, signal.

It's all Nantes, Nantes, Nantes. The home crowd have gone

quiet; tension emanates through the stands of this little stadium as the Cork City players tire.

Another lofted ball by a Nantes defender, sprayed with precision from the back, the ball falls for an advancing attacker in space, a substitute. The defenders are too slow, can't adjust their feet, he only has the keeper to beat. He chips the ball and it floats into the net.

One–all on the night, four–two on aggregate. The home side now effectively out of it.

You follow, run, stop, chase, dummy, point, shout, signal.

The ball bounces up, by the halfway line, an invitation for two players to go for it, a fifty-fifty.

Boots are high, studs are showing, it's an ugly-looking coming together and both players lose their heads, aggrieved at how the other one has gone in.

They push and shove, go face to face and lock horns.

Other players get involved, sprint from all angles of the pitch to protect their teammate, turn the situation into a mass confrontation unnecessarily.

You're in the middle of it all, trying to use every tool to keep it under control. Your assistants run on, offer extra security. No punches thrown yet, just bodies and words and accents and emotions intermingled.

You blow and blow, try to maintain order, and soon enough, after a bit of argy-bargy, it simmers down.

Players are dragged away from the kerfuffle by other players and after a few moments only the culprits remain.

You call the two original offenders over, decision made, yellow each.

You know already, as does he, that the Nantes player involved has already been booked. He knows he is just seconds away from being sent off.

You brandish the first card for the Cork City player. Your yellow card drops but the Nantes player is already walking off. He's swears at you in a language you don't understand.

You follow, run, stop, chase, dummy, point, shout, signal . . . and then blow the final whistle.

Final score: Cork City one, Nantes one (Nantes win four–two on aggregate).

Final score: Uriah Rennie soon-to-be-forty-five (and forced to retire from FIFA).

2005

The fact that you can be taken off the Select Group list, booted out of the Premiership and down the divisions like what happened to you a few years ago, shows that you are always accountable as a top-flight referee.

You're a professional now, and the threat of demotion is always there looming large; like most people in most jobs, you go through the usual performance review and monitoring, appraisals if you like.

But you like it here at the top and intend to stay here to hopefully, to put it bluntly, referee the cup final.

It's a question of dedication. You're no night owl, you're in bed by nine-thirty on a Friday. There is no smoking or drinking, you stay as sober as a judge in the days leading up to a game.

You still train hard; you know if you are not fit, you get tired, and tiredness leads to mistakes. When the pressure's on, in a powder keg of a game, things can go wrong to knock you down a peg.

Your belief is that referees are there to enhance the game for players and supporters, not upset the apple cart. No referee wants to be an integral part of any match to the extent that it's all about them.

It's true to say that if you go unnoticed, you've had a good game. But equally, sometimes it's important that you're told, 'Uri, you were rubbish today, sort it out', because it helps you realise that you weren't 100 per cent. And from there you can work to ensure you rectify any problems.

Starting today.

Your development is methodical.

January.

A1.

The North East.

St James' Park.

Sunday.

Alan Shearer.

Newcastle United vs Southampton.

Referee: Rennie, U. (You).

Newcastle United:

Given

Taylor   Bramble   Boumsong   Babayaro

Dyer   Jenas   Bowyer   Bellamy

Shearer   Ameobi

Southampton:

Niemi

Telfer   Lundekvam   Davenport   Higginbotham

Delap   Prutton   Redknapp   McCann

Crouch   Phillips

It's the team in twelfth (Newcastle United) versus the team in nineteenth (Southampton). It's you in the middle versus them all.

Shearer starts, widow-peaked thirty-four-year-old Alan Shearer.

You saunter into position: blow, point, glare, gesture, smile, scowl.

The seconds tick on, three minutes on the watch and it looks like you already have a big decision to make.

The Southampton defender Davenport is doing something he shouldn't as Ameobi bursts into the box from a booted ball from Bramble.

Heart rate increases as you stroll and then sprint into a position to see, knowing you're seconds away from having to make a potentially contentious decision.

Ameobi's shirt is being pulled, tugged, yanked on, by the Saints defender and there's a big decision to give.

a) Penalty for Newcastle.

b) Dive (caution Ameobi for simulation).

c) Nothing. Play on.

d) Free kick for Southampton.

No phone a friend, no ask the audience, the final answer is all yours.

You blow and point to the penalty spot just as Ameobi and the onrushing Southampton keeper Antti Niemi collide, a merging of bodies: bones, faces, studs, skin, skull.

To the disbelief of some fans – the home fans who think you have an agenda against them and the away fans who think no offence has been committed – you award Newcastle United a penalty.

You-riah Rennie: the enemy of the Geordie people, now a North East saint, a Tyneside saviour.

The Southampton keeper is down injured, crumpled in a heap, worse off from the accidental coming together.

The medics come on and the stretcher is called. A bucket, sponge and some smelling salts won't do. It's clear he won't be able to continue and will have to be substituted.

Shearer steps up to take the penalty that you gave. Shearer smashes it home. Shearer, on his return to the team after two months out, makes it one–nil to Newcastle United from a penalty that you gave.

All Newcastle, pass, pass, pressure. Southampton can't get a kick.

Southampton's stand-in keeper, Paul Smith, denies Kieron Dyer from twenty-five yards.

Déjà vu: heart rate increases as you stroll into position knowing you're seconds away from having to make another big decision. Davenport dives in on Ameobi.

a) Penalty for Newcastle.

b) Dive (caution Ameobi for simulation).

c) Nothing. Play on.

d) Free kick for Southampton.

Another quandary. No phone a friend, no ask the audience . . . no penalty.

'More than a fucking penalty than the first one!' Shearer laments at your linesman, you hear.

Thirty-seven minutes gone and you award Newcastle United a free kick in a promising position.

Babayaro's cross into the near post is met by Titus Bramble who makes it two.

Just before half-time, three minutes till the forty-five, Davenport knocks the ball down for Phillips who heads the ball against the bar. Peter Crouch turns it in from the rebound to get a goal back for Southampton. A goal back right before half-time is the best time to stage a resurgence.

Then a quick dash, a clash, a flashpoint, Newcastle United's Lee Bowyer and Southampton's Neil McCann tangle off the ball, a scuffle, but you're in there quick, to get in between them as they tumble to the floor, all arms and legs, all swear words and spit, all veins and venom.

No cards needed this time, a stern telling-off will do.

Just after the hour mark, the one and only widow-peaked thirty-four-year-old Alan Shearer is substituted and replaced by Patrick Kluivert.

You blow the final whistle and Newcastle have held on for the win.

Demons diminishing.

Another Shearer goal. Another Shearer landmark. The 400th goal of his career, you hear someone say after the game, an impressive feat.

●   ●   ●

January, February, March, April, **May** . . .

You must say, you've always felt it, Upton Park is a proper football ground.

It reeks of east London, of pride, of passion, of proper football fans chanting *We're forever blowing bubbles*.

Giant bubbles from giant bubble machines greet you as you saunter onto the Upton Park pitch.

Today, you're in charge of the first leg of the Championship play-off semi-final: West Ham United vs Ipswich Town. Winner of the tie over two legs gets to Cardiff. Winner of the game in Cardiff gets to the Premiership.

Ever-increasing Premiership TV rights mean the Championship play-offs have got bigger and better occasions every season. There's millions of pounds up for grabs these days.

This is not the FA Cup final, but still an appointment you are proud of.

This game will need to be well refereed and as far as you are concerned, you are just the man to do it.

There is not a slither of doubt about this as you blow that first whistle and get the game going.

A long ball is pumped forward by the West Ham goalkeeper, Jimmy Walker, you run backwards, get into a position to spot the aerial challenge, the two players jumping for the dropping ball, making sure it's clean.

It is, so you keep moving, keep padding across the Upton Park pitch.

The ball is flicked on by Bobby Zamora, Matthew Etherington has got in behind the Ipswich defence, he sprints down the wing, you sprint too, try to keep up, the crowd noise rises, sensing an opportunity.

You run and run.

Etherington centres the ball for Harewood who is there,

unmarked somehow, to tap it in for the easiest of finishes to give the Hammers an early lead, with just over seven minutes gone.

The home players rush to Etherington, acknowledge his good play in the build-up. The Ipswich Town defenders rush towards your assistant on the far side. Their offside appeals falling on deaf ears. The goal stands.

West Ham dominate, knock the ball about nicely, every pass evading the blue shirt of an Ipswich Town player. The home side look particularly dangerous on the left wing, the Ipswich right-back, Fabian Wilnis, is being exploited for fun.

Etherington, number twelve, runs at the defence again, plays a neat one-two with a West Ham player infield, gets to the byline and looks for Harewood like he did for the first goal.

The Ipswich defence have learned their lesson and block the cross before it can reach him, but the clearance is a poor one; the loose ball only goes as far as Bobby Zamora who strikes the ball into the bottom corner with his left foot to double West Ham's lead.

You're there and in position, no decision to make, instead just wondering as the goalscorer is mobbed by his teammates how many goals will West Ham score this afternoon.

The proper football fans go proper mental; they are off to a startling start.

The ball is pumped forward and you're on the move again: running, rotating, slipping one way, slipping the next. Shifting, tilting, teetering, oscillating, doing what you can, to be where you need to be.

The high ball is contested by the West Ham defender, Řepka, and the Ipswich Town striker, Kuqi – a battle between two Championship heavyweights.

Two of the heftier, battle-scarred footballers in the division.

You give a foul, against Řepka, award Ipswich a free kick in a dangerous area. The home fans aren't happy, the home bench aren't happy, the guilty player, Tomáš Řepka, definitely isn't happy. Neither are you about his unsporting reaction to your decision, dissent you do not tolerate at this level, and never have.

You give him a yellow card, a reminder that you are in charge, not him.

And, as the laws state now, you then allow Ipswich Town to take the resulting free kick ten yards further forward, ten yards closer to goal.

Tommy Miller's side-footed free kick is deflected, comes off the post and bounces off the keeper and Ipswich have a goal back, right before half-time to make things interesting.

For the fans, at the sound of half-time whistle, it's time for a piss and a pint.

The Ipswich players and coaching staff want to have a few words as you head down the tunnel, words to the tune of a foul in the build-up to West Ham's second goal are voiced, but ultimately ignored.

Harewood on Naylor they say, an incident you can't recall.

Half-time. A time for both teams to take stock. A time for you to take stock: a think and a drink. An interesting forty-five gone, an interesting forty-five to come.

Into the second half and Ipswich look for an equaliser.

There's a mix-up in the Hammers box, Walker and Ferdinand get themselves in a tangle, and Shefki Kuqi taps it in.

After a blistering start by the home team, Ipswich have equalised.

The game finishes two–two, and given the occasion, you consider it a job well done.

It's never easy coming to Upton Park, but you have done what you came to do and for that you are pleased.

West Ham beat Ipswich two–nil in the second leg at Portman Road, Steve Dunn the referee. Bobby Zamora scores twice.

West Ham beat Preston one–nil in the play-off final in Cardiff, Mike Riley the referee. Bobby Zamora scores the only goal.

You watch it at home, alone.

• • •

You wouldn't have noticed out there in the middle: running and blowing and pointing and bee-lining, but here at Boundary Park, as you referee a League One match between Oldham Athletic and Yeovil Town, someone in the stands has just shouted something they shouldn't have.

It's the first game of the 2005–2006 season and a young Old-ham fan, aged seven or eight, is watching the game from the upper tier of the Lookers Stand with his uncle. He spent pre-match at Boundary Blues, a sort of social club for kids, and made his way to his usual seat in time for kick-off brimming with new-season excitement.

After two goals in quick succession, Oldham went two–nil up after just twenty-six minutes, Chris Porter and Paul Warne the scorers. For a short while at least, Oldham were probably top of the league.

After the break, and even though the home side are still win-ning, many of the fans think you're not having a good game, or in other words, you're not giving them every decision they want.

One man in particular was particularly livid. Just moments ago, sat one row in front, and slightly to the left of the young fan, he belted out 'You fucking black bastard!' at the top of his lungs, loud enough for everyone in the upper tier to hear.

Terrell Forbes, Oldham Athletic's centre-back is black, and so are some of the Yeovil players, but there's no doubt that his anger was directed at you, Uri, the match referee.

The young boy, aged seven or eight, was stunned, mouth agape, that was the first time he'd heard racial hatred to that extent here before.

The fans in the vicinity all looked at each other awkwardly

but no-one spoke up, so the young boy's uncle, thinking about what to do for a moment or two, took it upon himself to report what was said to the nearest steward.

Moments later, as you continued running and blowing and pointing and bee-lining, the guy sat one row in front, and slightly to the left of the young fan is asked to leave: first a quiet whisper in his ear, then carted off by a couple of hi-vis-clad staff down the stand stairs and out of sight.

The game finishes two–nil, the home side take all three points.

2006

Alan Shearer played, and scored, against bitter rivals Sunderland on Monday night but hobbled off with an injury in the seventy-first minute.

They say he's torn his medial collateral ligament in his left knee.

They say he is now out for the rest of the season and will not play any part in Newcastle's remaining three games. They say he has already refused a new contract and so has decided to retire.

You refereed him a few weeks back at St James' when Newcastle played Wigan. He scored twice, one of his two goals from a penalty that you gave.

So, after a career spanning eighteen years and scoring 283 top-flight goals, thirty-five-year-old Gosforth-born local lad Alan Shearer has retired.

They say he snubbed Fergie's Man United to join his home-town club in '96. In ten years, Newcastle's number nine didn't win any trophies for the Magpies but will still go down as one of the greatest players ever to don the Toon top.

Football up there is like a church and he is a god. Darling of Geordie hearts to all the lads and lasses and their bairns.

You've had your moments down the years; you are two people doing two very different jobs, but he is loved and you are not. He is celebrated and you are sworn at. He is losing his hair, yours has already gone. He gets paid more than you do too, much more; he is the real Angel of the North.

One day, Newcastle will be great, properly great, with the right owner, with the right level of investment, they will be one of the top teams in the world and maybe he might come back, but for now, Alan Shearer has retired.

The one and only Alan Shearer.

Auf Wiedersehen, pet.

• • •

Final game of the season, final ever game at Highbury.

You're going to miss this place, a proper football stadium this is and you're sad to see it go.

You're sad it'll probably be replaced by fancy new flats with soulless cladding and a tiny postage-stamp balcony overlooking what was the field of play.

Open-plan kitchens, wall-mounted flat-screen televisions and off-white walls.

New homes for young London professionals who work in the City, who probably don't even support Arsenal and might not even like football.

It's sad that Arsenal's newly built stadium, just around the corner, won't have the same atmosphere as here.

Some call it old school, but the game needs places like these. The game will miss old-school stadiums like these, with the fans – who have spent their hard-earned wage to watch their heroes – just inches away from the field of play.

As you are driven down the familiar residential streets of north London and pull into the Clock End car park, you remember some cracking occasions you've had officiating here down the years.

You remember the FA Cup semi-final back in 1992. Liverpool vs Portsmouth here at Highbury. You, assistant referee. You remember the stands festooned with balloons and the bells and the paper strewn across the pitch. You remember shuffling into position and soaking up the atmosphere of what was the biggest game of your career back then. You remember being a history-maker and feeling the warmth of pride emanate through your body.

You remember the League Cup fixture here back in 1997. You, in your first season as a Premiership referee, sending off Arsenal's young defender Jason Crowe in a match against Birmingham City. The uproar it caused. A high-ish tackle just thirty-three seconds into his first-team debut. Still the quickest dismissal in Arsenal's history.

You remember the FA Cup quarter-final replay you did here back in 2002 against Newcastle, still the furthest you've got in the competition.

Today is another big day, the last game in this little stadium.

Everyone is putting in the effort to make today's send-off special. But this is no damp squib, it's a game that matters too, with a much-needed European spot up for grabs. Arsenal have Wigan, Spurs have West Ham away, no easy game for either in the battle between north London neighbours for bragging rights and a route into the Champions League.

Pre-match, you stride pitchside and take it all in. You stare up at the clock at the Clock End, watching and waiting for the hand to move, imagining you could pick it up and clasp it in your palm like the pocket watch your old man gave you for your very first game on Concord Park all those years ago.

You know, much like this stadium, you haven't got long left in this league, you're long in the tooth now at forty-six.

Not long left to take charge of games like these, enjoy occasions like these, on days like these.

Memories etched into the brick; moments of ecstasy and deflation oozing from the seats, from the stands – soon to be turned into distant figments of memory.

Millions of little stories, generations of anecdotes, magical moments from magical players uttered from here to the Bank of Friendship on Blackstock Road soon to be displaced, replaced.

You will miss this intimacy. You can picture the old faces in the empty seats.

. . . he's had a season ticket since he was ten.

. . . she was first brought here by her old man as a toddler.

You shove your hands into your suit trouser pockets and walk on. The stewards are busy fiddling with the last little bits, making everything perfect, and for a moment you imagine all this fuss is for you as the clock hand moves closer to kick-off.

Changed and ready, for the last time you shuffle down the sloping steps that lead out onto the Highbury pitch. It's a tight tunnel, it always has been shoulder to shoulder.

The atmosphere is highly charged, emotions run high, chants louder than you've heard from the home crowd here before, tears and tissues.

The Arsenal fans are in good song and there is a tenderness to their chants, a palpable sense of togetherness. Flags are waved and the weight of the occasion reminds you of the FA Cup semi-final you were assistant on, here, all those years ago now. In many ways, this must be what an FA Cup final must be like.

Barely ten minutes gone on your watch and the Wigan keeper fumbles at the ball, lets it slip from his grasp and Pires, the Frenchman, taps it in from a few yards like you've seen him do many times down the years. *One–nil to the Arsenal.*

You stand back, wait for a protest from the Wigan defence – an offside, a handball, a foul somewhere in the build-up – but nothing, this goal is not your fault, and Pires wheels off to celebrate with the red-and-white-flag-waving crowd. It's a scrappy goal but it's enough to delight them. The crowd who are puffy-eyed and teary.

Free kick. Wigan. Near the corner flag.

You get into position, scuttle somewhere to have a good look, see if anybody is doing something they shouldn't. The ball is whipped in at pace. You're stood where you can see.

The ball in is a good one, right into the danger area, a headache for the defence, a grey area for the keeper. Does he come – or does he stay?

A Wigan defender, Paul Sharner, up from the back, gets a glancing head to the driven-in ball and Wigan have an equaliser. One–all.

The Arsenal defenders, the redcurrant-coloured players, look around at each other perplexed, someone has failed to pick up their man.

They look towards you, in desperation, with pleading eyes, but you shimmy backwards and point in the direction of the centre circle, the goal is a good one and now there's a blue-and-white blotch on the scoreboard.

The Arsenal players look a little rattled. All composure gone. They concede silly fouls, fouls that you give without hesitation, decisions you make without doubt.

Another Wigan free kick, further out than before, probably too far out for an attempt on goal.

Bodies gather in the box and await the ball in: defenders facing one way, attackers the other.

You edge towards them, the melee of bodies in the box. Let them all know that you're there and watching.

Arsenal goalkeeper Jens Lehmann edges off his goal-line, yells at his defenders to push up and hold their line. You edge closer, let the players know you're about.

Lehmann edges out some more, further and further away from his goal, anticipating where the ball is likely to go.

The kick is taken from behind you but the trajectory is all wrong, you can see it in the players' eyes, the way their heads follow the ball, it's not going towards them in the middle, it's heading straight towards the goal.

Now Lehmann is scrambling desperately towards his unguarded goal-line.

The defenders helpless, the keeper even more so, as the ball curls towards the Arsenal goal.

Lehmann dives for it but he has no chance. He has edged out too far and the ball is in the net.

Again, the cluster of Arsenal defenders turn to you, need you to give something, but there is nothing to give. They've only got themselves to blame.

Wigan Athletic have the lead, on Arsenal's special day. This wasn't in the script, nothing in football ever is.

The atmosphere has gone a little sour. For once, for now, you are not the bad guy, the villain of the piece.

Wigan play the ball about, over-confidently, complacency

perhaps, the midfielder turns in the centre circle, takes too many touches, you're in position close by, no need to run.

The Wigan player dallies, hesitates, flounders, retreats back to his own goal and you've seen this enough times to know that this spells trouble.

He has no options, he can't play it back home, and so the Arsenal players pounce. Predator on prey.

A foot goes in, cleanly, no foul, the ball is poked away and Arsenal now have possession in the Wigan attacking half.

A few nice passes and the ball is played forward to Thierry Henry, slicing open the Wigan defence, just outside the penalty area.

You look across, no flag, he's onside.

Onside and in space. You break into a jog. Henry contorts his lower half, bends himself into shape, angles his right leg, shifts his weight and unhinges his hips. As soon as it's hit you know the outcome: two–two.

Relief reverberates around this little stadium.

Of course you are impartial, you have to be, you always have been, but you can't help but admire the quality of Henry. Such flair, pace and skill, such infectious exuberance.

He's won all the awards he can this season, they were presented to him before the game.

As you warmed up, he was the star.

Wigan still level, the final game of the season party poopers. Now into the second half and Arsenal need a goal. Need to win. You, despite the emotions and the drama, still have a job to do. You are not just a minor character in this, you have a bigger part to play.

The Highbury crowd have fallen silent, you sense 'bad' news from Upton Park. As it stands, with under forty-five minutes to go, you can feel it around the place that Spurs will take fourth and qualify for the Champions League.

You jog left, turn back, jog right. Follow the ball, read the play, anticipate what is coming next.

Wigan play the ball about, confidently, too confidently. The Arsenal players hassle and surround and chase and force Wigan into a mistake. A big mistake, their winger, the goalscorer, David Thompson, number twenty-seven, plays a risky pass back towards his teammate at centre-back.

The ball goes askew; straight to the player you wouldn't want it to, from a Wigan perspective: Thierry Henry.

Henry receives the gift, first touch perfect, obviously, and strides head-on towards the Wigan goal.

You react quickly, anything can happen in football, you gallop behind, try and stay close enough to see if something significant needs seeing.

He's one-on-one with the keeper with a decision to make. And, as he so often does for fun, Henry gives Pollitt the eyes and casually shimmies past him, around him, as the keeper goes to ground, but no contact is made, no foul is committed, no penalty needs to be awarded. Henry is just too quick, too smart to be caught. The guarantee of a goal is better than the possibility of a penalty.

With the open goal gaping, Henry, Arsenal's famous Frenchman, number fourteen, the captain, side-foots the ball over the line. And you're right there, just yards behind, as he runs off celebrating, king of his land.

Arsenal have regained the lead. Three–two.

After the shock of going behind, Arsenal look more dangerous than ever.

You award them a free kick and the ball is whipped in dangerously towards the penalty area. You breeze into position, no need to rush.

The searching cross is met by an Arsenal head at the far post, knocked down to Henry who does something clever, who always does something clever, always thinking two steps ahead; he dinks the ball towards the newly brought-on Arsenal substitute Freddie Ljungberg who has snuck into the penalty area, towards the Arsenal substitute who is being held by the Wigan player.

You watch and wait. You can see Ljungberg's arm is being tugged at, you know a decision needs to be made. You're in a good position, no-one can doubt your credibility. You blow. You point to the spot. You give the penalty. You send the Wigan player off, the substitute, the player who has been on less than two minutes. You apply the laws. DOGSO: Denying an Obvious Goalscoring Opportunity.

Wigan are down to ten men and Arsenal have a chance to extend their lead by two goals from the penalty spot.

As Johansson trudges down the tunnel, Henry converts the penalty to extend Arsenal's lead. Four–two.

Henry celebrates by bending down in front of the dewy-eyed fans and kissing the turf, a fitting gesture, you think.

The news reverberates that Spurs are now losing at West Ham and now the party can really start. Arsenal have qualified for Europe.

For the final time here at Highbury, you blow the final whistle, and even you are moved by the occasion.

As the players shake your hand, you feel drained: physically and emotionally.

The Wigan manager, Paul Jewell, isn't happy, you hear, says 'Uriah Rennie likes to make history, something was bound to happen' to the TV cameras post-match.

You don't take it personally, you can't. Even today, a poignant day for many in this little corner of north London, the fault for applying the laws of the game is yours.

But you don't take it personally, you can't.

• • •

The start of a new season, new kits, new players, new managers, new teams, new grounds, new goals, new expectations, new dreams. Same stench of shit, sweat and muscle rub. Same shoddy 'Match Officials' changing rooms.

It's early November now and you're in Essex, the breezy Essex coast, for a fourth round Carling Cup tie between Southend United and Manchester United.

Roots Hall, the home of Southend United, is an old-fashioned stadium; a little run-down, a little rickety. Tight changing room. Tight tunnel. Tight pitch. Slightly tight hamstrings. Old ground, old stands, old seats. Old-fashioned cup tie. You: the referee. You, in green, at the centre of it. Tower blocks of brown-bricked council flats overlooking one of the stands, dingy net curtains and dirty England flags blowing in the breeze. Tracksuit bottoms drying on clothes horses.

You were here a few months ago, refereed a Championship game back in September, a three–all draw vs Norwich but tonight couldn't be more different.

On paper, it should be a straightforward away win – Southend United bottom of the Championship, the current Carling Cup holders Manchester United top of the Premiership – but football isn't played on paper, and you expect to be busy.

It's completely sold out: Roots Hall is packed to capacity, fans in full voice already. They've finished work, had a few pints and a meat pie, and made their way to their seats.

There's a sea chill in the air, a November sea chill, but you know this won't dampen the home crowd's sprits, their desire to cheer their team on in the hopes of causing an unlikely upset.

Come on Southend! Come on Southend! Come on Southend! they shout, the whole stadium shaking with anticipation. Fans just inches away from the players.

Southend start brightly. Play with the heart you expect when underdogs face favourites, David takes on Goliath.

But Rooney looks dangerous.

And Man United's David Jones has just skied a shot into the stand.

Most of all, as you shuffle from position to position, you watch and admire Manchester United's Portuguese winger, Cristiano Ronaldo.

Like most places he goes, you imagine, he is booed with every touch, a low and sustained jeer by the home faithful.

Unlikeable to many maybe, but his quality is unquestionable. For once, so far at least, he is tonight's pantomime villain instead of you.

There is something magical about the way he caresses the ball, the clever touches, the darting runs into the box, the way he evades hapless defenders with speedy step-overs and jinking runs and clever flicks, holds back and pushes on at different times off the ball to shake off his marker, outfox the fullback and slide the ball into dangerous grey areas. His desire to always want the ball, despite the crowd's hostility, despite the threat of being hacked down by the over-zealous Southend defenders.

He shoots on goal whenever he has the chance, decent efforts too, forcing decent saves from the Southend keeper.

Every time he cuts inside, he looks a threat, deadly with both feet.

He is fouled once, twice, and then again by Jamal Campbell-Ryce with a slightly high foot. Not enough for a caution just yet. Not tonight. Not for that, just now.

Different Southend players do what they can to stifle Manchester United's star players. It's your job to keep a tally, tot up the numbers and make sure no player gets away with something they shouldn't on too many occasions.

Against the run of play, Southend have a sniff, a free kick. Thirty yards out from goal.

Campbell-Ryce fouled by Jones, the United midfielder, just outside the penalty area.

A couple of blue shirts stand in front of the ball to blindside the United keeper, then sidle out of the way when the signal is given.

Eastwood curls it goalbound, a powerful yet dainty side-foot instep. It soars over the Manchester United wall, past the diving Tomasz Kuszczak and into the top corner.

The old Southend stadium erupts into roars of pure joy.

Home fans' limbs flailing in delight in the old-fashioned stands of this old-fashioned stadium.

The underdogs have taken the lead with a wonder strike with twenty-seven minutes gone on your watch.

Eastwood runs over to the home crowd and slides along the Roots Hall turf on his knees. He is consumed by his ecstatic teammates and you are yards away, watching.

The game is resumed. Decibels cranked higher. Southend fans in the Southend stands bouncing and singing.

The mighty Man United try to get back in the game, try to salvage something.

Jones has a shot which hits the post.

They play it out wide, cut inside, ping it long, blast it goalwards but the Southend defence stay strong: throw bodies in front of shots, commit clever fouls, run down the clock by keeping the ball in the corner. All very clever, legal actions.

It seems you've got a cup upset on your hands.

Into the second half and against the odds, Southend still lead. Manchester United players grow more frustrated, lose composure. Commit flagrant fouls.

Rooney challenges the Southend keeper, the heroic Southend keeper, unfairly. You have no choice but to show Rooney a yellow card. Things aren't going United's way tonight and even their substitutes aren't effective enough to turn the tide.

Southend United hound and harass and harangue and . . . hang on to win.

At the final whistle, some of the home fans run onto the pitch, appear from all four corners of this old-fashioned stadium to hug their heroes.

The favourites, the holders, Manchester United, have been dumped out of the Carling Cup in the fourth round, and you are there, to run back into the changing room before you become lost in the middle of it all, like you so often are.

● ● ●

It's late November.

As you blow the half-time whistle, gather up the loose ball and trudge down the tunnel, you hear the boos from the home faithful; to be expected of course, football is a pantomime at the best of times.

There's anger in the air, there's anger in the tunnel, there's anger in the press boxes, there's anger in the boardroom, there's anger in the stands, there's anger in the commentator's gantry, there's anger in the pubs: has football become too angry?

You were raised in Yorkshire; you're made of tougher stuff. No matter how bad it gets, or how bad it was, you've just got to dust yourself off and carry on. Even if they say you've lost control, you've got to puff your chest out and go again because there's twenty thousand people out there who've paid good money to vent for the full ninety.

Sweat drips from your forehead. Your hammy twinges. Your muscles ache. In your Deepdale dressing room, it's hard to escape the voices of the two moaning managers either side of you: verb, cuss, cliché, verb, cuss, cliché.

Peter Taylor (Crystal Palace) to the right, Paul Simpson (Preston) to the left. Chirping away like angry birds they are. Vultures.

Fly away Peter (Taylor), fly away Paul (Simpson).

The walls are shaking. The liquid in your cup trembles. You are reminded of that song by Stealers Wheel: here you are, Stuck in the Middle.

In the stands, you tried not to look but you could see the hate in all the faces of the rabble-rousers: coffin-dodging fogies sucking on Murray Mints and Werther's Originals, the school-children, teachers, lawyers, doctors, their cheeks all puffed up and red like over-inflated balloons ready to burst.

They swear, every offensive slur under the sun, gobbets of spit flying out their mouths like a faulty shower, veins protruding from their neck, from the centre of their foreheads, from their temples.

You see their gestures too: wanker-tossing, middle-finger-flipping, V signs.

An impressive range: thousands of eyes, thousands of erect fingers all aimed at you.

Smell that familiar Saturday stench, football fumes: armpits and sweat and Deep Heat and testosterone and hairspray and last-minute shits in blocked bogs, you breathe in and it nearly chokes you.

Preston have had two penalty shouts and you've dismissed them both, to the dismay of the Deepdale crowd. They wanted a red for an alleged elbow on the Preston centre-back, Sean St Ledger. You dismissed that too, it was six of one, half a dozen of the other.

It doesn't take long into a game of football as a referee to know if the teams are going to work with you. Sometimes, once in a blue moon, you give a tight decision, a hearty fifty-fifty tackle or a shot that might have taken a nick off a boot in the last minute and you're not sure which way to give it, and your senior assistant on the far side gives you a blank look and you have to go with your gut. Use your inner instinct.

The players know you're unsure, the fans know it too, your face gives it away. And the players don't moan, or swear, or argue. You like those games.

This is not one of those games. You've got a bit of a battle on your hands here for the next forty-five with the score still nil–nil.

The players are ready to resume. The sound of studs against the concrete signals the impending start of the second half. You look at your watch and nod to your assistants.

Quick slash and it's time for Round Two.

Boots laced up tight, socks pulled up, ball in hand, ring the bell and go again.

As you walk out for the second half of Preston North End vs Crystal Palace, the Lilywhites vs the Eagles, north vs south, Lancashire vs south London, whites vs red-and-blue stripes, over the tannoy you hear the stadium announcer say something that doesn't sound right, that affects you more than it should, slicing your insides open, leaving you exposed to the Deepdale crowd like a rotting carcass: 'Enjoy the second half of the Uriah Rennie Show.'

The echoes are heard across all four stands, followed by a chorus of smirks and then outright full-blown laughter by the mickey-taking spectators.

For a big man, on hearing the words uttered over the tannoy, you feel all of a sudden quite small. You try to shrug it off. You push out your chest and straighten your shoulders, force a smile . . . but it hurts a bit.

You're doing your best.

The Uriah Rennie Show, eh?

Your show?

You can't let churlishness affect you.

You dig deep at Deepdale. Dig deep and hit a rock. You run your diagonal and penetrate the penalty area when you need to, get into your drop zone and position yourself to see any shirt-pulling or flailing elbows.

It's one of those games: twenty-two muscly, hairy, sweaty, swearing men, kicking lumps out of each other.

You're proactive, you use your voice: *watch those arms lads, keep it tidy*, keep it tidy, Uri.

It's cold, so cold, but not long to go of 'your show'.

You try to let the game flow. You tell Clinton Morrison of Palace to 'keep it tidy'. Keep it tidy, Clinton. Keep it tidy, Uri.

If Preston win they go top of the league. But Turner, the Palace keeper on loan from Everton, is keeping the away side in it with a string of decent saves.

Not long to go now of 'The Uriah Rennie Show', their words not yours, but your job is to make sure everyone behaves themselves for the full ninety.

James Scowcroft nearly nicks it for Palace but the score remains goalless.

One booking: Scowcroft. The crowd wanted a red. They saw an elbow. You gave a yellow.

Final score: nil–nil.

The players haven't scored but another game well managed feels like a win to you.

The Uriah Rennie Show? Damn right it is.

2007

Like a bad smell, you're back. Back up the A1. Back in the North East. Back refereeing a Newcastle United game at St James' Park. Back walking out of the tunnel to the saxophonic sound of 'Going Home: Theme of the Local Hero' blaring and topless blind-drunk Geordies cheering. Back among the fans chanting to their boys in black-and-white stripes. Back in the centre of it all, a criminal returning to the scene of the crime.

Despite the Saturday-night pints and punch-ups, football fans have long memories.

Life is too short to hold grudges, but up here you are remembered as the referee that first sent off Alan Shearer. Here, you are the attention-seeking showman that sent Sir Alex to the stands. Here, you are the referee they love to see the back of. The referee they love to hate.

Well, tough luck, you're here because the FA have appointed you, and like always you mean business. It's ten years now since you first burst into the Premiership, and like the first game, and every other game you have done since, you have a job to do. Laws to implement, instructions to impart and free kicks to award (certainly). Penalties to give (maybe). Distances to march out and cards to brandish (probably). Players to warn (definitely). Games to referee to the best of your ability (always).

Today will be no exception.

Today, Newcastle United play West Ham United and you are the referee.

Newcastle United:

Given

Carr   O'Brien   Huntington   Ramage

Solano   Butt   Parker   Dyer

Milner

Martins

West Ham United:

Carroll

Dailly   Ferdinand   Davenport   McCartney

Benayoun   Quashie   Reo-Coker   Boa Morte

Harewood   Cole

It's strange in many ways, you being here and Alan Shearer not. You feel a little bit lost, maybe even a bit lonely. He has retired now, at the back end of last season, did so as the all-time highest goalscorer in the Premiership: 260 goals in 441 games.

No doubt about it, he was a special player, an old-fashioned sometimes short-fused centre-forward: brave, loyal, tenacious.

A leader in every sense. Versatile too: the ability to blast the ball into the top corner from a free kick outside the penalty area, volley the ball sweetly from thirty yards out or score a tap-in from two. Not to mention that he was good with his head too.

Yes, hard to referee at times, he had his bad-tempered moments, but the better players often do.

You think you might miss him, the battles you had, the disagreements, the silly spats, if you're silly enough to call them those.

It's crazy to think that he never won a trophy while at St James' Park, it's a bit like you not refereeing the FA Cup final, yet.

There's talk of him being a manager here one day, you'd like that. You can picture him on the touchline barking out instructions in his suit and tie. You think he'd be great, would understand the players, the fans, the city, the weight of expectation.

No, no Shearer today. You are the captain now.

Today it's you vs Given. You vs Solano. You vs Ramage. You vs Huntington. You vs Carr. You vs Milner. You vs Butt. You vs Parker. You vs O'Brien. You vs Dyer. You vs Martins.

Out you walk onto the sloping St James' Park pitch, again: that song, that smell, that feeling, your whistle to signal kick-off.

Sloppy start from the home side, not woken up yet, not at the races.

West Ham corner, whipped in by Yossi Benayoun. Met by Davenport. Volleyed in by Carlton Cole, past Milner who stands on the goal-line. Eighteen minutes gone and West Ham have the lead.

The home fans voice their discontent, mood fractured.

West Ham come again, full of confidence, McCartney rolls the ball forward, Marlon Harewood with a clever turn and shot at the edge of the box makes it two. Two goals in five minutes. Two–nil West Ham.

The home fans voice their discontent, mood worsened.

Newcastle stunned, muster a response, try to get themselves back in the game: Martins blasts a shot over, O'Brien hits the post.

Minutes to half-time, minutes to keep control. Keep your eyes peeled. Think two steps ahead. Apply the laws.

Out on the right wing, Newcastle's James Milner cuts inside and whips one in at pace with his left foot. The ball squirms its way into the bottom corner, through the legs of a Newcastle player who's stood in the middle of the penalty box, through the legs of midfielder Scott Parker.

The home crowd celebrate: joy, relief and belief all infused.

A goal back right before half-time is the best time to stage a resurgence. But they, unlike you, haven't seen Nigel Bannister, your linesman with his flag hoisted high. You felt the buzz on your arm. Heard the words in your ear too.

Newcastle players hurry to retrieve the ball, desperate to get the game going again, desperate to get an equaliser.

When you look over to Nigel again, the flag has been dropped but it's too late, the West Ham players have seen it and a cluster of them – including their goalkeeper, Roy Carroll – converge around you and then your assistant, protesting against the goal: outstretched arms, flailing spit and pointed fingers.

You have a big decision to make. You jog towards the touchline, towards your assistant, usher the players away, give yourself a moment to have a conflab, confer and clarify, give yourself a moment to think

A moment to think.

Think.

Here, at St James' Park, you have another big decision to make. You give yourself a moment to think.

The goal stands.

West Ham are furious, the players, the managers, the coaches, the fans up in the heavens here, it's clear they feel Scott Parker impeded their keeper's view and interfered with play. You think otherwise.

The goal stands.

The Newcastle fans roar their team on.

Moments later, you blow the half-time whistle and the West Ham United players voice their discontent.

You saw what you saw and laws are laws.

Into the second half, Newcastle United now the better side. Milner free kick from the right touchline, hits Boa Morte's hand and you know what you have to do.

You do not have an agenda, you do not take sides, you are not a ch**t. You are an honest referee who makes honest decisions. That's right, you award Newcastle United a penalty.

Solano sweeps the ball home from the spot and Newcastle have their equaliser with still over half an hour of the game to go.

You shimmy and shuffle, do everything you can to get out the way, not interfere or be a nuisance; do everything you can to get into a good position.

Despite chances from Obafemi Martins and David Edgar, the home side fail to score the winner and the game ends two–all.

West Ham are still livid.

Again, at this stadium, something goes awry. This time a big key match decision goes in the home team's favour but in the grand scheme of things, that'll do little to change what the home faithful think about you.

Uriah Rennie: the so-called scene-stealing shiny-headed showman.

• • •

Are you still in with a shot? It's hard to say.

It's been a hellish few months, probably the most testing times you've experienced in your whole career as a referee. People have cast you aside, called you dead in the water, have said your career is finished.

They probably think you've gone off the grid for good, at home with your big fat feet up watching *Bargain Hunt* and *Homes Under the Hammer*. But instead of packing it in, you packed your bag. You pulled up your socks and stood tall.

At times, you've thought about throwing in the towel and letting the young ones have their chance, but here you are: a fighter, surviving, playing to the final whistle.

It's November now, you haven't refereed a game since April: brighter, warmer, fitter, stronger times.

The first game of your injury-interrupted season takes you to Glanford Park, Scunthorpe for a Championship fixture between newly promoted bottom-half side Scunthorpe United and play-off-chasing Hull City.

You're a little apprehensive, hoping you will be up to the job, not just lumbering about, but up with play; keeping control, making correct key match decisions, you're in zero doubt that you will but, you also know, it's been half a year since your last match so probably bound to be a little rusty.

Bags dropped, pitch inspected, match programme skimmed.

You've missed this pre-match buzz. The hubbub of activity: ghetto-blasters blaring, meticulous warm-up routines, mugs of tea, stilted small talk, small sips of Lucozade Sport, checking undershorts, checking sock tape.

You've missed the football lingo, the language, the idioms: *up his arse, on your bike, on your shoulder, get rid, stick it in the mixer.*

At 14.53 you ring the bell, send your assistants off to fetch the two teams and head to the tunnel where both teams are already lined up.

With nerves of steel, Sheffield steel, you strut out onto the Glanford Park pitch. Back doing what you love to do, ball in hand, thousands of fans: a cape-less superhero with all the power again.

Hull City's Dean Windass scores for the visitors in the fourth minute, then again on the sixteenth, two–nil. The favourites have started strongly and the home fans you see in the stands shake their heads dejectedly.

You're about, doing what needs to be done, running where you need to run. You're not feeling as mobile as before, but that's to be expected, you're refereeing professional players in the second highest division of English football, it's going to take more minutes to run off the rustiness.

Scunthorpe grab a goal back just before half-time.

It's two–one to Hull at the break.

It's an ugly second half, one that requires good refereeing. A good referee. You issue four yellows, including one to Sam Ricketts for dissent.

Puffing on until the ninetieth minute, you keep going, moving your tired legs from one end to the other.

At the full-time whistle, you're blowing out of your big black backside but you've done it.

Scunthorpe manager Nigel Adkins isn't happy. Complains you missed something. Calls it a 'clear' penalty on Paterson.

But as far as you are concerned, given the circumstances, you've done a decent job. As far as you are concerned, with this game under your belt, you're ready for the big boys and being the best again, you have an FA Cup final to referee, and on a wing and a prayer, you'll get there.

2008

Hamstrung: your had-it hamstrings have hampered progress. Before, during and after every game these days, you're starting to feel the instability of your ageing body, a twinge followed by a wince, an unreliability of sorts, like a second-hand car with too many miles on the clock. Your legs just don't have the same spring, the same strength, the same capacity to do what your brain is telling them to do when you want them to do it.

You know where you want to be to give a decision, but getting there isn't as easy as it once was. In more or less every game these days you're fighting through innocuous niggles, and you can't get as wide as you once did with the same alacrity.

For the first time in your career, you might not always be where you need to be to give the correct decision. Luckily, you've been in the game long enough to read the play, predict what'll happen next, sort of know where the ball will bounce. It's the mark of an experienced referee. You're a bit like a central midfielder dictating the play from the centre of the pitch, a midfield maestro, a Scholes or a Gerrard, a Pirlo or a Zidane.

It's mid-January now: freezing cold weather, faltering New Year's resolutions and credit card bills from Christmas to pay. Today, back in the North East, back at St James' Park, back at the home of Newcastle United, for once, is not about you, the referee.

No, today is not about Uriah Rennie. Not about sending off Alan Shearer for a flailing elbow against Villa in 1999. Not about sending Sir Alex to the stands for calling Jeff Winter a ch**t in 2003. Not about letting Milner's goal stand versus West Ham in 2007. Tonight, the fans, the players, the whole of Newcastle are celebrating the return of their prodigal son, King Kevin Keegan, who just hours ago was reappointed as their new manager.

The Tyneside Messiah will soon be back in the Newcastle hot seat after eleven years.

Tonight, King Kev will watch from the stands as Newcastle United play Stoke City from the Championship in the third-round replay of the FA Cup. A trip to Arsenal the prize. You, the referee.

The news was only announced a few hours ago and there's a real buzz about the place, a smile on everyone's face, from the stewards to the groundsman to the tea lady. Some are in such good spirits they are even happy to see you.

The third round of the FA Cup, the promised land to many, the round where the big boys enter, and the minnows dream of a big-money tie to pay their overheads for a few extra months. You still harbour FA Cup dreams yourself, an outside chance you might referee this season's cup final. To get there though, you must prove that you are good enough, fit enough.

You are no fan favourite around these parts but you put that to one side and prepare to referee the game how you would any other. Professionalism till the very end.

Tonight, ideally, you need a controversy-free ninety minutes.
A game where you drift into the periphery. Barely in shot. A
cameo role.

Newcastle United:

Given

Carr   Taylor   Caçapa   José Enrique

Milner   Emre   N'Zogbia   Duff

Viduka   Owen

Stoke City:

Simonsen

Zakuani   Shawcross   Cort   Delap

Lawrence   Eustace   Pugh   Fuller

Cresswell   Parkin

The managers merge into one: this is sacked Sam Allardyce's
team, selected by caretaker Nigel Pearson as King Kev watches
on.

You run and blow and wince and shout and Michael Owen
makes it one–nil to Newcastle after just eight minutes. Duff's
left-wing cross, Milner's knock-down and Owen stabs it in
from close range.

King Kev watches on.

You're in position, watching and waiting. Keeping your shoulders supple, shifting one way and then the other to keep the ball in view, anticipate the next phase of play, be proactive and spot the next infringement.

The ball gets stuck, tackles fly in, no holds barred, battle lines drawn: black socks and white socks intermingled, but every lunge is fair, clean. Northern tackles, Northern soul.

You run and blow and wince and shout, Stoke City's John Eustace catches Emre, Newcastle's Turkish midfielder. But you let play go on, you let the game flow, this isn't a tie that needs a big Uri intervention, not yet at least. No foul, no card.

Ranting and raving, Emre is outraged, at you and at him, utters profanities in half-English, half-Turkish tones and shows you a lump on his shin. These things happen.

Emre seeks retribution, lunges in late with his studs up on Stoke City midfielder John Eustace.

You know what you have to do immediately, it's beyond reasonable doubt. You dip your hand into the back pocket of your shorts and hoist the red card high for all of St James' Park to see. After just twenty-nine minutes on your watch, Newcastle United are a goal up, but now a man down.

The crowd roar at you, another Newcastle United game, another Newcastle United red card. Uriah Rennie: the so-called scene-stealing shiny-headed showman.

If only they appreciated that laws are laws.

More running, more blowing, more wincing, more shouting, and Caçapa makes it two from a corner.

At half-time, Newcastle are two–nil up. Despite being a man down, Newcastle look too strong for shot-shy Stoke.

Into the second half, Stoke City's Rory Delap goes close. A header that goes into the side-netting.

Newcastle resort to route one, boot the ball long and far down the sloping St James' Park pitch. A Mark Viduka flick and a low Milner shot makes it three.

Damien Duff makes it four.

It's one-way traffic, Newcastle are playing well, very well. The Championship side are on the ropes, being outplayed in all areas of the park and looking exhausted.

Liam Lawrence does curl in a consolation in the ninetieth minute but it is nowhere near enough and Newcastle United win. They will play Arsenal away in the next round.

Your progress less clear.

As you shake the players' hands, as you walk down the tunnel towards your changing room, you think how, not for the first time at St James' Park, you are forced to go into your back pocket and show a Newcastle United player a red card.

Tonight, a controversy-free ninety minutes was what you needed.

• • •

You referee three FA Cup ties in January. But as time ebbs away, it seems you are needed no further and you are not appointed to any of the fifth-round ties.

The letter unsent. The phone call unmade. As your career slows, it seems that despite your best efforts – the history-making, the records, the accolades – you will not referee the FA Cup final.

The one thing you have wanted since becoming a Premiership referee all those years ago will now not happen.

FA Cup Final Referees:

1996: ~~Uriah Rennie~~ Dermot Gallagher

1997: ~~Uriah Rennie~~ Steve Lodge

1998: ~~Uriah Rennie~~ Paul Durkin

1999: ~~Uriah Rennie~~ Peter Jones

2000: ~~Uriah Rennie~~ Graham Poll

2001: ~~Uriah Rennie~~ Steve Dunn

2002: ~~Uriah Rennie~~ Mike Riley

2003: ~~Uriah Rennie~~ Graham Barber

2004: ~~Uriah Rennie~~ Jeff Winter

2005: ~~Uriah Rennie~~ Rob Styles

2006: ~~Uriah Rennie~~ Alan Wiley

2007: ~~Uriah Rennie~~ Steve Bennett

> *Que sera sera*
> *Whatever will be will be*
> *You're **not** going to Wembley*
> *Que sera sera*

It makes you think, your role, a paradox: the forgotten man in the middle of it all. Even after a good job you are not given the credit you deserve, after maintaining everybody's safety and applying the laws to the letter for years, you are abused, stigmatised, ridiculed, scoffed at.

The players get the glory, the plaudits, the accolades and the love.

After decades, too many to count just now, you are still pigeonholed; you are a figure simply seen on TV, the bald black card-happy referee. Not a real human but a character. A bit part, an extra, now being directed out of frame.

It's the end of February and you referee three games in League Two, the lowest division in the Football League.

You do Chester City vs Accrington Stanley.

You do Stockport County vs Bury.

You do Shrewsbury Town vs Hereford United.

No airs or graces, football is football, no game is beneath you, and every fixture needs a referee but it feels as though your time at the top is coming to an end; sand slips through your fingers.

You feel a little out of favour. No longer flavour of the month. You've only done one Premier League game so far since the new year and only four since the beginning of the season in total.

Injuries and an ageing body have made things harder recently, no doubt about it. Top-level football is getting faster too, the players are getter better, fitter, they want to get on with the game as quickly as possible now, unlike back in the day when some, a little worse for wear from the night before, were happy for the game to be stopped to receive a telling-off just so they could rest their palms on their knees to catch their breath for a moment.

You remember the days, not so long ago, when, like Keith Hackett said, you were the fittest referee of the lot: fast, flexible, agile; sprinting, then crouching to look for illegal contact. Now, you're getting through games, watching the action unfold around you, a pedestrian at times, using your brain more than your legs to read the bounce of the ball, to anticipate and predict what might happen next like a round in *A Question of Sport*. Operating on autopilot, using muscle memory to stay one step ahead, telegraphing a player's next move. Before, you were the same age as some of the players, but at forty-eight now, you are older than some of the managers.

It's late April, the twenty-sixth, you go to Upton Park, a proper East End football stadium. They're at home to Newcastle

United. A decent game between two decent teams in the middle of the table, you, in the middle.

West Ham: Mark Noble volleys it home to make it one–nil (tenth minute).

West Ham: Dean Ashton makes it two (twenty-third minute).

Newcastle United: Obafemi Martins gets a goal back (forty-second minute).

Newcastle United: a George McCartney own goal levels things (forty-fifth minute).

Despite West Ham pressure in the second half, the game finishes two–two.

Time ticks on. Your career nearing an end it seems. Powers waning. The next game could well be your last. It's starting to feel that way. The series finale of some long-running drama.

You've sucked and seen it all, you either retire a hero or live long enough to see yourself become a villain.

It's the eleventh of May, today: Tottenham vs Liverpool. A sunny Saturday in north London as you blow the whistle and the game kicks off in this, your last game of the season. Maybe ever?

Voronin scores halfway through the second half to give Liverpool the lead. The Ukrainian slots the ball home past Radek Černý from a Fernando Torres flick-on.

Torres then bamboozles the Spurs centre-back Michael

Dawson with some clever trickery, a couple of cute and clever touches and side-foots the ball into the corner.

The game ends two–nil to the visitors, and as you exit stage left, languidly head off the sunny White Hart Lane pitch you pause, allow yourself a little smile, a little nod to your career and your achievements down the years. Not many of the thirty-six thousand fans here will care about your special role this afternoon, but as far as you are concerned, it's another job well done.

And for now, this is the end, the final curtain. Years of being on first-name terms with the country's finest footballers, soon to be over, just like that, on the sound of three short peeps of your whistle.

The end of the swear words and squabbles, flashpoints and mass confrontations.

One hundred and seventy-five top-flight matches, 543 yellow cards, thirty red cards. You definitely did it your way.

As far as many are concerned, you are:

the best referee not to referee in the Champions League (properly)

the best referee not to referee at the World Cup

the best referee not to referee an FA Cup final

You tried, you did what you had to do.

Cards are there to be used, so when needed, you used them.

You can't be everyone's friend, issuing sanctions to players who have done something wrong is part and parcel of the role of being a referee. A negative reaction to these actions is also to be expected.

But as wrong as it is, disrespect and abuse towards the officials is the norm in the life of a referee.

You hope it's easier for the next black referee coming through the ranks, you hope the systems are rejigged, you hope they are given a fair chance, a fair crack of the whip, not just by the FA, but by the fans and the media too.

You, a paradox: the forgotten man in the middle of it all.

Here at White Hart Lane, this is no fairytale ending; this is no glamorous cup final, no fanfare, no big dance number, no last hurrah, no guard of honour, no commemorative plaque and a bunch of flowers, no slew of awards, no rapturous round of applause, no standing ovation, no open-top bus parade, no shedding of tears. Your retirement won't go down in folklore. A sticky damp squib of a game is your last outing as a professional top-flight referee.

But this isn't the last the world will see of you, you have ambitions left, many of them. For a start, you would like to see football doing more with the profile it has, and you believe you have your part to play.

Community involvement is very important and you think it has more to offer than it currently does.

These are the thoughts that run through your mind as you

troop down the tunnel for the last time, unsure of what will be thrown your way in the next chapter of your career but ready to face it head-on.

FA Cup Final Referees:

2008: ~~Uriah Rennie~~ Mike Dean

3

Feels different than before, coming back here. Not Newcastle-under-Lyme, Newcastle upon Tyne. Back up the A1. Back in the North East. Back refereeing a Newcastle United game at St James' Park. Back walking out to the saxophonic sound of 'Going Home: Theme of the Local Hero' blaring and topless blind-drunk Geordies cheering. Back among the fans chanting to their boys in coal-black and ivory-white stripes.

It was originally meant to be Peter Walton on this game today, but he's been drafted in to officiate the Community Shield so in a slight change to the billed episode, you've been drafted in as his last-minute replacement. Some thought you had retired, hung up your hat somewhere, but here you are, back again defying expectations.

It's Newcastle's final pre-season game of the new season and you're the referee for today's friendly.

A game of football is a game of football. If given the chance to, players will try to pull the wool over your eyes, get one over, blindside you, but you're old enough now, wise to their tricks, despite their flailing spit, their indignation, their arms, swear words and dirty looks.

Before every game, that familiar feeling, that nervous energy that sits in the bottom of your belly, anticipation coursing through your veins: the butterflies kicking in, he's kicking him, studded down the shin. The Monday morning appointments are in, your eyes roll down the page, you look for your name, look across at the two teams, look for the ground, think about games from before, what might have happened last time you were there.

Sometimes, in some stadiums, the ball is big and you see the situation clear.

Sometimes, in the same stadiums, your sight line is broken, the ball is incessantly lost in a tangle of legs and the same bad things seem to happen.

But you go where you are told to go, referee the games that need to be refereed in front of the cup-of-tea-swillers and the pint-of-beer-spillers.

As a referee, not the most beloved position on the pitch, you need to have eyes in the back of your head. These days, thank God, at this level, you have assistants who are your extra eyes and ears, you, him and sometimes her: one symbiotic being.

You arrive, head into the Officials' Room with your kit and flags, you've gone from handling plastic bags, to holdalls, to wheelie suitcases; you get out what you need, two of everything and line them up ready, like animals boarding an ark.

Working on the weekend like usual, there's life in this old dog yet, you've gone from rain-slicked dog shit on the pitch to being the dog's bollocks fending off dog's abuse in the biggest stadiums in the country to be best in show, your show. From grumpy groundsman reluctant to put the floodlights on in the peak of winter, to Old Trafford and Wembley. From scratchy loo roll and mushy peas and Hendo's, repeatedly kicking a tennis ball against a wall, playing football with your mates till it got dark and you've lost count of the score, to being back at St James' Park and saying a little strength-giving prayer in a quiet little corner before kick-off.

Between your finger and your thumb, the squat whistle rests; snug as a gun.

Air sucked in from the bottom of your lungs, up through your chest, and out through your lips. B R E A T H E.

The whistle is mightier than the sword.

The first ten minutes are crucial for game-management, bag them and you have the game in your pocket, safe from the crafty players who want to take the law into their own hands.

Sometimes you know as early as the first five, refereeing a real pig's ear of a game, whether you'll need to bang out an early card or not. A game where there'll be no turning a blind eye, no benefit of the doubt, no cutting them some slack, no cutting out the middle man, not when *you're* the middle man; you can't afford to let your guard down, the buck stops with you.

You, the so-called cock of the walk, a black Grant Mitchell, versus the big-hitters giving it the big *I am*, uttering their well-versed excuses. Players with unchecked egos taking a tone and spouting obscenities, and you, showing fleetness of feet, shooing the shouters away or intervening in between futile fisticuffs, some fraught off-the-ball fracas between lager louts at loggerheads spoiling for a fight.

Scowl at the mardy bums from afar, an unerring glare, adopt the trailing eye, give the players who are trying your patience evils, keep them in check, check the ball hasn't gone over the line. Run, run, run from pillar to post, and then stop, avoid getting hit by the ball, skip over it, jump over it, let it roll through your legs. Stand in front of it, stop the quick free kick; the game needs to be played at your tempo, with all due respect this is your game and you dictate the pace.

Refereeing means respect, the two words should go hand in hand. Without giving and garnering the right level, you're nothing more than a bloke in black with a whistle and perpetual pressure from all angles, at constant risk of being crucified and pilloried and poked fun at; heavy is the head that wears the crown.

Call it a calling, nothing can beat that five-to-three feeling, stood in the tunnel, heart pulsing and pulsating. It's very different to scoring a goal, or a world-class assist, or winning a fifty-fifty tackle. In the heat of the moment, you're ablaze, under-fire Uriah. This is professional football, and it's live, happening right now, no going back, no going again from the top, no quick breathers, you can't afford to fluff your lines. There is no post-production cutting it up or scene slicing and dicing.

Need to make sure you're in control, even when those around you think you've done something wrong, even when they call you pedantic. You set the tone, either let the game flow or slow it down, hit the whistle quick. In being too lenient you run a risk, run, run, run, run into position, run from end to end, run your fingers along the net before the game, visualise situations to come, push away the pointed fingers from your face, a referee of colour awash with colourful language.

Give a free kick and after a quiet word, give the defender time to get back in.

One second to make a decision, one angle, one chance: careless → reckless → excessive force? Wipe the sweat off your brow and blow, dripping with the emotion of it all.

A game of football is a game of football . . .

Newcastle's a one-club city. The capacity here down the years has gone from thirty-two thousand to over fifty-two. It is undoubtedly one of the best stadiums in the country and even though there's been tough times, you were here, in the middle, at the centre of it, refereeing the best players in front of some of the most passionate fans in the country. In front of the it's-only-a-little-bit-of-rain bat-shit-crazy fans.

Many a year here, you've been the talk of the town. The talk of the Toon. The shit sticks like tar. Thick black tar.

They can be hard ones to judge, pre-season friendlies. Things normally not allowed on a matchday are permitted: fans chat to their mates, check their phones, skim through the match programme to read about their new signings, all while the game's going on, because the result doesn't really matter. It's about fitness and minutes and perfecting tactics, and players and managers and referees refamiliarising themselves with what it means to be in the spotlight again, but at the end of the day, when all is said and done, laws are laws. A penalty is a penalty. A yellow card is a yellow card. A red's a red.

You, yellow Umbro top with the embroidered FA logo, three lions on your shirt. You get changed and tool up. All your refereeing bits and pieces in an old plastic Chinese takeaway box: whistle, Argos pens, Argos pencils, cards, watch, spare whistle, spare pencils, spare cards, spare watch. 70p worth of 10p coins.

Valencia are in town and on another day, this could be a Champions League game, an all-important tie where you are the referee.

Spain won the Euros a few months back and the away team is made up of world-class internationals and managed by newly appointed, Unai Emery. They've even got the tournament's top goalscorer, David Villa, on the bench.

You watched Howard Webb referee at the Euros this summer, a chance you never got of course. A South Yorkshire lad on the biggest stage, pissing off the Polish, but making his country proud on the beginning of his journey to being one of the best referees in the world.

Newcastle United:

Given

Beye   Caçapa   Taylor   N'Zogbia

Gutiérrez   Butt   Guthrie   Milner   Duff

Martins

Valencia:

Hildebrand

Albiol   Helguera   Moretti   Miguel

Joaquín   Albelda   Baraja   Vicente

Silva

Morientes

The rain has stayed away today and St James' Park remains dry as you take to the field of play.

Big Uriah Rennie is now BIG Uriah Rennie. The belly rounder and your body shape a little out of sorts, to some you do not quite look like the referee you once were.

That familiar song plays in your head as you walk out onto the field of play, no not 'Return of the Local Hero', not this time, not today, the tune in your head is the beginning of 'Young, Gifted and Black' by Bob and Marcia. The song makes you smile, puts you in good spirits, reminds you of your younger days in Dalvey, your younger days in Sheffield.

St James' Park is only about two-thirds full as you the blow the whistle to start. Is this the last time you will referee here? The last time you will see these fans, be centre of their attentions. The fans who wear their hearts on their sleeves and grumble at the players who wear long sleeves.

Shorts in all weathers, not afraid to whip off their top and get their bellies out. Get on the Tyne & Wear into town and have three rounds of triple vodka and Red Bulls. Head down to Quayside, Pitcher & Piano, order at the bar, clutch four over-spilling pints at a time as they waddle back to their booth ready to a sink a skinful.

Newcastle: Fog on the Tyne is all yours, all yours, Ant & Dec and the back pages of the *Chronicle*.

Valencia, the visitors, attack the Gallowgate End. They start quickly, clearly good on the ball, comfortable playing out from the back. European quality wins them a free kick, Vicente is fouled by Milner.

As a referee, you need to be like the Mona Lisa, your eyes following the players wherever they go. The ball is pumped into the box by the Valencia centre-back and is headed on by Morientes.

You say it with your chest, handling the head honchos going at it hammer and tongs, unsavoury slurs uttered from their tongues, and haul them over the coals. In the middle, you can't suffer any fools, you can't let the scoundrels built like barn doors walk all over you, you gotta give as good as you've got, glowering at goalkeepers encroaching and giving outfielders doing the wrong thing a ticking-off with daggers. Placating the pugilistic over-passionate players going primal with stern eyes and strong hands, coming down on them like a ton of bricks when they're being pricks. If looks could kill . . .

No FA Cup final appointment (yet) is a kick in the shins but you take it on the chin, you have to. Life is too short to hold grudges; life is too long to make no plans.

How do you sleep at night? Just fine.

Valencia are first to the ball and it's tucked into the corner by their tricky winger Joaquín to make it one–nil to the Spaniards after thirty-eight minutes.

Crossed arms and rolled eyes from the home fans; muted cheers from a smattering of away ones.

Like life, the game goes on and the ball is kicked and the memories shift: folded newspapers for shin pads, shorts were shorter and hair was longer and hardnuts watched through concrete-barriered high-wired fences.

You think about the fans too, sometimes, schlepping from stadium to stadium. The journeys they've taken to get here, the Saturdays they've sacrificed through the rain, and the sleet and hail, aquaplaning on sodden motorways, eating shitty sandwiches in shitty services in the middle of nowhere, grimacing in the stands for just ninety minutes of escapism.

A restricted view, frozen fingers, Newcastle Brown Ales, an incessant urge to piss. Nails bitten to the quick, ripped skin, bloodied nailbeds.

It's hard to see when you've been blinded by the lights for decades now; been on the frontline, carrying the weight of so much shit on your thick-skinned shoulders. From jumpers for goalposts – the ever-moving goalposts – to refereeing in the Premier League with the wise heads and their wisecracks.

You've done the *let's have a good clean game, lads* days, ref-ereeing podgy Sunday-leaguers who 'could have gone pro'. Local park players hard as old boots who look like bulldogs who've chewed on a wasp giving it both barrels.

No win guaranteed, same fee.

Soon you will not be in the middle, the decision-maker with the whistle and the power, dealing with red mist and red cards; a lashing out, swear words, thick greenish-white spit on the ground, studs down shins.

You're no spring chicken, in all truth you're long in the tooth. Your days seem numbered, your legs knackered, Father Time has well and truly caught up with you and told you what for too.

Damien Duff ghosts into the penalty area unmarked and heads home a goal with thirteen minutes left on the clock. Arms in the air everywhere.

There *is* colour and there *is* sound in this black-and-white town. The tune in your head is still 'Young, Gifted and Black' by Bob and Marcia.

Under fifteen minutes to go and you signal for a Newcastle corner. Creeping into position like a slinking cat, waiting for the ball to float in, as players jostle in the box, yell out 'ref!' to bring to your attention a shirt-pull from the defender.

In position, you stand and watch and remember. The thou-sands of times you've stood in similar positions on football pitches across the country. From no-seater council-owned municipal playing fields with paint-flaked goalposts to all-seater world-famous stadiums with the big-time pleased-as-punch title-winning Premier League players.

Jack-of-all-trades, you've refereed all sorts down the decades, cobbled-together teams made up of: the steely-eyed, the thick-thighed, the gangly-legged, the loud-mouthed, the over-zealous, the wide-chested, the big-headed, the bad-breathed, the beer-bellied, the neck-tattooed, the cheeky-chappies, the stud-happy, the prima-donnas, the attention-seeking, the middle-finger-flipping piss-taking sharp-fanged Sunday-leaguers to the world-beaters.

Steven Taylor heads the ball onto the post.

And your knees will need icing after this, kept elevated on a footstool or a pouffe. Newcastle score a last-minute goal to win it at the death through James Milner and you blow the final whistle, blowing, blowing . . .

Post-match, you scrub the mud off your boots, thick clunks flake off under the pressure, bearing the imprint of your sole.

If you have nothing to hide, you have nothing to fear; you have girded your loins against criticism down the years, grinned and borne it all. The dissenting voices that say you are not good enough, not white enough, to get where you got to. But you did.

King Kevin Keegan, Kenny Dalglish, Ruud Gullit, Sir Bobby, Graham Souness, Glenn Roeder, King Kev again, Sam Allardyce, you've outlived them all here. At the centre of it all, in the Premier League, on this famous field of play, here at St James' Park.

All the glory to God, you know it's all Him.

●   ·   ●

It's June 2009 now but back in July, nearly a year ago, there was an article written about you in the *Mirror*. You read it while working out on your exercise bike trying to get fit for the new season.

'RENNIE HOT FOR FINAL HONOUR' the headline read, written by Alan Biggs, a Sheffield-based sports writer you know well.

The article was a rare fair one, you recall: 'Uriah Rennie is the earliest ever favourite to referee the FA Cup final as his career goes into extra time,' you read, your 'Sheffield: National City for Sport' sweatshirt billowing, body fat jiggling.

It was a line that made you think, you've never felt like the favourite of anything before, suddenly your dream to referee the famous end-of-season Wembley showpiece somehow felt alive once more.

'Rennie – 49 in October – has been retained beyond the retirement age of 48 after winning an appeal to stay on,' it continued.

That was true, there had been a significant development last summer, a U-turn of sorts, your retirement postponed a year, your career at the top given one last chance by the powers that be. This really was the last dance. The last throw of the dice.

You read on as you pedalled, tiring, trying to strengthen your hamstrings enough to pass any test needed to prove your fitness, to referee in the big league again, to throw your name in the hat come May for the FA Cup final that you were so desperate for.

'The appointment takes form into account but, if he is on the top of his game, few insiders would bet against Rennie crowning his career in style.'

Things looked brighter back then definitely. When you were allowed back on the Select Group list, for a time you felt like Dirty Den in *EastEnders* coming back from the dead. You refereed the Newcastle vs Valencia friendly in August and it went well enough and you were raring to go. But little did you know, your legs had other ideas.

You read on as you pedalled and pedalled, wiping the sweat off your furrowed brow, the article giving you renewed belief. Hope (the only word on *that* Obama poster).

And you were pedalling and pedalling, putting in the hard yards trying to get fit, really trying, your hamstrings niggled a bit, but you powered on, your sweat poured like tears.

But as tirelessly as you worked, as quickly as you pedalled, eating up the kilometres with semi-flexed knees, muscles at mid-range, the pain lingered like guilt.

The season went on, and you pedalled bedevilled with envy, and the days went by and you were still sidelined, watching and sweating and wincing.

And even after surgery, and physio, and long lengths of the Olympic-sized Ponds Forge pool and encouraging words from friends, family and other referees, you were not able to officiate a single game in the 2008–2009 season, never quite fit enough to attempt the fitness test.

Then the news broke, the 2009 FA Cup final man in the middle will be a referee from South Yorkshire . . .

Howard Webb from Rotherham, thirteen years your younger, was appointed.

Credit where it's due, Howard's a great referee undoubtedly, but he's not you.

They say you're only as good as your last game, and for you, competitively speaking anyway, that remains Tottenham Hotspur vs Liverpool at White Hart Lane in May 2008 and not Chelsea vs Everton at Wembley in front of ninety thousand fans.

Instead, you gingerly watch José Mourinho, the self-styled 'special one', lead the Londoners to cup glory at home on the TV. The exercise bike gathering dust in the corner.

4

Dead tired, you rub your eyes, yawn, indicate, change gear, check mirrors, switch lanes, toss and turn half asleep, the soulful melodies of 'Joy and Pain' by Maze featuring Frankie Beverly are heard like background music . . .

From one big game to the next, for years, you graced stadiums with your presence like a fragrant car air freshener dangling from the rear-view mirror.

Suddenly, without knowing how, you're stepping off a team bus with tracksuited teammates you only vaguely recognise, wireless Beats headphones wrapped around your neck. You quickly sign a few autographs for freckle-faced young fans in fat-soled Air Forces and pose for a woman's iPhone camera with your arms behind your back like a player in a Panini sticker book, or a bobby on the beat. She wears high-heeled open-toe 'going out out' shoes.

Impossibly, from the back pocket of her high-waisted denim jeans, this woman, who ages a year by the second, retrieves a copy of Alan Shearer's autobiography *My Story So Far* and hands it to you to hold. A well-thumbed hardback too big to have been in her skin-tight jeans. The picture on the front depicts a young-ish Big Al in an old-ish England top with a full-ish head of hair.

Somehow, without realising, you're now walking down the tunnel of a stadium, twirling your car keys around your index finger, it could be Elland Road, it could be Saltergate, and with each step it's getting darker, like someone from above is fiddling with the dimmer switch and soon the only light is the light at the end of the tunnel that is bright lime green. But too green to be the green of a football pitch. Everything feels strange, one minute you're in your old Official Sports ref kit, clip-clopping on the concrete in your old pair of FILAs, the next you're in a short-sleeved check shirt and chinos.

As you near the end of the corridor, which narrows as you get closer, becoming so tight you're touching each wall with each of your shoulders, there is no roar of a crowd, just the inside heat of a tiny lime-green television studio. The next thing you know, your hands are being shaken vigorously by a familiar face, old pal, local football reporter, Alan Biggs. His head looks disproportionately bigger than his body, like a lollipop, or a pencil with a cartoonish pencil topper. He looks delighted to see you, beaming like a yellow-faced emoji, as he adjusts the little mic that sits on your chest and pats you affectionately on your shoulder before ushering you into a seat.

He is wide-smiling now to try and make you feel comfortable, and rambling on about something that isn't coming through clear. The studio is small, not lavish like Graham Norton or Jonathan Ross, there is no audience, just cameras, and lights, and you look left and the seat next to you is free. You look away and then look left again and you're suddenly sitting next to another Alan, Alan Shearer. His sudden appearance beside you goes from making you feel alarmed to normal in seconds. From the side, he looks like the TV version of the ex-England striker, not the hero-worshipped talismanic centre-forward you refereed in the nineties and noughties.

Your tongue is sticky and coarse, the roof of your mouth rough like Velcro. There is a jug of water on the table in front of you but you do not know which glass is yours, and now, you've realised, every time you look away and back again, the table has moved further and further away, then eventually completely out of reach.

Shifting in your seat trying to get comfortable, not sure where to put your hands, not sure why you are here, your head feels hot. You and Alan Shearer sit shoulder to shoulder, seat-sharing the smallest of red sofas like two plants growing in the same pot, two pigs in the same pen.

Completely disorientated, without warning, Alan Biggs starts giving a little introduction to the camera; he makes a tension-easing comment about the rising temperature in the studio. Shearer laughs but you can't. It suddenly dawns on you then that this must be his dream and your nightmare.

You're trying to listen carefully as he consults his notes, reeling off facts about your career like a Wikipedia page, his words are out of sync though, like a poorly dubbed kung fu movie. He swivels slightly to face you and adopts his best Michael Parkinson voice, looks you squarely in the eyes and begins to speak, this seems to be the start of some kind of set-the-story-straight interview.

An incident that stands out, he begins, is from 1999 at St James' Park, where you, Uri, issued Alan here with his first red card, he glances down at his notes briefly and then looks up again. When I researched it today, it was for persistent use of the elbow. It wasn't just the one elbow then?

Your heart thumps like a drum.

Well, look, the point is, you scratch your face and slide your hands along your thigh, you're not sure whether this is going out live, I had to do what I thought was right as a guardian of standards. No means no in anyone's language and from the estate where I came from, if you're told not to do something, you don't do it. Those who won't hear, will feel . . .

I think perhaps there is something personal there, Shearer interjects suddenly, tilting his head towards you with a raised eyebrow and a cheeky grin, equally as amiable as unsettling. If you go through the years you've refereed Newcastle, you've given me very little.

An awkward laugh is followed by a short pause. Your mouth feels bone dry and your right arm hangs limp on the side of the couch, the much-too-small couch. I saw what I saw, you say. Faltering. You clasp and then unclasp your hands, you feel the sweat spread across your body, behind your ears, under your chin, around the back of your neck.

Well, Shearer pauses to formulate his words, he has learnt from his punditry on *Match of the Day* to think before he speaks, I respect that being a referee is a difficult job and everyone makes mistakes. He's speaking like a seasoned television presenter, enunciating the syllables, trying to be pragmatic, it's clear to see he's a natural. You expect him to say more, to argue, to accuse, to reaffirm an agenda, but he doesn't. He says his bit and leaves you to fill the silence.

Clearly, you say, the top of your nose now wet with sweat, it was the clenched fist, if you look at it again, there was an element of something quite deliberate there. You're speaking more with your hands than your mouth, unable to articulate the right words quickly enough to defend yourself. Shifting in your seat, trying to get comfortable, still not sure what to do with your arms, interlocking your fingers, palms as if in prayer. This dream suddenly feeling much too real.

Your head feels fiery.

Look, Shearer strokes his bald head slowly, I respect that being a referee is a difficult job, I expect the odd mistake, every player does. For me, I think we need to incentivise ex-players to train as match officials for when their playing days are over, and by that I mean, former players who have played at Football League and Premier League level, players who may have finished in their early thirties and are looking to stay in football.

His words, uttered in a television-friendly toned-down Toon twang, are heard clear, but you don't think this is a good idea, too short-sighted, and there would be issues of supporter bias to consider, fans of rival clubs for example, but you're unable to speak, your tongue is stuck, lips glued shut, instead, you're fingering the hem of your shirt collar waiting for this night-mare to end.

Shearer continues apace.

It's harder because most referees haven't played the game at a high level. I do also understand that players are also responsible for making things more difficult for the officials, with over-reactions, diving and the way they roll around and pretend to be in agony . . .

There are nods all round, including from you, involuntarily. You are really thirsty but the table with the water looks thirty yards away now.

Alan Biggs seizes on the lull in conversation to change topic slightly, the mole on his face looks as big and bulbous as an avocado seed. Well, moving on, we can all agree you've both had your run-ins with a certain Mr Roy Keane.

At this mention, both you and Shearer share a sincere glance, and laugh. Bottom-of-the-belly laughter. You seem to over-do it though, and both Alans look at each other quizzically.

Shearer speaks again, energetically recalling his bust-up with the hot-headed Irishman.

He punched me in the face once, at St James' Park, didn't he? He got that red card, he walked off the pitch, it was the last minute of the game and he'd been given the red card, and he was waiting for me at the top of the tunnel. Of course, we tried to get each other and we couldn't, it was like *hold me back, don't hold me back*, but we couldn't get to each other, it would have been interesting.

After pausing to sip from the glass of water he has luckily managed to get from somewhere, Shearer speaks on.

He tried to take a quick throw and I tried to slow him down as there were only a few minutes left and we were winning, he adds. He got the hump at that and threw the ball at my head. I can't remember what I said, but he tried to throw a punch at me and got a red card. Minutes later, I'm walking down the tunnel and there he is, waiting for me.

Time moves fast, as Shearer speaks you're twiddling your thumbs, staying quiet for fear of saying something stupid.

He has moved onto VAR, speaking more passionately about this than any of the topics before. If we are not careful, he says, I really do think it will cause more harm than good, with the effects on the flow of the game, the change in dynamic and momentum, while still not eradicating mistakes.

You're not particularly keen on VAR either, but either you're not given the opportunity to speak or you've forgotten you already have, because the interview is over now, you presume.

And off camera, in the green room of the lime-green studio, Shearer playfully slaps your belly like you are old school chums and says, Me and Les, and some of the other lads are playing in this charity golf thing this weekend, you should get involved, big man.

The invitation feels like a genuine one, he's smiling warmly as he unclips his mic with the ease of someone who has done it a thousand times.

You presume the Les he's talking about must be Ferdinand. You doubt it's Dennis.

You match kindness with kindness.

Thank you, and if you ever want to sign for Hallam, you can wear the number nine shirt, you joke, hoping something or someone will wake you up soon.

2015

As you've said before, it can be lonely in the middle. Often, you cannot think about anything else except your next decision, the next move and whether you think it's right or wrong in the eyes of the law. Your brain constantly ticking over, thinking relentlessly about your positioning and reading the next phase of play and whether you're standing in the right place at the right time.

There were times when you thought about jacking it in, packing up your troubles in an old Umbro kitbag and burying them beneath the sea. But even through the worst of times, you remained resolute, determined to not give up.

Despite all the qualities needed to be a good referee, this is probably up there; the one thing taking you far out of your comfort zone. This isn't appearing at a charity function or your role as a magistrate on a weekday or telling an irate Wayne Rooney to calm down at a packed Old Trafford; this is new territory, taking method acting to the next level: television studios, contestants, presenters, scripts, cues, make-up. It's a step out of what you are used to, but you are ready to dip a toe in anyway.

This might seem out of character to most, might seem like typical attention-seeking Rennie to some. But on paper, the role suits you, plays to your strengths, you think.

'Freeze Out, the quiz show where £10,000 is up for grabs if

players know their general knowledge and they can get to grips with this slippery surface. A table covered with six inches of solid ice.'

Not quite *The Uriah Rennie Show*. No, not quite your show.

It has been a while since you've felt so pampered, so looked after. A team from ITV make sure you have a face for TV. You are given your costume, not quite the Umbro kit you are used to. Instead, the black-and-white striped top resembles one of the intimidatingly trendy teens from Foot Locker, or, dare you say, a Newcastle United player.

You are well looked after, cups of tea and M&S sandwiches.

Durks did *Simply the Best*. Jeff Winter did *Superstars*. It seems there's a place for you refs after the final whistle. What's the worst that can happen?

You meet Mark Durden-Smith, the presenter. He puts you at ease, well, tries to at least.

You've read the rules, rehearsed your lines, met the contestants. Diane, Keith, Michael, Phil, Mike, Jo, Richard, Denise, Hannah, Alan etc. Names from across the country, their odd facts divulged to the rest of the nation.

In many ways, this new role is just like a game of football.

There are rules, right and wrong, and interpretation.

Here, in this studio, you are not Uriah Rennie, you are Ice Judge Rennie. A pantomime character with a whistle and an unforgiving stare. An actor stepping in from the wings.

TV loves a baddy.

Ice Judge Rennie: a fitting name, when you think about it. You've played the judge before, and not just on the football field of course.

Like you do when you're on the pitch, here you will have to make direct eye contact, look down the barrel of the camera and stiffen your body to come across as tough and uncompromising. This is what the camera crew and the producers will expect.

You do what you are told.

The show's format is a simple one really. Contestants have to answer a series of quick-fire general knowledge questions and then skim sliders along an icy surface.

You're introduced as the former Premier League referee accompanied by an ear-splitting guitar riff. You give a cold nod in response; play the part you have been told to.

Round One: Smash Out

– *What is the square root of sixteen?*

– *When applying for a job, what does the acronym 'CV' stand for?*

– *What is the German name for a motorway?*

– *How many months are there in a trimester?*

– *According to the proverb, the 'what' is mightier than the sword?*

You've refereed cup finals and all the big names in English football and here you are in a television studio playing the big bad guy trying not to smile when the camera is aimed at your face and Mark asks you something silly.

You won't eat scorpions on *I'm a Celeb* or pretend to be a cat on *Celebrity Big Brother* but this you can do, this role you can play, these rules you can enforce.

CLEAR! You shout. The sliders have been successfully bull-dozed out of the ring and it's your job to confirm how many seconds it took.

Round Two: Centre Slide

– *How many wheels does a Reliant Robin have?*

– *Which football ground is home to Leeds United?*

– *What is the capital city of Australia?*

– *In which century was William Shakespeare born?*

– *'You can't handle the truth!' is a famous line from which 1992 film?*

Round Three: Ice Breaker

– *Sofia is the capital of which European country?*

– *Haggis is a dish most associated with which country?*

– *What is the official language of Brazil?*

– *What was the first name of Nelson the famous admiral?*

– What is the county town of Suffolk?

It's a double. The slider straddles two pieces, good news for the contestant.

You've refereed big derbies with the most ferocious fans baying for blood, and boundary-pushing players and their bad-mouthing managers who are uncooperative and don't want to listen to your explanation that laws are laws. Now you're here playing the bad guy on tele.

Round Four: Face Off

– On which continent is the Serengeti National Park?

– Which number does the Roman numeral 'M' represent?

– Kate Hudson is the daughter of which actress?

– Who wrote the novels The Grapes of Wrath *and* Of Mice and Men?

– On what date is US Independence Day?

You blow your whistle and exclaim: IT'S GOOD.

The winner is crowned and the credits roll.

Episode four, five and six.

Episode seven, eight and nine.

Episode ten is the last, before the show is discontinued, axed.

Your television career (as Ice Judge Rennie) is short-lived. The papers have had their laugh, as have some of the former players you refereed too, probably. Water off a duck's back.

It was refreshing to be out your comfort zone for a bit, yes, but could you see yourself being a TV personality forever? Probably not. You can't let TV eat into your legacy.

You have bigger, more impactful, things planned.

Rennie was yesterday unveiled as the new patron of Sheffield's Weston Park Hospital Cancer Charity

+

At Hillsborough Leisure Centre, celebrated former football referee Uriah Rennie is set to host his second walking football challenge. All the money raised during the 15-hour all night sporting marathon will be donated to St Luke's Hospice

+

Former top level football referee Uriah Rennie officiated, helping to raise a final total of £13,000 for the charities

+

Football United Against Dementia is pitting the world of football – including old foes like Robbie Savage and Uriah Rennie – against its toughest opponent yet: dementia

+

Great to have the @sheffREDSVBLUES #Charity match refereed by #Legend Uriah Rennie

+

Uriah Rennie, retired England football referee, is among those raising funds for vital research during February – National Heart Month – with the Take the Stairs Challenge

+

Uriah Rennie, one of the most renowned referees in British football, has signed up to become a member of Sheffield Health and Social Care NHS Foundation Trust

+

In its third year, Uriah Rennie's overnight walking football fundraiser is an event not to be missed. This year all players will play for six hours through the night and they will raise sponsorship to support St Luke's – Sheffield's Hospice

+

Sunday 9th June, kick off 2p.m. sees Hallam FC annual charity football match being played at their Sandygate Ground. This year it's in aid of Sheffield Children's Hospital Charity and their "Build it Better" Appeal. There will be celebrities on show and keeping the whole event under control, Club President and former FIFA referee Uriah Rennie will be this afternoon's referee

+

Happy Birthday to our good friend and community champion Uriah Rennie from everyone at Pitsmoor Adventure Playground! @SIV_Social #sheffieldissuper

+

Trophies after the football tournament were presented by ex-England referee, Uriah Rennie, and the winning team, South Yorkshire Police took home this year's main trophy

+

Sheffield Mind is holding its first ever fund-raising ball at Baldwin's Omega. There are two tables of 10 still available, at £450, so why not join us? Uriah Rennie, former Premier League referee, will be guest speaker

+

The race was started by retired Premiership referee Uriah Rennie who also got the 1.3-mile fun run underway. All those youngsters completing the course received a certificate signed by Olympic swimming star Rebecca Adlington

+

The popular racecourse venue brought together guests including retired football referee and Hallam FC president Uriah Rennie to raise over £6,000 for Weston Park Hospital

+

Former football referee Uriah Rennie, who is now community liaison manager at Sheffield City Trust, said: "We are committed to getting kids involved in sports and physical activity so we are delighted that the funding will support the further development of Grenoside Park Bowling Club."

+

The marathon match, organised by former Premier League referee Uriah Rennie, will see players from local walking football teams join forces to play through the night on Friday June 10

+

Many of you new members signed up to the Trust at a recent SHSC street nurse event which was held at Crystal Peaks Shopping Centre. We hope you enjoyed the event and many thanks to Uriah Rennie who attended the event and became a member on the day – what a result!

+

Mr Rennie, former FIFA referee, will take the stair challenge alongside other fundraisers. He is also President of Hallam FC and has taken part in the BHF's Santa Jog previously

+

Plate winners were Bretton Hall Tigers and the Uriah Rennie fair play award went to Steve Dwyer from AFC Massams

+

A big thank you to Nick Frith Tiles for loaning us a truck, Bev Nunn and Uriah Rennie for supporting us throughout this challenging moment in time. Play packs and books have been delivered to children and you have helped us to create miles of smiles! @SIV_Social

+

Celebrities and sports stars including Jo Brand, James Cracknell, Meera Syal, Robbie Savage and Uriah Rennie are backing the biggest ever campaign from Alzheimer's Society calling on people to come together to defeat dementia

+

"Uriah was great. He's an ex-student so he came back to talk to the children and give them one or two pointers."

+

Former top flight football referee Uriah Rennie is backing a South Yorkshire wide push to encourage free smoke alarm sign ups amongst black and minority ethnic (BME) communities

+

CONGRATULATIONS to our enthusiastic PE department who were presented with the Moss Award at the Sheffield Town Hall on 3rd December with guest speaker Uriah Rennie

+

Retired Premier League referee Uriah Rennie has attended the opening of a new tyre swing at Pitsmoor Adventure Playground

+

He is brilliant with the disabled kids we work with. He does a lot for charity, or out of goodwill, so it wouldn't surprise me if he was reffing that game as a favour to someone

+

When I say "big man"… this is a "real big man!" The only black referee in the UK football Premiership League, Uriah Rennie. He came out, to support Leyton Orient Legends v Men United Charity Football match to help raise awareness of

Prostate Cancer UK, as the official referee for the game. What a man! I salute you Sir for your works, as you are an inspiration

+

The presentation was made by well-known football referee Uriah Rennie (far left) on behalf of the Federation of Disability Sports Organisations

+

Leading the draw alongside Uriah Rennie, a former Premier League football referee from Sheffield, was a real privilege

+

Lovely story for Will & his u11 team. He met Uriah Rennie yesterday at @HallamFC1860 & told him he was playing today... Uriah came to watch!

+

The awards, which are held annually, celebrate the achievements of athletes and volunteers throughout Britain. The awards were supported by Nationwide, First TransPennine Express and Lancashire County Cricket Club and was attended by guests such as Premiership referee Uriah Rennie and Manchester City player Danny Mills

+

Uriah said: "I fully support SHSC's work within the city and I am pleased to be a member. One in four people will suffer from a mental health problem in their lifetime – which is a very high statistic and indicates just how many people are affected by mental health issues. This is just my way of helping."

+

Thank you To Asda ADC3, Queensbury Jewellers, Philips Hairdressers, Redcats, Hoops-a-daisy Bridal, Uriah Rennie and David Sztencel for donating the fantastic prizes

+

A FORMER Premier League referee visited Chesterfield College to introduce a new generation to the game. Uriah Rennie was at the college's Clowne campus to launch a new Referee Academy

+

Chairman @BasfordSteve secretary @kevinscottsport and president Uriah Rennie all sporting #RainbowLaces today!

+

Great to see No.2 son playing at Neil Baldwin's charity match this afternoon @Buxton_FC refereed by Uriah Rennie!

+

When you go to watch your local non league footy team play and the half-time entertainment is mascot on a stag doing dizzy penalties. In case you're wondering who's stood by the spot dressed as a TV detective, it's Uriah Rennie

+

A great day today in Sheffield raising money for st Luke's charity with celebrities such as david hurst ex england and sheffield Wednesday player, uriah rennie ex premier league ref, also jon mcClure frontman for reverend and the makers

+

Wake Smith will be taking on Sheffield Medics at Bramall Lane on 28th May, 6:30pm. Raising money for Cardiac Risk in the Young, refereed by Uriah Rennie. The football match is free to attend, there are plenty of seats available in the stadium so please come along and watch. #syb

+

Top Ref Uriah Rennie gives house fires the Red Card with a home fire safety visit – watch the video from SYFS

+

My old Uni @sheffielduni & Uriah Rennie, yes Uriah Rennie, raising money for @TheBHF running up the horrible Arts-Tower

+

Listen to what our charity patron, Uriah Rennie, has to say about the Charity Unleashed Gift Books. Buy yours today!

+

Greening Grey in Super Sheffield with the Royal Horticultural Society! On a sunny spring afternoon Gavin Hardy from the @The_RHS and retired Premier League referee Uriah Rennie lead from the front and planted vegetables and a diverse selection of flowers with families in Pitsmoor

+

Uriah Rennie with @WillBayleytt who'll be joining us for Uriahs All Night Walking Event for @StLukes_Sheff

+

The learners who took part really got involved and stretched themselves over the sessions, and at the end they received their certificates from the national football referee, Uriah Rennie

+

Referee against Lincoln or Bury when I was mascot for @LaticsOfficial. Can't remember which as I was mascot twice that season but Uriah gave me a fiver, a copy of Shoot magazine and was a total gentleman

+

We had a lovely evening with the Lord Mayor @Anthony-Downing1 the lord mayoress Val Downing, Mark Aston, Uriah Rennie and Anne Murphy celebrating the success of the @SheffieldEagles on their fabulous cup win. @theBMessenger @SheffieldStar

+

Uriah Rennie cut the ribbon on Thurs 4th May to the brand new multi-use games area (MUGA) at Owler Brook Primary School. Men of all ages (fathers, uncles, cousins and brothers)

supported children in five-a-side football matches – the league was umpired by Uriah and by Chair of Governors, Ian Annis

♥

Thoroughly enjoyed this morning meeting Uri Rennie to hear his story and explore ideas about helping kids get moving #movemoresheff

♥

Uriah Rennie did his apprentice here as well, never seen such a fit bloke, he'd come off the pitch and wouldn't have broken sweat. Used to see a lot of top refs back in the day

♥

We were guests of Uriah Rennie that eve, top bloke, and finest ref around then

♥

Uriah Rennie was one of England's top referees. At his peak, he was described by Keith Hackett (head of the Professional Game Match Officials Board) as "the fittest referee we have ever seen on the national or world scene"

♥

Uriah Rennie is up there with the best there's been for me… handy with the martial arts in case matters got out of hand

♥

I watched Uriah Rennie in lower leagues. He was always

excellent. He communicated constantly with the players

♥

Uriah Rennie was an outstanding referee, Application of the laws, Control, Decision making…yes he was also a very fit referee

♥

Uriah Rennie with a top engine to get with the play. Modern refs would struggle with that

♥

That was a crazy atmosphere both inside & outside the ground … Uriah Rennie had a decent game as ref under the circumstances

♥

Uriah Rennie reffed me in the North West Counties league 1990's……was one of the best and had thighs like tree trunks! Nobody messed with him or saw him as 'black', he was just the best ref in the league

♥

Bring back uriah rennie he was a quality ref #Unit

♥

Would love to have a pint with Uriah Rennie…Just to see how his mind works…Decision making of the highest order!

♥

Uriah Rennie with the wheels to keep up though, under appreciated pace

♥

Need Uriah Rennie back he was a top ref!

♥

uriah Rennie was one of top premiership football refs few yrs ago, he was massive and a kickboxer I think

♥

Promotion on the pathway to the top is fair and is performance related. I had the pleasure of managing Uriah Rennie who was a brilliant referee and rightly reached the top level

♥

met the guy a few times, he's now an assessor, top bloke & very intelligent!

♥

Just trying to compile a list of decent refs I have seen. So far come up with Uriah Rennie & Collina. Not a very big list!

♥

Uriah Rennie was the best referee what a g

♥

Uriah Rennie was the GOAT

♥

Uriah Rennie set the bar for other to follow. We are lucky in South Yorkshire he is the Chairman of the Sheff and Hallam CFA Referees Committee

♥

Can we just appreciate the speed Uriah Rennie had to keep up with the play here! Class reffing that

♥

Rennie kept control of the game superbly

♥

I believe Rennie to be the most impressive referee I have seen all season

♥

I think Uriah Rennie handled the game very well indeed. He is perhaps the best official that I have seen at Goodison Park this season

♥

Rennie has deservedly earned a reputation as one of the Premiership's fittest, sharpest-eyed and most sensible referees

♥

Uriah Rennie is probably the best referee in the Premiership

♥

Uriah Rennie was a top ref back in his day

♥

A lot of football fans shudder when they see the name Uriah Rennie on the team sheet but I'm not so sure they should. He's as good as any, and better than most

♥

Referee Uriah Rennie has established himself as one of the leading match officials in England through sheer endeavour and application

♥

Uriah Rennie was as fit as most of the players, to be fair!

♥

Been a long time since big Uriah Rennie. He was a brilliant ref as well. No ego, honest and well liked in the game

♥

Seeing Uriah Rennie referee at the top of the game inspired me

2018

It's hard to know who you can trust when you are who you are, have done what you have done, been who you have been. You've been the victim on too many occasions. Lied about, left hung out to dry: wronged.

People wonder where you are, what you've been doing since hanging up your whistle and sauntering off the field of play for the last time, and you are reluctant to divulge; you are a private man really, a man of few words.

And you have never met a journalist who wants to give you a fair hearing, allow you to say what you really want to say without misconstruing or over-interpreting your words.

You think of Twitter and the damage it can cause.

Despite what the papers reported, you do not have Twitter, you did not have a spat with the ex-Crystal Palace chairman Simon Jordan last year, @TheRealUriah was a fake account, but some people believe what they want to believe.

You think about privacy settings, Facebook and Cambridge Analytica. You think about clickbait headlines and the media who love to spin some sham story to sell papers. You know of many two-finger typers who have lost their jobs because of reckless tweeting. People in positions of power who should know better, people with questionable views who should know better.

Now somebody new wants to tell your story, some young man from a university somewhere. Somewhere not in Sheffield, somewhere you can't remember. You've had this before, young writers wanting a bit of Uri. You remember one from a few years back, just as you got promoted to the Premiership when everyone wanted a piece of you.

You say 'a few years back', must have been a few decades ago now, a university student wanting to write your story. Sell your history. An ill-informed warts-and-all exposé maybe. Very rarely do *they* want to hear about the good things you do, but you come here with an open mind, today; someone new wants to hear what you have to say, and you want to hear from him before you agree to anything concrete.

It could work: Clive Thomas has a book. Keith Hackett has a book. David Elleray has a book. Jeff Winter has a book. Graham Poll has a book. Pierluigi Collina has a book. Mark Halsey has a book. Howard Webb has a book.

You like to give everything a try, and you like helping people, giving back to the game you love, so you agree to meet this young man desperate to meet you, who's emailed claiming to be a friend of a friend. He's a referee too, he says. You have your doubts, boundaries and disclaimers you want to make clear as you head towards Ponds Forge Sports Centre, a home from home, a place you know just as well as the four corners of a football pitch.

It's November outside, Sheffield November. Let's-get-a-Costa-it's-cold November. The real warmth you can be sure of is the humidity of the building as you walk in.

You think about what he might want to ask, what he might choose to write about, what aspects of your life he is interested in retelling. You think about your career, the journey you've taken to get here. You've certainly travelled the miles; driven back and forth along every motorway in the country, ten times over and more.

Sheffield to Scunny, Derby and Donny, Portsmouth, Port Vale and Plymouth. Millwall to Macclesfield. Watford, Wigan and Wrexham. Liverpool to Luton. You've refereed in the FA Cup, the League Cup through all its various name changes: Coca-Cola, Worthington, Carling and whatever it was called before then and before then again. You've seen it all, but this meeting makes you nervous, what will your friends and family think if he gets this wrong, or former referees, the FA, or the old players.

You wonder too, briefly, what he will think of you now? Are you still the hero that he claims you were?

As God is your witness, you are no hero, you have made mistakes, have a few regrets – but everyone has their cross to bear. You are just a man who was in the middle once.

Despite what the shrieking middle-class curtain-twitching *Mail* readers felt, you were not just a hard-lined, heavy-handed, self-indulgent, whistle-wielding, card-waving black-hearted headline-hogging bald-headed busybody, you never felt out of your depth while at the top, while refereeing the nitty-gritty of a tricky game made up of brawl-ready players in front of die-hard fist-pumping fans. You did your best.

Life in the middle is a full-blooded high-pressure double-edged sword sometimes; you're yards away from head-scratching sitters, missed clear-cut point-blank gift-wrapped chances, skied follow-ups, mistimed split-second last-ditch tackles from hot-headed no-nonsense centre-backs or battling box-to-box midfield dynamos, but it's *you* who gets the blame during a big bubble-bursting game when the promotion-chasing team loses to the so-called second-rate bog-standard giant-killers, it's the likes of *you*, doing the after-dinner circuit with a pot-belly in front of long-suffering double-chinned pot-bellies or on television shows with Mark Durden-Smith.

It can be self-destructive sometimes, strutting your stuff in the spotlight, being so hell-bent to be the best – but your story is no whistle-stop, coming-of-age stream of consciousness.

You're no longer at the centre of it all: in the papers, on the television, the subject of some online fans' forum, interviewed while topless on a Harley-Davidson or mentioned in *FourFourTwo* magazine. You imagine most people have forgotten about you already. The impact you had. Forgotten the games you refereed, the big names you kept under control and, on occasion, man-handled.

No longer are your decisions widely scrutinised, played in slow motion, shot by shot, frame by frame. No longer the butt of the joke. You are no longer victimised and vilified. No more put-downs and quips. No more post-match 'shit sandwiches' in cosy dressing rooms from FA assessors who stutter and stammer trying to find the right words:

Good (bun):

You had a good presence out there, your match
control was exemplary, your authoritative style
was never really compromised.

Shit (meat):

You looked rusty at times. Your positioning needs
adjusting from some set pieces. I think you missed
a yellow card or two.

Good (bun):

You did well to spot the penalty. It was a bold
decision but a correct one.

Despite what others might think, Alan Shearer is not your
bête noire. Different skin but similar within. He was a passionate footballer. You were a passionate referee. What others saw
from the stands or the settee were two sportsmen doing two
very different jobs. He scored goals, you applied laws.

His eight games as interim Newcastle manager back in 2009,
for whatever reason didn't work out. Newcastle United were
relegated.

They're back in the Prem now and Big Al is a straight-talking
well-respected pundit you watch on *Match of the Day* on a
Saturday. But if he wanted it, he surely deserves another shot
in the hot seat.

Like Keyser Söze in *The Usual Suspects*, you walk with a bit of
a limp now. The subject of made-up stories. The villain of the

piece; the villain of the peace. Your years of contact sport have caught up with you, taken its toll on your papier-mâché knees. Not quite the strapping specimen you used to be.

You look older than you did, older than he expects, you imagine. Wider too. Your body isn't what it used to be but your mind's still sharp. You still have the memories: the cup finals and the top-of-the-table clashes, the relegation six-pointers, the accolades, the European ties, the honour of being in a position of authority overlooking the best teams and the best players – just inches from the megastars – in some of the best grounds in the country.

Little Uri has done OK, Little Uri has done just fine.

The world you thought you knew is different now. No more lino flags with wooden handles. Linos are now assistant referees. Assessors are now observers. Hurlfield is now Sheffield Springs Academy. A Getty image of you sending off Shearer against Villa costs up to £375.

It's all Snapchat, Bitcoin, Fiat 500s, tattoo sleeves and cocaine off car keys, men necking pints in overpriced PSG tops yapping on about Mbappé and what could have been in the summer, in Russia, if football came home again, and fold-up Brompton bikes, Apple AirPods, tinny grime music, Gen Z snowflakes, sliders with socks, half-and-half scarves, pubes in the pisser and pictures taken in 'portrait mode', podcasts, Netflix, *Fleabag* reruns and vulnerable boys being sucked in by the lure of county lines. And flipping new-fangled self-checkout machines – humans must cost too much these days apparently.

The 4-4-2 is now a 4-5-1 or a 5-3-2.

Today's team sheet is barely legible:

Paper straws

Love Island   *Playing out from the back*   *VAR*

Trump (C)   *'Oh, Jeremy Corbyn!'*

Universal Credit   *Brexit*   *Toxic masculinity*

Knife crime   *AFTV*

Subs:

Climate change
GDPR
Rainbow-flagged tote bags
Birkenstocks and white nail varnish
Sam Fender
Bad Bs coming to the niz
R.I.P. Mac Miller

From what you have seen, there are more homeless people in the city than you can ever remember, and from what you have read, there are more Tory-tired people than ever relying on foodbanks. Police numbers have been cut and there are fewer bobbies on the beat; you question everything and everyone that has made the world this way today. You shudder at the thought of the victims of the Windrush scandal, forced to return to a country they barely know. What about Grenfell? The injustices make you dizzy.

You think of Sterling and the way he's mistreated in the media, one of England's star players. The same player, fans from across the country were cheering on in Russia when, against the odds, we got to the World Cup semi-finals.

You think the authorities must come down harder on the culprits of racism in football or they will drive talented Black players and coaches and referees from the game.

Your lad Jordan plays a bit of football too, you want to protect him from ignorant fans with backward views, teach him to be bigger than the bigots. It's part of the reason why you're here this morning. That's why you agreed to meet, to chat, to discuss, to unload.

It shouldn't be unusual to see a Black referee. Before you get too old, a long-forgotten name from the past, you want to leave a legacy to encourage more young people, young Black boys in particular, to take up the whistle and forge a career in refereeing. You want more young Black boys to come up through the system, have their turn in the middle, to smash through the glass ceilings.

You want to see more Black refereeing mentors, referee tutors, referee observers and better procedures in place to facilitate their progression as referees. You want to play your part in breaking down the barriers to provide equality of opportunities to all disadvantaged groups, who at the moment don't have the opportunity to achieve their potential.

You're a flag-bearer, you walked so others could run, spearheading the way for:

Akil Howson, Sam Allison, Paul Howard, Aji Ajibola, Jamaal
Horne, Harrison Blair, Joel Mannix, Farai Hallam, Kennedy
Kikulwe, Reuben Simon, Ari Mendonça, Ayesemuate Agho,
Bruno Gaisie, Conor Griffin, Deryll David, David Lunani, Dele
Somitirin, Dylan Ossei, Eugene Robinson, Jacob Viera, Jide
Ogunba, Jordan Whitworth, Marlon Williams, Paul Agboola,
Reubyn Ricardo, Silvester Aina, Val Anekwe, Wally James.

Credit to Trevor Parkes and Phil Prosser and Mark Tweed and
Dave Bushell and Joe Ross. They did their thing too, Black
beacons who shone their light.

The story behind the men in the middle is the story you want
to hear; the men on the spine of David Peace's *Red or Dead*,
the bit-parts, the scapegoats, the forgotten ones . . .

The almost unbearable warmth, like when you open a pre-heated
oven, hits you as you walk in, smack right in the face. A fleeting
flashback to Jamaica and being young and dancing and running
comes and goes like a single sneeze. That familiar chlorine smell
jolts you back to today, to right now, with the makeshift signs
and Katy Perry's 'Firework' playing in the background.

This is a big meeting. You chat to the staff a little, the cleaner
and the people behind the counter of the café.

Everyone knows you in here, you're a familiar face, have been
for decades.

In here, you're the boss to some and a friend to many, by hook
or by crook, you've got to know every nook and cranny, the
name of every cook and granny.

You see *him* sitting down, that must be him, over there, thirty feet or so away, sitting down at one of the table and chairs. Younger than you thought.

Before you can get to him, you are cornered by the familiar face of the old dear who's just come back from Hong Kong and is desperate to tell you about her newly born grandchild. You manage the small talk, smile and ask the right questions, because you are genuinely interested, enjoy hearing people's stories, things that make them happy, or aggrieved, or need help with.

Like you were as a lad, you are still a community person, you believe in the good in people.

Three or so years ago now, you appeared in *Marvellous*, a film about the life of much-loved former Stoke City kit man with learning difficulties, Neil Baldwin. It was quite the honour; his story, for you, epitomises the kindness of humanity, of acceptance. You are proud of your cameo, your role as Uriah Rennie, the referee at the end of the movie.

Down the years, you've bumped into former pros, top-tier players, names of yesteryear you refereed at a decent level, victims of their excess, surviving now as security guards, postmen, couriers, midday supervisors in secondary schools, bin men, some are sofa-surfing or slumming it on the street. Men that played at Wembley, now in prison or signing on, struggling to make ends meet.

You've even attended some of their funerals, their deaths not treated as suspicious, God rest their souls.

Not many have a nine-foot bronze statue outside a stadium (as much as they might deserve it).

Life today can be tough for too many in the margins, and you just want to do your bit. Play your part.

Even though these days you are no longer the man in the middle, front and centre, the one given a complimentary post-match pint and pat on the back, you're just a person surviving now yourself, watching from somewhere in the distance.

No longer running the show, merely observing it, wearing a big puffer coat with an embroidered Sheffield and Hallamshire FA logo on, shivering and shuddering, hoping, when all is said and done, something will give, hoping attitudes will shift.

You approach with caution.

'Can I get you a coffee?' you say.

ACKNOWLEDGEMENTS

Thank you to Uriah 'Uri' Rennie for allowing me to tell this particular version of his life story. I regularly pinched myself blue knowing how lucky I was to have the honour of writing this novel based on his inspiring journey to the top. He is a hero to me and the many others he continues to generously serve in the Sheffield and South Yorkshire community.

Thank you to Professor Andrew Cowan for his regular words of wisdom. In addition to his early feedback, his thoughtful 2019 novel *Your Fault* was, and forever will be, hugely inspirational to me.

Thank you to Professor Alison Donnell for her constant guidance and support. I am forever indebted to her for her kindness, generosity and positivity.

Thank you to CHASE for funding my PhD study at UEA and the professional support offered throughout the time it took to complete this novel.

Thank you to Deryll David, Gavin MacFarlane / MAD Sports Network, Pappy Mattis and Ralph Hedley for their help researching various bits of pieces over the last few years.

Thank you to Nick Bradley and David Peace.

All my love to Elisabeth, always, for her love.

At Faber, thank you to Angus Cargill, Kate Ward, Hannah Marshall, Josh Smith, Rachel Darling and Connor Hutchinson.

Thank you to Ian Critchley (copy-editor) and Paul Baillie-Lane (proofreader).

Thank you to my agent, Philippa Sitters of David Godwin Associates, for doing all the important bits behind the scenes.

Love to **all** my family, Mum and Tyler especially. Miss you Grandad.

R.I.P Jermaine Wright, 'Mr. Hackney Marshes', Referees Secretary of the Hackney & Leyton Sunday Football League who sadly lost his life to Coronavirus in April 2020.

RESPECT to every football referee out there.

Unsurprisingly, this work of fiction required quite a bit of research; the following books in particular were of a great help to me:

- *Alan Shearer: Fifty Defining Fixtures* by Tony Matthews (2016)
- *Wybourn Black: Life on the Wrong Side of Town* by Julian Antonio McKenzie (2012)
- *The Man in the Middle* by Howard Webb (2016)
- *Who's the Bastard in the Black* by Jeff Winter (2006)